# In Crocodile Waters

Judith M Kerrigan

All correspondence and inquiries regarding any written works by Judith M. Kerrigan should be directed to:
judirose@tds.net or jkerriganwriter@yahoo.com
See also the contact page at
www.judithkerriganribbens.com

The Anna Kinnealy series:
Book 1: *Betrayal by Serpent,* published 2012
Book 2: *In Crocodile Waters*, published 2014
Book 3: *The Jaguar Hunts* scheduled for publication in 2016

Published by Judith M. Ribbens
Golden Moon Studio
W2445 Main Street
Bonduel, WI 54107
ISBN 10: 0985706627
ISBN 13: 978-0-9857066-2-3
LCCN: 2014931795

Cover design by Paul Beeley
Create-Imaginations
www.create-imaginations.com

# COMMENTS AND REVIEWS

The first book of the Anna Kinnealy series, *Betrayal by Serpent*, was published in 2012. *In Crocodile Waters* is the second book of this new series of suspense novels.

## Comments on *Betrayal by Serpent*

"Simply stated, *Betrayal by Serpent* is a terrific mystery novel that holds the readers total attention from beginning to end. Superbly crafted characters, an imaginative plot, and detailed backdrops mark Judith M Kerrigan as a master storyteller."

excerpt from Midwest Book Review

"I was pleased and proud when Judy asked me to read her book...and a little apprehensive. First books can sometimes be painful. I can honestly say that painful is NOT one of the things this book is.

"*Betrayal by Serpent* is a complex and riveting thriller. Beginning with Anna's heartbreak upon the unexpected death of her husband ...I was drawn into the story and didn't want it to end.

"I am eagerly looking forward to the next book."

Dawn Gray

"I don't even know where to begin! This book is one of the most riveting books I have ever read! From the very first chapter you are sucked into a world of intrigue and suspense until the very last word! Incredible attention to detail and clever twists to the story keep the reader on the edge of their seat, and unwilling to put the book down until the very last page is turned! If you are looking for a great read, this is most definitely the book for you!"

Jeanne R.

"Kerrigan has crafted a novel heavy with suspense and mystery ...The story is intricate, racing between Wisconsin and the Yucatan peninsula.

"Her descriptions are detailed and very visual. You get a good feel for the places she takes you...

"It will definitely keep you interested. It will keep you guessing. It will make you look for more books by Judith Kerrigan. I recommend it to anyone who likes a suspense novel."

Jim C., Texas

# ACKNOWLEDGEMENTS

Once again I could not have finished this book without the aid of my faithful pre-readers. They have the task of scrutinizing the unedited manuscript looking for errors, such as the one I made in the first book where I killed off Anna's son, AJ, and then resurrected him in a following chapter. Thank you, Arica, for seeing that.

Without these patient and long-suffering friends and relatives, I'd have pulled even more hair out, and I can ill afford that.

Here they are--

Jeannie Kerrigan, author of *Layla;* founder and executive director of Ricky's Revolution, a 501c3 non-profit dedicated to aiding the homeless and abused to find help. Jeannie is my daughter and has written a stunning book of her story of recovery from addiction and abuse.

Arica Johnson, primary editor of my books
and granddaughter.

Lois Bergman, proofreader for several
authors

Dawn Gray, reader, critic and preparing to
write her own fantasy fiction

Joseph Ribbens, reader, son

Bev Nelson, reader

Jane Coleman, reader

Sara Marie Remmel, reader

# DEDICATION

To all my children, John, Jeannie, Joe, Jeff, Jacob John, and Julie
For a lifetime of learning so much from every one of you.
Love, Mom

# Part One

# Green Bay

## One

"If I wanted to, I could kill someone. Yes. I could kill."

The boy's eyelids narrowed to slits. Hate hardened his face. Rage poured from his body into the hot air around him.

"I could pick up a gun and shoot them, or stab them with a knife, or pound someone to death with my fists or kick them until they died. I wouldn't care. It would be so easy. Then I'd kill myself because I would never let them put me in prison. Never.

"Except maybe, if they caught me and I went to prison, I might get to see him, my first lover. My only real lover so far. He's not in prison yet. I don't know where he lives but I'll find out."

Liam sat on the lowest step of the back stairs leading to Alex's room, his slight body bent forward, arms grabbing his knees, and head hanging down. His voice, half child, half teen, was a sibilant whisper as he muttered to himself.

"They all think it was awful. They all think I was so abused. It did hurt at first but he explained that to me. He showed me everything. He prepared me. He told me if I had a dad, that my dad would have taught me all these things. I don't have a dad. I didn't know that.

After a few times, it didn't hurt anymore. It felt really good, his stroking, his holding me, his saying that he loved me. He did. He loved me. They don't understand.

"I pretended I felt bad when they questioned me. That's what Ma wanted to see. I'm not afraid. I'm not. I want more. He always told me not to be afraid.

"They won't let me see him but I will. I will.

"I've found another one like me. Cory is just like me. He wants it just like me. His dad died long ago. He doesn't have a dad either. I can make him love me. I will make him love me. He turns away now when I give him my special look, the look Daddy Clayton taught me. But he'll see. He'll find out how good it feels. I can make him like it."

Liam Fitzgerald pushed himself two steps higher, closer to the sound of the voice within. In the wet muggy heat that permeated the top floor of The House, sweat beading on his skin, he crouched outside the door at the top of the stairs that led to the attic room.

Waiting.

After a while he reached up very slowly and silently turned the handle.

Locked.

A wave of rage swept through him again and he shook with frustration. He raised his fist to pound on the door but stopped himself just in time. Behind the door he could hear the murmur as Cory Kinnealy spoke to someone on his cell phone.

"Another boy. He's got a boyfriend."

Jealousy followed impotent rage into his muscles, to his bones, eating away what little self-esteem he had. Hopelessness ripped at him with sharpened teeth and he nearly collapsed in tears. Only the fear of being heard stopped him from dissolving into sobbing. Obsession gnawed at his mind, driving out all reason, all sanity, and tearing apart his fragile façade.

"He'll never love me, never really love me. I'm too short and too small and don't even look like I'm fourteen, not like the other boys he knows. How will I ever get him to look at me?"

He sat and waited while self-pity ate him alive.

4

Inside the attic room Cory Kinnealy lay sprawled across his brother Alex's bed, shirt off, in shorts, scarcely noticing his sweat as it soaked into the sheet under him.

"I'm hiding out in my own home, and I'm pissed as hell," he told Alex, who was on the phone with him.

"He creeps me out, man! He's always staring at me when he thinks I'm not looking. I don't know what he wants but I think he's sort of trying to flirt with me. It's crazy. He's crazy! I feel like I'm a prisoner in this house. Right now he's on the back stairs, waiting to pounce, like some stalking animal. Alex, I've got to get Mom to come home. It's June. When is she coming back? I know she's recuperating but it's been almost a month and I can't talk to Liam's mom, who, by the way, wants me to call her Cait. Yeah! Right! Like after all these years of having to call her Mrs. Fitzgerald I'm really going to do that.

"And that's another thing. She's still working in Mom's office and I know it's ok with Mom, but she's still living here too. With Liam. And Andrew. And Seamus. They were supposed to be out of here a week ago, just after you left for camp, but the renewal work on their house isn't done yet, and she's screwing that detective, Klarkowski, in Mom's bedroom and I know it's just until their house is fixed up but shit, how long does that take? How would I tell Mrs. F. what Liam is doing? She'd never believe me. She thinks he's getting cured because he's in counseling."

One hundred miles to the northwest, Alex paced back and forth in the summer camp crafts room.

"I hear you. He's always been kind of weird, different, but I never would have thought he'd be like this. I can fix it up for you to come here for a week, maybe more. We lost one counselor already and could use the help. I think Mr. B, our head counselor, would go for it."

"I'd do it in a minute if the band didn't have gigs set up all summer. I have to be here. We're practicing three times a week. That's the one good thing going for me right now."

"How bad is the cyber-bullying?"

"I don't even go on the internet, don't even read my Facebook page or even Twitter. If I didn't have the guys in the band, I'd have no friends left. All the publicity about what Dad—damn, I hate even calling him that— what he did makes it impossible to go anywhere. There are reporters at every gig we have.

"That guarantees us an audience, but even Harry, my eternally-present bodyguard, thinks it stinks. How's your tail doing? Boring him to death with accounting and sports facts? I drown Harry in music and art and even got him dancing once.

"Geez, Alex, when is this going to let up? What if this is still going on when school starts again? How will I get through my senior year with a bodyguard dragging at my heels and everyone thinking I'm some drug lord? Will it ever be any fun again? How come Mom isn't coming home yet?"

Alex knew the answer he wouldn't give to his brother right now. Mom was also screwing a man, Ramon Aguilar. Well, maybe screwing wasn't the right term for that relationship. Ramon was pretty much in love with her. AJ had told him it looked like a pretty deep relationship, but still...

"Look, Cory. You have to call her and let her know about the bullying and the paparazzi. Maybe she's ready to come home now. Her arm must be healed from the shooting. I talked to Jake and Jim Bradley just before I called you and their dad said he's going to call her because she has to do something about all the investments like, well, yesterday. Mrs. Bradley said she's needed for consulting about C & C Decorating too.

"You call and then I'll call," Alex said after a brief pause. "I'll tell her I need her to help me get ready to go to Belize. Just tell Liam to f... off. They'll be back in their own home soon and he can't creep around our house then.

"Listen! You can always go stay with Marthe to get away. She loves Harry, your guard dog. Too bad he isn't a real dog. He'd be more fun I bet. Dancing, huh. That must have been great. I wish I could get mine to loosen up. He's gonna die young of hypertension if he stays on alert like he is now."

There was a short pause and the sound of derision in the background.

"Pete just flipped me the finger. Look, I gotta go. Call Mom. Go get Marthe to feed you both and stay there overnight. Schedule extra practices with the band. I'll call again tomorrow after I get hold of Mom."

Liam sat up and glued his ear to the door.

"He's off the phone. He's quiet now. I wonder who the other boy was he was talking to. I could rip that boy's little balls off!"

When Cory finally unlocked and yanked open the door, Liam was gone. Cory sighed with relief, ran down to his room, called Marthe, brought Harry up to date, and they packed bags for three days and left.

Liam, watching from behind the door to his mother's bedroom, crumpled to the floor.

"He hates me," he whispered to himself.

The tears came as he stood up and ran into Cory's room and threw himself on Cory's bed, his pocketknife in hand, stabbing at the pillow.

# Mexico

## Two

I'm nervous. Tension is growing. Some threat hangs in the air.

It was just after lunch today when Jorge Aguilar burst in. He began pacing the length of my living room like a jaguar, a fierce and determined pacing, his handsome brown face reddened by his anger and frustration.

"They were in the swamp."

He spoke in Spanish. Another indication he was angry. When he was being courteous to me, he used English. Now his anger spilled into his staccato words.

"They have found a way in around los cocodrilos that wait there. Julio saw and heard them. Why they did not come all the way from the sea to the house I do not know. Perhaps they were not equipped to scale the steep side of the hill. It is just like a cliff. They were there and they are not our friends."

"We could not pursue them?"

Ramon's question hung in the air, sounding almost like an accusation, an unstated criticism of his brother's security precautions.

Jorge turned on him, eyes steely, giving off dark sparks.

"Do you think I have not done enough? Could you do more? What would you do? What is to be done? We are not enough yet and our men are frightened. They believe the cartel will kill their families like they did to Arturo and Simon. Why do not you join us? Why do you hold back?"

He turned his glare on me and then quickly turned his head away.

I know why he is so angry with me. Our relationship is keeping Ramon from participation in defending their people. Jorge has formed a group to fight the cartels. He wants Ramon to join them.

I wanted to speak but could think of nothing to ease the situation. I knew if word of their secret group got out, there would be even more violence from the cartels. They would also become targets of the local police, perhaps even of the Federales, of the many officials who have been bought by the cartels. I am terrified at that prospect. We hear news of killings every day now, of cartels burning people to death, of a cartel that uses tanks, even of cartel members who have turned to a form of religiosity complete with ceremonies. Horror does not even describe it.

Ramon looked at me, his eyes worried, sad and loving all at the same time. We can never look at each other now and be separate. We are always one. I've never known anything like this. My heart and body are in strange territory. When I walk, he walks: when he moves, I move. When he thinks, I hear it. When I feel, his feelings are there too.

"Were there any other signs of intrusion? What about in the gardens or out on the road leading here?" Ramon asked.

"I sent men north and south and had the rest of the grounds searched. Nothing so far. No signs. But if they can get through that swamp, they can breach here at any time with the right equipment."

He swallowed, looking reluctant but still determined.

"It must be said. She brings us into even greater danger."

He was unable to look at me as he said this.

Ramon became very still. His fists were clenched, knuckles pale white against his brown hands. I could feel

9

the effort he made to control the anger that piled up inside. He took several deep breaths as the room filled with even more tension.

I found my voice.

"Stop, both of you! You must not argue, not over me, not over any of this. You have to be united or your family will suffer terribly. This is not the first intrusion they have made here."

Both men looked at me, Ramon surprised, Jorge defensive.

I spoke with hesitation, unsure of the Spanish words and then, trying to make myself understood, switched to English.

"I think someone has come in when we were gone. I have sensed it, a darkness, a change in the feeling in the house. Jorge, even with the guards you have set, someone has been here. They wait until Adelina and I go to Puerto Juarez, or to the hacienda, until Ramon is at work, and when you are not here to supervise."

Jorge looked skeptical and began to protest.

I interrupted him.

"No, wait! Not at first did I feel this. Not for most of this month. It was last week that I sensed something wrong. When Adelina and I got back from the school three days ago I felt it again. I thought it was my imagination but just now, hearing what you discovered, I don't think so."

I turned to Ramon.

"You know my sensitivity to color. The colors in the house changed when it happened. They became," I searched for a word to describe what I had seen, "dirtier, a dirty gray film hung over everything here in the downstairs and in my office upstairs too. I saw it."

"Why did you not say anything to me?" Jorge said, his voice an accusation.

"Because I came in tired and sometimes the same thing happens when I'm tired. I can't control it. It just happens. Those times, I could not have told you if it was from inside me or from outside, but now—now I think it was not inside me."

My housekeeper, Adelina, had been in the kitchen. I felt her come in. I don't have to turn to know she is in a room. She wears her long black hair pulled severely into a bun at the back of her neck. In contrast, she wears the colorful skirt and blouse of Mayan women. She is so short, so tiny, yet her energy flows into the air around us with a subtle but powerful force. Her energy announces her presence.

When she speaks, it is with firm authority. Now she supported me.

"She is speaking truth. That day we were both very tired. We had long meetings to interview teachers for the school, and many decisions to make. We had to buy food supplies and then wait for evening when Ramon was free from the tour he was guiding. The time was after ten when we got here. There was a change. I felt it too."

"It is also a reality that some of the men you leave here to guard this place are not loyal, not committed to this cause. They are afraid. They leave if you are not here, or they do not watch carefully and become careless. Anyone can get in."

Adelina motioned for us all to sit down with firm authority. I know by now that means she has something she will say that none of us want to hear.

Melissa, my bodyguard, paced back and forth along the wall of windows, her eyes continually scanning the landscape outside. Ramon and I sat close to each other on the long couch. Jorge paced briefly and then sat on one of the straight chairs.

I knew what was coming. Adelina didn't hold back and I realized suddenly that it's because she has an urgent sense that we must now act.

"Anna, you are healed. You must go home."

Ramon looked shocked and I knew he wanted to protest but I stopped him. I put my hand on his arm.

"Mi amor," I said in Spanish, "she is right. I must go. We have known this must come and it is time."

I tried to say those words lightly but I couldn't. I will have to tear myself away from him. It will feel like I'm tearing myself in half.

Ramon's face melted into anguish. I know the source of that pain. Again, a woman he loves will be torn from him. His wife, hopelessly mentally deranged, can give him no love, no companionship, no passion. Now I, too, must leave him.

I've pushed this moment away all the time I've been here, reveling in our love-making, drowning in it, giving myself to him in ways I never believed possible a woman could give to a man or man to woman, for I have gotten as much as I gave.

I took a deep breath and set out all I knew.

"I've ignored for the last week the growing knowledge that my own children, even though nearly adult, are in trouble they can't handle. I can feel it. Cory is scared, angry and hurting, Alex worried, Marnie withdrawn again, and AJ has thrown himself into his medical work and wants, with great impatience, to begin to set up his clinic.

"My accountant and friend, Robinson Bradley, concerned about my inattention to all the money I inherited, has left several phone messages which I have ignored. Caroline, his wife and my so-very-close friend, wants me to pay attention to our home renewal and decorating business.

"Caitlin Fitzgerald, my childhood friend, called earlier this month and is worried sick about Liam, her son, who was sexually abused by the man who was part of the group up north, the group which was, and is, dealing drugs.

"In addition, there is still the trial of that man, who also tried to murder me. I will have to be there to testify at that trial."

I looked at them all.

"I've known, we've all known, that the time must come when I have to leave. I don't believe I'm the only cause of the intrusion into this house, but I may be part of that. Ramon, you and Jorge have opposed members of at least one cartel and you may be the targets, but you will never know if they are after you or me until I leave."

Adelina nodded in agreement again. She and I have grown closer and I discovered there is far more to her than I had imagined. She is much more than my housekeeper and eldest cousin to Ramon and Jorge. She has an ancient wisdom and almost supernatural knowledge of what is to happen, or should happen, or...I don't know what "or".

I returned a nod to her, just a very slight inclination of my head. She slowly blinked, her sign she saw it.

"The sense of my children needing me is almost overwhelming, especially Cory's need. He won't admit how scared he is, even to himself. I must go. I've asked Melissa to book us a flight from Cancun to leave in three or four days."

I saw Melissa nod vigorously.

"She feels I would be safer back in Wisconsin. She knows that territory better, feels more competent there, knows we can rely on police there. Here, we just can't know who owns the police or any government officials."

Ramon sat with his head in his hands. Jorge looked away, but I saw his face. The longing on his face was as strong as that on Ramon's.

That's the other reason I have to go. Very early this morning, when the light was breaking over the house, when Ramon and I had finished making love on the roof which looks out over the garden and down to the far sea, I stood at the railing which edges that outdoor room. In the soft dawn light, I saw the bright red shirt Jorge is wearing now, saw him standing on the far raised platform a hundred yards away overlooking the swamp, half-bent over. I saw the passionate colors whirling around him and I felt his deep hunger to be inside me, as his brother had just done.

I've made up my mind. I will not come between these brothers. I'll return to my northern coolness where maybe, just maybe, the passion I can scarcely control here will ease, where I can think straighter and with more rationality than I can in this hot sensuous climate and this erotic house that Conrad left to me, this house where he must have met his own lovers.

But not tonight. Tonight, one more time, I know I'll dissolve into the fierce love and passion that binds me to Ramon.

# *Three*

As if to emphasize Adelina's decree and my decision, more phone calls came all next day.

Alex was insistent.

"Mom, you've got to come home. It's getting bad. The cyber-bullying is fierce for me and Cory. I got us new pre-paid cell phones and different numbers and that's ok so far. Harry and Pete had us take down our Facebook pages today and I think someone has even tried to hack into our computers. Pete's running checks on that. It's from all the publicity about what my late father did."

I could hear anger and cynicism in his voice as he spoke of Art, and felt my own anger rise again, anger I keep telling myself is long gone. It's not. It simmers just under the surface of everything I do. With each new stress, I become more resentful of Art's cruel betrayal, of his lies.

"Are you well enough, Mom? Can you come, please?"

"I am. No more nightmares and all wounds healed. Will you be safe there at camp? Are you being harassed there? How do the camp leaders feel?"

"It's ok. No one has gotten to me here and I haven't even told the camp director. Pete fits right in. He's really good with the kids and they think he's just another counselor. No one knows. The camp director jus thinks I've got this really weird parent who is overprotective of her son. He's happy for the help as long as we both do the jobs he assigns.

"But Cory's not so lucky. He's going to call you today. He and Harry left the house last night and are staying with Marthe. He won't go back until Liam's gone.

"And holy crap! That's a whole other thing. Can you talk to Mrs. F? When will you be coming?"

"Adelina and I have the school just about set up and she can take over. I've a flight out of Cancun in three days. Melissa will be going to set up security there. I need to get all the art out of the house first and have it hidden. We're already crating it up and it will be gone in two days. Not to alarm you, but someone has been in this house when we're gone, in spite of the security."

Alex made sounds of worry but I reassured him.

"We're fine. Jorge has extra men on guard. I'll call Cait today."

I took down the boys' new phone numbers, programmed my cell phone and dialed Cory.

"Mom, I was going to call you. I'm at Marthe's and I'm staying here. I want to tell you about Liam but not over the phone. Mom, he's become really creepy. I don't know how to deal with him."

"You're right. Don't discuss it here. Wait for me to get home. Right now, I'm much more concerned about the bullying and the attempted hacking. Where is your bodyguard?"

"He's here and he's on it. His firm is setting up monitoring of all our computers. So that'll be taken care of. Our band has a gig in Oshkosh and the press follows us a bit but it's not too bad. The guys think the extra attention is cool and they amp it up a lot and I have to tone them down at times but, so far, that's not too bad either.

"Mom, I'm worried about returning to school. The band has my back but some of my classmates are coming out to our gigs and getting nasty, shouting about us selling drugs, and stuff like that. Detective Klarkowski has them watched when we're in Green Bay, and there's security, but it's embarrassing. What if this happens in school?"

"Cory, don't do what ifs. We'll deal with that when I get there. Meet me at the airport in three days. In the meantime, be safe. Tell Marthe thanks for taking care of you."

I gave him my arrival time and flight number.

"I'll call Cait right now."

I didn't have to call her. I took a break to go to the bathroom and she called as I was coming back. She was extremely upset and I just let her vent it out.

"Annie, I need you here. I got a problem I really don't know how to handle, and you know I can handle most anything. It's Liam. He's not any better for counseling. He's worse. I never thought I'd see the day when my own kid creeped me out but he does. He is absolutely obsessed with Cory, follows him around, sneaks up on him when told to stop, and it's sexual.

"I'm embarrassed even telling you this but I just gotta do something and I don't know what. He's fourteen now and he has the right to confidentiality so I can't even find out what his counselor is or isn't doing or if he's doing anything. All the guy says is that he thinks Liam's making progress. This is not progress.

"Yesterday Cory left. I'm so sorry. I don't want your kid chased out of his own home. We're just days from moving back into our house. It's almost done and is great and I'll be so glad to be there, but that won't make Liam's obsession go away. Every time I see him I get so damn mad at Clayton Foster I can hardly see straight and knowing that asshole is still on a bracelet and not even in prison yet just pisses me off."

She took a deep breath and blew it out.

"Then there's the business. We need to meet. We're at the next phase for expansion and we need your input. Caroline is her usual unflappable self but you can tell I'm not."

She paused for another longer breath and I broke in.

"I got a call from Cory. I know about Liam. I'll be home in three days. Don't move out of there until then. I want someone there at all times. Please, Cait, I mean it.

Alex and Cory are being cyber-bullied, and the band is getting heckled about drug pushing by a few of Cory's classmates. I need you there in case they need a fortress to live in. Marthe shouldn't have to deal with this at her age.

"Here's what you can do for me right now. One, thank Greg for his help with security for the band. Two, I'm very aware we need to start arranging for the buying trip to Ireland in August. Can you call a travel agency and get them on it? Three, tell Caroline to tell Rob to set up a meeting on finances for next week and a trip to the bank in Switzerland for me right after the Ireland trip. Does that help you a bit?"

"Oh, yeah! Whew! Sorry. I didn't even ask how you are. Still having a great time in the sack, I hope."

"To echo your phrase, oh, yeah. I really hate to leave but it's time. I'll tell you more when I get there. Just so you know, there's some threat here too. We don't know if it's aimed at me or the Aguilars or both and we'll never know if I don't leave. I'm fine. No nightmares. No aches and pains. Cory will meet me at the airport."

"Great. I'm going to try having a talk with Liam but he's become secretive and I'm damn worried. Greg just walked in and he wants to talk with you. I'm done, so here he is."

"Hi, Anna. Glad you're coming home. When?"

I told him. He continued.

"We're still deep in our investigation of this murder-drug thing. I want to bring you up to date. You remember Foster said there was a group involved in running this and someone would take over leadership if the current leader was taken out? Well, he has, or she has, depending on who took over. We still have no trace of Ardith, which is very weird and frustrating. Of course, we have her fingerprints from their office but she's not in any system. How can anyone just disappear like that? We can't even follow her money. She apparently cashed in everything immediately and that's it. $750,000 and no

18

trace. How can that happen? That's a rhetorical question."

"I can't imagine, Greg. I would have thought cashing that amount of money must take time and leave a big trail. Is she even the one? When Clayton Foster was gloating and bragging to me, he said it was other men."

"We just don't know. We do know there are more drugs on the street again. In case she might be the one who took over, I need you here to go over every memory you have of her, any interaction with her all the years you knew her. More picking your brain apart again, I'm afraid, but we need to do it.

"One more thing. Anna, I strongly recommend more security around Cory and his band. At least two on each boy for the band's gigs. Alex and Marthe too, and Cait and her boys. It's important you take no chances. Not to wish anyone harm but I'm almost hoping something does happen and we catch them. Maybe it will give us leads we aren't getting now."

Pictures of Ardith Seacrest ran through my mind as I replied to him.

"I can't think what more I'd know about Ardith you don't already know. I have been thinking about her though. One thing strikes me and that is, as Conrad Wentworth's executive secretary, she was in the perfect position for a very long time to build her own control over a lot of people and to know a lot of people's secrets. She certainly had opportunity, and means, too, but what her motives would be I can't imagine. She is definitely very smart.

"I'll call my security firm and authorize more help and make sure they give you full cooperation. I also know there are police who do off-duty security. If you need to go that way, do it. I'll make sure there's money available. Give Cait a hug for me and I'll see you soon."

Rob called with tentative meeting dates. Marthe called concerned about Cory. AJ called concerned about plans for the clinic. Caroline called concerned about me, just me. That was refreshing.

Aunt Carrie called from Chicago, thoroughly disgusted with Marnie.

"Your daughter won't listen to me anymore at all. She's become an arrogant brat. Modeling has gone to her head. I don't think she's using drugs or alcohol. I haven't seen it but then I don't go out with her to clubs and she sure does go to clubs. A lot. Mostly with other young girls as far as I can tell. I'm too old for this, Anna. I'll stick with her through Paris fashion week but I can't do more than that."

"That's more than I ever thought you should do, Carrie. She's a grownup. It sounds like she's sliding back into her addiction. I know that's painful to watch but if she's messing up her life, she'll have to face her own consequences and we can't rescue her. I'll make a try at reaching her when we get to Paris. If I can't, well, then, we'll both just have to let go. An Alanon motto—let go and let god."

"Carrie, I want you to come with me to Switzerland. I need some coaching in being rich. I haven't the faintest idea how to move in those circles and you at least have some experience. Want to come?"

"Oh, I'd love that! I want to see that chalet on Lake Como in Italy. I'm taking you shopping in Paris too."

"Italy? Lake Como's in Italy? I never even thought of that, or even looked it up. Oh dear! I have so much to learn. I'd better call the travel agency for us instead of having Cait do it. If I don't do anything else, I want to find out more about Conrad's life there. It's my greatest regret that I didn't do that while he was alive."

"You didn't know Lake Como's in Italy? Oh, dear god! You must take me. You are so unsophisticated. And yes, I bet there's a very fascinating story to be found behind that oh-so-cool exterior Conrad always used."

Carrie sounded almost as if she was purring. I could just picture her patting her perfectly arranged white hair and plotting out a French-Swiss-Italian sweep through Europe. I'll have to put her in restraints to keep her from running amok.

As I finished that call, Ramon entered my office, which I had created out of one of the upstairs bedrooms.

"So we have two nights left together."

He barely whispered that as he faced out the window that overlooked the north side of the garden. In four days at most, I would be thousands of miles north in a land he could not even picture, that he had never seen.

I rose and walked behind him and put my arms around him.

"No, what we have will be for all our lives. I could not ever forget this love we have, never forget what it is like to live inside you and have you live inside me. I have seen people who love each other deeply but I have never seen any couple who even appear to have this. Maybe there are such lovers, but..."

He turned and put his arms around me too.

"Es verdad. Es verdad. Our love is a very great love. We cannot be separated. Come. We will waste no time."

We went to the room of mirrors and undressed each other, and sank into each other's ecstasy again and again.

# Four

...two days later...

This afternoon the last of the artwork was taken away. The sculptures, the paintings, the Chihuly chandelier, anything of value loaded into armored trucks which sped them to a Mexico City vault recommended by Sothebys.

Adelina remained with us when Tomasita drove off to their family hacienda with the rest of the food. All that remained was our supper, a light one, and tomorrow's breakfast.

I wandered through the house, an empty shell now, tossed up here by invisible turbulence, stranded on this high hill, the sea far away across the vast swamp.

Jorge has been out at the edge of the cliff leading down into the swamp. He had his men setting some sort of traps but he said he didn't really expect any more problems. He makes it clear he believes I am the one who is attracting unwanted attention. We've seen nothing. I've felt no dirty energy disturbing this place again.

*Even with all his checking he's nervous. Why is he so tense? Does he know more than he's telling us?*

Instead of going to Cancun to work, Ramon remained with me today, our last together.

Now there's nothing left to do. I'm near exhaustion, already grieving the losses here, and on the edge of tears because I'm feeling Ramon's grief too.

Adelina sent them to check the whole estate again. I raised one eyebrow. She was getting rid of them.

"Señora Anna, we must talk."

She sat herself down in the straight-backed chair in her office, in her most dignified four foot, eleven inch upright posture. I slumped into a small cushioned chair near her window.

That was when I got some inkling of who and what she really is. I will not write of all she revealed to me but she is quite definite about who she believes I am. It's a measure of my immersion into the exotic atmosphere of Mexico and this house that I even listened to her strange tale.

She believes I am a woman chosen to be the representative of La Diosa in this existence and in this reality.

"From time beyond any memory there have been women who the goddess chose to enter, to become human for a brief time, women who are given a special task to carry out, a special role to play. You are one of them. This is not a Mayan belief although we have our goddesses, and in our history I have heard tales of one woman who seemed to have her power. That was long ago, and the place where she lived was far to the south of here.

"No. I speak of a time when the female was the one who moved all, before the time of male dominance. I have met many priests of the Catholic Church, and priests of the Maya and Aztec and from other tribes. Few of them know of this. Of those who do, most have tried to destroy knowledge of Her. Or they create Her in their image of what they think a goddess should be. They destroyed the truth when they did this. They are still destroying the truth."

She paused. Her voice held hints of both anger and sadness.

"Someone is trying to destroy you also. Perhaps it is just the drug cartel seeking revenge for whatever it was your husband did or did not do but I do not think so."

She became silent, with a far look in her eyes as if she was seeing another time and place. Before she spoke again, she lit copal in an abalone shell, sending the sweet smell around the room with a fan made of bright macaw

23

feathers which she drew from a drawer. Then she continued.

"Now we name her La Madre, La Patrocinadora. However, she has had many names.

"You have told me that even as a little girl you wanted nothing more than to be mother. Mothering is part of you, deep within you. Not all women have such intense desire to mother as you do. That is one of the signs. There are others—the loss of your husband, the suffering, most especially the attacks on you by men who resent your power. A woman chosen for this often suffers much.

"Ramon is the man who the god enters when you make love. It is why you have become so very close. He was chosen even as a child, perhaps even before his birth. We, the women who know, we saw this. Because they bonded so young and so easily, I thought his wife was the one to be with him. But I deceived myself, wanting it to go so smoothly. It did not. I believe her mind was not strong enough to take in the goddess without breaking. Her spirit is full of holes. It is a great tragedy."

She grew silent again for some time, remembering. I waited. Finally she resumed her story.

"There is more you must know but I will not tell you now. You have duties, as do all women who have children. You must fulfill those duties. You have powerful enemies also. Enemies still, from the time of your husband, and enemies because Señor Wentworth loved you. You must face them."

As she was telling me all this, I felt myself pulled into another place and time, standing with a large group of women, feeling myself existing in a mysterious world. But even as this happened, highly skeptical thoughts ran through my everyday brain. Caught between, I couldn't even ask the questions hurling through my mind. She read that in my eyes.

"Do not ask those questions now. You will be back. You will find answers then. For now, you will spend this night with Ramon. I will come for you when it is time to leave."

She rose out of her chair and, for an instant, she seemed to grow very tall, but then the moment passed and she was her usual tiny self.

She grinned, raising her eyebrows in a sassy leer.

"I think you will need much of my salve tonight. I have left it in the cupboard on the roof."

She began to leave, then turned back, her face again serious.

"You must know one more thing. There is another man who is also partner to the goddess. He is aware of you. Do you feel him?"

I stood for long moments, looking at her. The astonishing knowledge edged its way into my mind slowly. I nodded.

"Jorge."

"Sí. The spirits of Jorge and Ramon are like twins, very close. He and Ramon are bonded in this. He feels everything Ramon feels. Everything."

"But, what should I...?"

She was gone.

## *United States*

### *Five*

...journal...four days later...Missouri...

Four days! Four days it has taken to get me out of that country. Four crazy, frightening days! Finally I have some safety. Extracting me from Mexico has been like prying me from the locked jaws of some huge animal. I'm so very relieved to be here in this nondescript motel outside of down-to-earth Hannibal, Missouri.

On the day of my departure, Adelina woke us before the light came. We showered and dressed quickly, eating breakfast in the car on the way. Melissa called the night before from Cancun.

"You don't have to worry about a thing. Everything's secure. Now listen. Your reservations are under the name of Katherine O'Neill. Just go to the airline desk and say that she left your ticket for you. Only then will you have to identify yourself, so there's no chance anyone can look at the passenger list and see your name before that. OK? Got it?"

"Yes. No problem."

"I'll join you there."

Jorge left two men to guard the grounds but for all intents and purposes, the house is now closed. Driving south to Cancun we were silent except for some last minute business about the school. My mind was filled with thoughts about that beautiful home, these dear people and what they now mean to me. Loss and more loss. Will I ever be able to return?

Jorge chose to drive. Because of what we did last night, he would not look at me and kept his face a mask. Adelina watched him at first with raised eyebrows, then shook her head slightly and ignored him. Ramon kept his arms around me the whole way.

I hugged Adelina when we dropped her off at the school in Puerto Juarez.

"Thank you so much for your help with la escuela, mi amiga," I said. "I know it is in good hands now. Please call if you need anything more from me. I promise you will have it."

"It is I who should thank you. This is a dream of mine, that these children will have a school, and now it will come true. Please know that I will report everything to you."

Her eyes shifted quickly to the two men and then back.

"Everything."

She smiled and backed away.


I was due to leave on an international flight at 11:48a.m. It never happened. As we were parking, before we even got into the airport, we were surrounded by seven police officers and herded into a small room.

"Señora Kinnealy, Señores Aguilar, we have a serious problem. There has been a bomb threat against the flight the Señora is on.

"Señora, we must ask that you remain here. We believe this is related to you."

"When did this happen? When was the threat made?" I asked. "I have told no one I would be on the flight. I'm not even on the passenger list. How could anyone know I would be on it? No es posible. I had my personal assistant make the arrangements and they are not in my name. Where is she? She was to meet me here. Her name is Melissa."

"We know of no one by that name, Señora. We only know there is a bomb threat and your name is connected with the threat. The caller mentioned you specifically."

"So it was a phone call? Who got it? I received no threats."

I was not about to tell them of the prowlers at the house. I did not want the police crawling all over the house up north. The local police up there cannot be trusted. I can't begin to know who owns them, whether of not they are honest or have sold out to a cartel. I didn't trust these men either.

"Señora, we must act to prevent any destruction. The plane is detained until it can be thoroughly examined. There is a bomb squad on the way. You will please wait in the first class lounge. It has been cleared for your safety."

The lead officer turned to Ramon and Jorge.

"I am sorry, Señores , but you may not accompany her. We will keep her safe. You must leave the airport."

All arguments advanced by Ramon and Jorge were turned aside. I had one last look at both of them, seeing their fear for my safety and their indignation, as I was firmly escorted away to the lounge. It was completely empty except for two guards. My luggage was brought there ten minutes later.

Six interminable hours passed before anyone came. I paced. I sat. I tried to get the guards to tell me more or go for someone who could. Nothing. I went through rounds of fear, anger, and useless speculation as to who could be doing this. In anger and totally impotent frustration. I once tried to walk out the door. A guard grabbed me and sat me down and said only one word. "No!" At the end of the day, I was almost numb with exhaustion.

Finally, someone came in, an old man, in a shoddy blue suit, with a long gray and white beard. He looked me up and down and laughed, cackled actually.

"You will be flown out now."

He grabbed my elbow, and propelled me as fast as he could down corridors, a vise-like grip on my arm. Four police followed us. The place was empty. There was no one I could even ask for help.

At the farthest end of a long hall, he ejected me through a metal door and steered me across asphalt to a small propeller-driven plane far from any international flight gate. If we'd been any farther from the main building we'd have been in the jungle. The old man, about my height, seemed very spry and strong for his age. With grim determination on his face he shoved me into the plane.

"Fasten your seat belt," he ordered, shouting over the noise of the plane's engine, his voice grating close to my ear.

I shook with a terrible fear. My luggage was thrown in after me. The door was slammed shut. Two men sat in the pilot seats. No one else was on board. They did not turn around and said nothing to me. We took off into early evening and I could see the land slip by below, all solid jungle.

I was so frightened. I tried to stop shaking. I never succeeded. I believed I was being kidnapped. I cried silently, just letting the tears roll down my face. Agonies of time passed. My thoughts beat my brain to a pulp with if onlys and what ifs. *Why didn't I scream when I had the chance? Would anyone have heard me? What would the police have done to me if I did scream? I should have...I could have...I wish I had...* It was endless.

I thought of my mother, my dear Momkat, in an assisted living facility with Alzheimer's and felt relief she would never know what happened to me. I thought of my children and cried more.

I felt as if I had somehow failed Cait and Caroline and Marthe. Everyone.

An interminable time later we set down again in darkness. I could see, in the distance, signs of a very busy airport. Lights of a city glowed far off.

I had to go to the bathroom urgently and was extremely uncomfortable and hungry. We came to a stop and the door was jerked open.

I was so shocked. There stood Kevin MacPherson.

I burst into tears, slid to the floor of the plane, sobbing, and wet my pants.

# Six

"Why, Mac?" It was all I could gasp. "Why?"

"Anna, I'm so sorry."

He grabbed my arms and held me up.

"I couldn't explain then and I still can't. I'm sorry for all the discomfort, for all the fear and pain, but I had to get you out of Cancun and we have to leave here right now. These guys are safe. They work with me, but there are those who don't and I don't know who they are. I'm suspicious of nearly everyone and in this darkness we can't see them coming.

"Here." As the two pilots left, he opened my luggage, took out clean clothing for me and shoved it into my hands.

"Change right here. You'll be able to shower later. I've got a car waiting. Come on, do it! Fast!"

He turned his back but kept on talking. My entire body was trembling almost uncontrollably. I dropped the clothes.

"Mac, I can't stop shaking."

He turned around, grabbed my shoulders, leaned me against the plane and ordered, "Breathe! Deep breath...hold it in...now let it out slowly. Again. Five more times."

Slowly my shaking stopped.

"Ok, I've got control now. This is so embarrassing. This is terrible."

"Don't think about it. There's no time. Just change as fast as you can."

He turned his back as I pulled off my cotton slacks and underpants and got into the dry ones.

31

"We're at the edge of the Monterrey airport. I have us booked into a fancy hotel as a married couple on vacation under another name and I have passports for both of us. You are Jenna Wilson and I am your husband Tom. This is our private plane. We're on vacation. Don't let anyone get you in a conversation about what I do or about our family. I didn't have time to make up a long story. Let me do the talking. Play the sweet little wifey."

"Wifey! Wifey?" Irritation stopped my quaking, which had begun again.

"I know. You aren't. Just fake it.

"I'm ready."

I stuffed my wet underwear and slacks into an extra plastic bag from my suitcase, shoved my feet into my sandals and took off almost running as Mac grabbed my bags and began walking at top speed. He kept right on talking.

"Now listen. Monterrey is not totally cartel territory but it's getting there. Police here are pretty honest. Maybe. There's a cartel trying to bully its way into this place and there have been some bad incidents. I think we can get you out of here and into the states but I don't have all the arrangements finished yet."

As he spoke he hurried me into a Range Rover. We left quickly. He drove out of the airport and through streets that were, at first, lighted mostly by a full moon. The lights of the city grew more numerous as we neared its center. I watched people going about their oh-so-normal lives and envied them. I thought of Cory, waiting for me at an airport and me not arriving.

*He'll be frantic. I know it.*

"Mac, what's going on? I'm not involved in any cartel. I'm no threat to anyone. Where is Melissa? She called and said all was secure. Why is this happening?"

"Melissa is the one who got word to me. She was nearly killed in Cancun when someone tried to take the briefcase she was carrying. She flattened him, then called her supervisor who called someone I know who called me. Pure luck, actually, that I was there.

"I couldn't tell you anything. I didn't dare show up as me. I can trust only some of the police there. They weren't the ones on duty when I came in. I had to wait for the second shift so I could get you out. I was the man in the beard. Great disguise, isn't it? I flew out on another plane to preserve my anonymity, to make sure no one made a connection. I'm in the middle of a sting operation and I can't risk it."

"Anna, I'm sorry!" he said as he heard me catch my breath in anger. "I didn't mean to scare you so. I couldn't explain. I had another matter to see to and then my own ride to catch so I could be here. I couldn't be seen there as me.

"I don't know why anyone is after you but there are two possibilities. Either someone has it in for you personally, or someone is thinking you're helping Ramon and Jorge. My best guess is that what you told law enforcement agencies up north ruined someone's very lucrative income and he's pissed as hell and has vowed to get you for it. What you revealed to police up north became very public. That makes you his target. Believe me, revenge is hard-core religion with these guys."

"Cory must be waiting for me at the airport now. He'll be terrified when I don't show up."

"No, he won't. I sent them a message, from you, of course, that you'd be delayed three days. At least, I hope it will be only three."

We pulled up at a huge luxury hotel. I was clearly not dressed for it and said so.

"Yes, you are. We've been 'out in the jungle'. Watch and learn. This is another lesson in survival, just a different setting where we have to act like the natives. In this hotel the 'natives' are wealthy tourists."

He jumped out of the Rover, grinned a big smile at the valet, thumped him on the shoulder and slipped him the car key and a bill which the valet quickly evaluated, grinning at Mac in return.

Mac began a loud patter about our time out "roughing it" and how "the wife" wanted a "fancy place now" so she could get into a hot tub and get a great massage. He gave a wink-wink and bill to a porter and our luggage was on the way to the front desk. Put off by his phony behavior, I succeeded only in looking sour and rumpled, which definitely added to the impression Mac wanted me to make. He got us registered in our room with more phony camaraderie and we were soon alone, after Mac had slipped another bill to yet another valet or porter or whatever they are called.

I looked around. I'd never been in a real luxury hotel. The décor was a decorator's idea of what a rich person's home should look like if it was to be featured in a high-end travel magazine. There was nothing really wrong with it except it was all beige. It had one piece of supposedly authentic artwork which was an abstract of blues, greens and a bit of red, the only color in the room. I don't know why some decorators love bland so much.

The bath was better. It was a luxurious pale orange-gold color, with gilded accents, and a huge tub with jets. I couldn't wait. I smelled like pee.

There was only one bedroom. I thought of all the sex I'd had this last month, of the two men whose sexual intensity had poured around and through me, and of Mac's declaration months ago when I was in the hospital that he'd like to marry me, and I just couldn't face myself or my own sexuality. Or his.

"Mac, I..."

"Anna, I'm sleeping on the couch. I know you're Ramon's lover. I'm OK with that. I would never pressure you into doing anything you don't want and I know one bedroom might seem like pressure but it's not. It was all I could get on short notice."

"Oh, thank you. You have no idea what a relief that is at the moment. I need to crash. This has been too much. Just let me take care of my needs, get my head on straight."

"Great idea! I'm going to find us some food. Any preference?"

"Edible. Just edible. I don't care."

I picked up my bags and headed for the bathroom, then stopped.

"Do you need to use this before I go in? I'll be a while."

"No. I'm going downstairs to check out this joint. I always want to have my escape routes planned. Don't answer the door."

He left.

I ran a tub and dissolved into it, trying to scrub the terror of the day away. I only partially succeeded.

I am mystified as to why anyone could want to harm me. Art's life was so long ago, so insignificant now to me. I have changed so much and lived so much more. Nearly eight years now since he was killed. Why would someone carry out revenge after so long? Maybe it really is because I deciphered the codes they used and gave them to police. I don't understand revenge. It's such an exhausting and stupid emotion.

I let myself sink under the water over and over, holding my breath each time for as long as possible.

Cleansing. It's cleansing. Adelina told me to use water like this for cleansing. She's right. It works.

## Seven

Mac returned with a wonderful Mexican feast. I ate with great enjoyment.

"I've never seen you eat like that. You were starved."

"Yes. I ate just after 5 a.m. this morning. Yesterday morning. It's long after midnight now."

"I'm sorry. I didn't know you had no food all day. It's fun to watch you eat with so much enthusiasm."

His eyes never left me. I thought he was hoping for some romantic mood. He was disappointed. I was not on that wavelength at all. I was having none of it.

"Where's Melissa? I sent her ahead so she could check it all out and we could get out of there easily."

"She's safe but she was wounded. Her outfit extracted her as soon as I got you out of police custody. She can take care of herself pretty well. She put the guy who assaulted her in the hospital.

"Don't worry! She'll be OK," he said when I looked upset. "Her wound was superficial."

"Good! I've grown to like her. I want her with me in Ireland, France and Switzerland. I've learned I have to go to Italy as well."

I told him about the chalet on Lake Como.

"Green Bay too, if I ever get there," I added.

"You'll get there but don't be surprised if your security firm sends someone else to guard you. Now listen up. We leave early tomorrow and I'll have you on a plane again from here to Dallas. Same guys. You'll be flying very low, under the radar until you get over the border. Then you'll have an escort to Dallas. You can easily catch a plane home from there."

"I hope so. How come you were in the area? Or can't you talk about it?"

"I can but I won't. I'm following drug trails from here to Canada for my government. That's all I want to say. It's a never-ending battle."

"I don't want to know then."

I was growing uneasy. I could feel Cory's distress growing and I wanted to call him and knew I couldn't. Mac noticed.

"What's wrong?"

"I can feel Cory's anxiety. It's always been that way between my children and me. I know when they're hurting. Things aren't going well for them at home. Cory and Alex have been the targets of abuse because of the publicity. I want to call him but I know it's safer if I don't, for him and for me."

"Can you sense when you yourself are in danger?"

"Sometimes. I know now that I sensed the danger from Clayton, but I ignored it for months. I truly thought he was my friend. I minimized my deeper feelings. Also, it felt strange, unfamiliar. I couldn't label it. When he finally came to the house and threatened me, he oozed out a part of him that was so distorted, so sick and malevolent that I couldn't help but feel it intensely. I'll certainly never forget that kind of sick threat again."

"So you can't make it happen, or control it?"

"No. Except I always know if my children are in trouble."

"I bet they didn't always love that."

I laughed.

"No. They didn't. Still don't. I always know where they are, what they're doing. Well, almost always. I'm losing touch with Marnie. She's withdrawn from me. She started drinking and AJ got her into treatment and as far as I know, she's now sober, but there's a barrier. I don't really know why. She won't talk to me about any of it. I think she blames me for her father's betrayal somehow. She was always her father's girl and really looked up to

37

him. I'm not sure she believes, even with all the evidence, that he was involved in drug trafficking."

Mac got up and began cleaning up the leftovers. I could sense more than my children's moods. I knew he wanted to make love with me. I couldn't. Ramon was still inside me.

I got up, collected my things and turned toward the bedroom.

"Anna."

"I can't, Mac. I just can't."

"You know I hope for some day."

"I know."

# Eight

We left early and quietly, driving back the way we came to the same plane.

On route he gave me instructions.

"Get your intuition in high gear today. I hope your senses are very acute. There's Plan A and Plan B. Plan A is—you land at Dallas, go to a domestic flight desk, get a flight to Green Bay and all is well.

"Plan B. If all does not go well or even seem well, you leave the Dallas airport by taxi, go to this Howard Johnson—here's the information you'll need," he handed me a card, "and you go to the last row in the west parking lot. There will be a Range Rover, dark blue, waiting for you. The key is on top of the left rear tire. Get in and drive out of there and go north on the fastest interstate you can find. There's a map in the car. Don't stop unless it's for gas and coffee. Check to be sure you're not followed when you leave Dallas but I'm pretty sure you'll be safe. If you don't think you're safe, at least you can trust U.S. police and get help. You can also drive to another big city and get a flight to Milwaukee or Chicago. From there I'm sure you can get home. How are you set for money?"

"Not much. I need to visit an ATM."

"No need. I've got some. I have a very liberal expense account. Don't, I repeat don't, use any ATMs. Your credit card can be traced."

"Mac, thank you so much. Will you let me know if the passengers on the plane left safely? If you find out?"

"Definitely. I'll be in touch. I want to connect with that detective from the Green Bay Police. What was his name? Krakowski.?"

39

"Klarkowski. I spoke to him just days ago. He said someone has reorganized the drug trade in northeast Wisconsin. Drug-related crime is already rising again. It could even be a woman."

I told him about Ardith.

His eyes narrowed. "Wow! That's way too fast for reorganization. Something was already in place. Damn! You be careful, Anna."

At the plane, he strapped me in and leaned over and kissed me on my cheek.

"I'll see you as soon as I can. What you told me worries me. It's too easy to use the Green Bay corridor to move drugs up to Canada. I have to check it out, set up more contacts there. When do you leave for Ireland?"

"The third week in August I hope. Arrangements aren't final yet."

We flew out of Monterrey and did fly, literally, under the radar into the United States. I felt like I was contraband goods being smuggled in, except that we had a DEA plane escort as soon as we hit the border. They checked my passport in Dallas and escorted me to the domestic flights area and left me on my own.

All did not go well.

My uneasiness grew as I walked down the line of desks. Something was off. I don't know even now just what triggered it or why I felt so spooked. I made a spur of the moment decision to use Plan B, walked right out of the airport, got in a taxi and left.

At the Howard Johnson's I found the Range Rover, the key, the map, the route to the interstate north and got out of there, too.

I was passing through Oklahoma when I stopped for gas and coffee. An overhead TV was on in the C-store. There had been an explosion in the Dallas airport, the section which housed the domestic flight desks. American Airlines. They go direct to Milwaukee. I would have chosen them.

I kept driving north.

Now I'm at this cheap unremarkable motel in Hannibal. I'm tense, on guard but hope I can get some sleep.

I sent a telegram to Marthe which said only, "arriving by car stop two days stop".

I hope she and Cory understand.

I won't answer my cell phone, voice or texts.

For now, I'm determined to remain under the radar.

There is another reason I'm glad I'm gone from Mexico. I'm embarrassed to even write this but if I'm to be honest with myself, I have to face it.

I don't know what possesses me when I'm there. Maybe it really is La Diosa. I'm certainly not the same person in Mexico that I am in Green Bay. What is it that overcomes me?

I went there thinking I was normal. Then I succumbed to an intense passion I've never felt before with a man who is still married to a woman who doesn't even know him anymore and lives in yet another world, the world of madness.

In addition to my harrowing escape, I've beaten myself up for the last four days because in less than one month there, my sexuality went completely out of my control.

Ramon and I spent all those days and nights of this last month locked in such intense sensuality that I lost every inhibition and I didn't even care where or when we made love. So we made love one night on a dance floor, when all the patrons were gone, way beyond midnight. A friend of his played erotic rhumbas for us on the piano, watching us and matching his music to our passionate movements. As Ramon lifted my skirt and slid himself into me, I became the most wanton of women.

We made love in bright sunlight out on the ocean, naked on the boat deck, laughing at each other as we poured champagne on our bodies and licked it off.

On that last night with Ramon, I could feel both Jorge and Ramon inside me though it was Ramon between my legs. When I woke during the night I became aware that Jorge had been standing near us on the roof all along and his passion was unsatisfied, pouring over us, reaching out to me. Without even a thought, my desire for him rose to a fever pitch and before I could reign myself in, I took him inside me and satisfied him, and Ramon accepted that! I've begun to think we all have some kind of sex addiction. The strangest part is, I just could not make myself regret it. When I was there it felt so normal, as if it's what I'm supposed to be doing.

Now? Now I feel embarrassed and ashamed and certainly not the woman I've been all these past years. I think I went flat out crazy.

# Green Bay

## Nine

The near West side of Green Bay still bears the obvious vestiges of an earlier age. Two- and three-story brick buildings with old-time Western-style facades line Broadway, the main street that runs north to south along the river. The old Larsen Canning Company, a huge building, has become partly refurbished office space, and a whole lot of emptiness. There is talk of a Wal-Mart going in on that site.

The majority of the smaller buildings, while holding businesses and taverns on the lower floors, have no tenants on second and third floors. Numerous upper windows are grimy, blank dirty canvases reflecting only the lights of the streets, never lit from within. If, somehow, there are tenants on those second and third floors, a close study reveals, more often than not, threadbare curtains and a quick glimpse of poverty.

In the midst of efforts at urban renewal, Broadway and its side streets now hold an odd potpourri of shops: a vegetarian restaurant with a gourmet cheese counter, a bead shop, at least two banks, a head shop, a pet store, a violin repair shop, a furniture store, a decorators' upscale showroom, two micro-breweries, numerous taverns, and much, much more.

Surrounding Broadway are streets with a few warehouses, small old buildings, and the houses that were once filled with the Irish immigrant families, even a Scotsman or two, and perhaps a few from other ethnic persuasions as well. Now people of all colors and ethnic origins walk the streets—African-American, Hmong, Native-American, and Caucasian predominate.

Poverty still stalks those streets. Wealthy people have their McMansions in more picturesque, countrified, and carefully landscaped settings on the edges of the metropolitan area. Except for a few whose roots are on the West side, those in the middle-class also prefer to live elsewhere if they can manage it.

Behind one of the brick facades, next to a dirty second floor window, a tall slim gray-haired woman watched as people below scurried, strolled, wandered, or stood still waiting for whatever was to come into their lives. Elegantly dressed in black tailored slacks, a pale pink silk blouse, and expensive black patent heels, she looked as out of place as Queen Elizabeth in a tattoo parlor.

On her cell phone, her right foot impatiently tapping the dirty floor, she finished the arrangements with the owner to rent the building: a contract that would include a thorough industrial cleaning of the three floors and repair and refurbishment of the old freight elevator that still rattled its way up and down at the rear of the building, all to be done yesterday.

"Yes, the company I represent is Design Imports and we'll be using the third floor as offices, the second as storage, and the first floor will be our showroom. I'll fax you our requirements by the end of today."

She listened briefly, then keyed the phone off without any goodbye. Once more she scanned the dirty, littered floor where only a few days ago homeless men had sneaked in to take shelter. Stout locks on the doors would now keep them out. She shuddered at the thought of coming into contact with them and stepped carefully over it all as she left.

She had one more task to complete. She must be assured of the whereabouts of Anna Kinnealy.

Somehow Anna had eluded all attempts to monitor her departure from Mexico. The last sighting had been at the Cancun airport where Anna had been separated from her lover and his brother and taken into custody by police.

*They are police I do not control. I need more contacts in the police force there. I must form an alliance with El Cocodrilo. He has the connections I want.*

Patting a strand of silvery hair into place, she moved quickly from the rear of the building to a small gray sedan, an unremarkable car, chosen specifically because it would attract no attention, and, of course, rented under an assumed name. Before driving away, she was again on the phone.

"Have you sighted her? Who is watching and where are they?"

The report was as thorough as her contractor could make it. Anna had not been sighted.

"Son Cory and his bodyguard are at the Allouez home, as is the old woman. Son Alex is at camp one hundred miles north. He also has a bodyguard. Son AJ is still in Guatemala with Doctors without Borders. He is now with a nurse practitioner, his lover. Her name is Sheila. This is recent. I have no last name for her yet. I have inquiries out. They met the last time he went to Minnesota. Daughter Marnie is on a photo shoot in Chicago.

"Anna has not been seen. I have runners using the path along the river, and someone monitoring any cars that park in or near her house. I'm running license plates to find out who comes and goes. Anna's mother is under surveillance in the nursing home by a CNA whose pay we have enhanced substantially."

"Very well. Keep on. Inform me if there is any change, any change at all."

Hatred had long been the white-haired woman's drug of choice. A surge of it flooded through her system, giving her a quick thrill, then a slow ride ascending to the ecstasy she felt when she thought of what she could and would do to Anna, what she had wanted to do and suppressed for so long, what she had never wanted so fiercely as she did now. She prolonged the ecstasy as long as she could, loving the throbbing in her body, the triumph, the satiation it brought.

As her orgasm subsided, she turned her attention to her other main concern, her other love. Accessing her Cayman Islands business bank account on her phone, she noted with satisfaction that a substantial increase had been deposited with delivery of the last shipment to Montreal.

"Now to make that grow," she thought. She put the car into motion.

One hour later she left on the private plane waiting for her at the Appleton airport.

Many hours after that she arrived at one of her homes on an unnamed and remote island in the Caribbean, where she disrobed, discarded her white wig, shook out her long blonde hair and slipped into a waiting tub of water and another orgasm with a handsome brown male she had hired for the occasion.

# *Ten*

Greg Klarkowski sat at his desk in the Green Bay Police Department staring at a pile of folders, puzzled, thinking.

*Eight burglaries or robberies in as many days. Ridiculous. Something's way out of order in this, but what?*

His partner, Myron "Iron Mike" DeLorme, looked up from his concentration on the computer keyboard.

"You'll never solve them by that evil stare, although you might want to keep that as part of your repertoire for grilling suspects. Looks good, that. Seriously threatening. You can be the bad cop next time we have to question someone."

Greg stretched, feeling sore muscles pull and twinge as he did.

*I'm getting too old for the kind of nights in bed I have with Cait.*

He tucked that thought to the back of his mind even as a remnant of his adolescent self would have preferred to brag about a night such as he'd had—about the many nights of intense sex he'd had since he'd bedded Caitlin Fitzgerald.

*More like she bedded me. She sure won't be denied when she wants sex and she wants sex a lot.*

He fought to keep the tomcat grin of satisfaction off his face.

"Just thinking how odd this is, eight in eight days and not a clue have we found. I don't like it. It hints of prior planning by someone organized and fairly smart and this is just this month. We had five in five days a month ago."

"I know. I agree."

Iron Mike reached both hands up and scratched his balding scalp vigorously with all ten fingers. He had read somewhere it would stimulate some hair growth.

"I've gone around to all the places from that first batch, followed up on any names that owners and workers could give me as possible connections. Blank. Just a blank. Always the same too. Nothing but cash taken. Whoever does it won't be caught for selling stolen objects or cashing stolen checks, and he appears to know just when to hit the places where there's a fair amount of cash to be had. Still, he won't get rich off these hits."

"So far," Greg stretched again to get kinks out of his back, "it's the same with these but I have more victims to see yet. Maybe we'll get a break. I'd better be at this or I'll be working overtime."

He rose and shrugged into his suit coat. Grabbing his notebook, he dropped everything into his briefcase, which also held a small computer. He had at least ten people to question and he tried to keep a running report on what he was doing on the device to minimize later paperwork. His cell phone rang as he began to leave and he stopped, set the briefcase down and held the phone to his ear.

"Klarkowski," he grunted and then listened for some time, his face growing more still as his attention focused on what he was hearing.

Iron Mike, although still typing, kept one ear tuned.

When he was done, Greg snapped the phone shut and looked at his partner.

"We might have a small break. An informant of mine says he heard something odd last night in a bar on Broadway. Something about a guy planning a series of 'jobs' to earn more money, and my informant says it sounds like it might be illegal. I'll be over there meeting with him and then go to question more of the victims. By

48

the time I'm done, it will be late evening and I'll just go home."

As Greg walked out, Iron Mike called after him, "Maybe you ought to ask for a massage tonight to help that stiff muscle instead of..." the sentence remained unfinished. Greg slammed the door.

Myron grinned for a long time as he finished his report.

He wished his wife of many years could make him feel as stiff as Greg was feeling.

# Eleven

...journal...

Finally home. After ten pm. Too tired to sleep.

It took me the better part of two days after leaving Missouri. I chose the back roads of Illinois and Wisconsin. I know southwestern Wisconsin roads well. I love that part of the state. I loved our vacations there. If anyone followed me, I've led them an odd chase through a lot of tiny towns.

I had to stop several times to nap or I'd have been asleep at the wheel. The stress of these days, the driving, the grief I still feel, the pull...

The pull from Mexico is extreme tonight. I've used these days to try to break away but Ramon is feeling as torn apart as I feel.

I never expected to have a problem, or any threat at all leaving Mexico. Now I question if I can ever go back. I believe now that the threat was aimed at me and not at Ramon and the Aguilar family. Realistically, though, they're in danger too, if only because they know me.

No. That's not the whole of it. Ramon and Jorge are involved much more in the opposition to the cartel than they chose to tell me. It was Jorge's remark about not having enough men "yet" that alerted me, but I was suspicious before that. I was unable to find out more from Ramon. He shut me out when I asked what was going on, what Jorge meant. He's never done that before.

I checked for news while at another cheap motel last night. Fortunately the motel had cable. The explosion at the airport in Dallas injured no one and was small, and is still under investigation. No news on any threat at the airport in Cancun. What if that was some sort of hoax? What if Max hadn't gotten the message? Who was behind that? There are just too many unanswered questions.

I put the Range Rover in the garage under cover of darkness. If someone watches, they might have seen me, but perhaps not. I used my keys in the locks and punched in the combination to the alarm, then set it again once I was inside. The main floor was empty except for our newest dogs Screech and Woof, who thankfully did not live up to their names.

The dogs sniffed, recognized me, licking my hands and trotting around me quietly, the only sound their toenails clicking on the wooden floor. They followed me as I went up the back stairs to Alex's room at the top of The House. I thought about keeping them with me. I'm still uneasy and on alert. Letting go of suspiciousness won't be easy. But I've decided against that and sent them away.

I have locked the door in case Liam is prowling. I don't want to deal with him. I'm so tired I'd likely blow up at him, which I'm sure would make things much worse.

Cait and Greg have gone to bed of course.

A cool breeze is moving through the room smelling of the river. Mexico is so far away.

I'm hot with hunger to touch and be touched, to feel Ramon's hard body lying on mine, to feel him moving inside me.

I thought the change in temperature from wet moist heat to the relative coolness of summer here in the north might help relieve my passion, my longing. Tonight it hasn't. I would take a cold shower if it wouldn't disturb everyone. I can't face them yet.

I woke up after eleven this morning, showered, dressed in jeans and a T-shirt and went downstairs.

Thankfully, Ramon's presence has receded to a manageable level. I want to cry with the grief of missing him but my tears won't fall. There's a dam holding them back because the demands of life here descended on me as soon as I walked into the kitchen.

Cait was getting coffee. She fell on me as if I'd been away for years.

"Oh, thank god you're home! I thought you'd never get here. Why in the world did you drive all the way from Texas when you could have flown? There's so much we have to talk about. Let me call Caroline. She wants to hear it all too. There's a stack of mail and emails and calls for you. We have to make a lot of decisions about the business. I want to hear all about you and Ramon. Wow! Are you tan! It looks good on you."

She pulled up my T-shirt and looked under the cup of my bra and down my back.

"Tan all over! All right! Sexy! Geez! For a fifty-three-year old woman you have awesome boobs."

I just had to smile. It suddenly felt more like home—a relief to hear her familiar down-to-earth voice, to feel her tough, gritty energy spill out all over, and, I have to admit, a relief to feel pulled farther away from Ramon and Mexico for a while.

The day has been one long series of meetings and calls. I haven't had time to dwell on Ramon.

Cait called Caroline and Caroline called Rob, who came bringing a large lunch from Panera which filled the dining room with smells of garlic, cheeses, chicken salad, and chocolate, caramel, and vanilla lattes.

I brought them up to speed on Mexico and my scary flight home as we sat around the dining room table.

"Anna," Rob said, "this is serious. Where is Melissa? Where is any bodyguard? You could have called your security firm and had them send you someone else. They're probably tearing their hair out as we speak wondering if you're going to sue them for not fulfilling their contract."

"I was safer on my own, Rob. I kept to the back roads and places no one would look for me. Remember, I grew up as one of the working poor or middle class. I can blend in when I have to. No one could watch all the many motels and C-stores along the way. Mac gave me plenty of cash to get home. No trail at all. I'm in more danger in this house than on the road. So are all of you, by the way, just because you know me. It's here they'll pick up my trail, if anyone is actually looking for me."

Cait was squirming in her chair. She'd been uncharacteristically quiet while I told my story and it was wearing on her. I thought it was because she wanted the details about my relationship with Ramon, but I knew she put that in the "girl talk" category and wasn't about to bring it up while Rob was with us.

"So. We have some news for you," she burst out, looking at Caroline, who nodded and smiled. "The business is looking very good. Caroline got us a contract to decorate a luxury hotel in Ashwaubenon near Lambeau Field. We're going to need a new office and a warehouse to hold our purchases until they're installed.

"My house is done and it's just darling. I've shown neighbors and five homeowners through it and everyone loves it and several want to have their homes done too. Two couples made offers on homes for sale in the neighborhood and then came right to us to have them made over. Wait until you see my house!"

"Anna, you're going to love it," Caroline said, looking as pleased as Cait. "We've got some high end customers too. They love what we've done with the Allouez house and we'll be getting your investment back within the year if this keeps up. I think we can confidently say we have a good business going."

"They're right." Rob added. "It was a good decision and these two" he pointed one thumb at Caroline and the other at Cait, "have been working their tails off all month to make it happen."

He stood up.

"Now, having given credit where credit is due, as an accountant should, I have to go back to work so these two can learn all about your sex life."

Cait and Caroline tried to look embarrassed.

"But not before I firm up that appointment to meet with you. As a matter of fact, it's set up for a week from today. Your newest lawyer will attend, as well as representatives from your new investment firm. Be there!"

"Yes, Sir! I will."

I gave him a mock salute. I was quite sure if I wasn't there, he'd come and pick me up and carry me.

"I do know I have decisions to make, Rob. I'll be there."

He left.

We never got to discuss my sex life. At this point Liam entered. I was sure he'd been listening from the front stairs. His face was a picture of diffidence and carefully arranged arrogance. His energy seeped outward from him and filled the room and it was sticky, sickly, crawling with hate.

*His mask. That's his mask. Behind that bravado is one angry young boy. I can feel the terribly sick distorted rage, the twisted sexuality willed into and forced into him by Clayton Foster. Oh, god! He's become his abuser. He's become Clayton.*

He knew instantly that I recognized what he is, what he feels. His defiance was palpable, pouring out of him into the air, daring any of us to challenge him. I feel so sad. He was a magical child, white innocent magic, and now it's all gone dark and sour.

"Are you packed and ready to go home?" Cait asked.

He nodded, never taking his eyes off me.

"You can take your things to the car then."

I heard the fear and sadness in Cait's voice. She looked at me.

"We'll talk." I said.

54

Liam interrupted me.

"Not about me you won't. I don't want any help from you. You're the one who messed it all up. Leave me alone."

He stood defiantly, hands on his hips, glaring at me, a corrupt caricature of Peter Pan.

"Liam! Don't talk like that to her!" Cait barked.

If there is one thing I know, it's how to handle a defiant fourteen-year-old. In a very quiet voice I let him know he could not dictate to me or his mother. I fixed my best Mother stare on him and spoke.

"Liam, whether you feel you have been harmed or not, you have, by any standards, legal and moral. We care about you and we are the adults in charge. You are the minor so you will be cared for by us whether you want to be or not. It is our responsibility and obligation and our decision, not yours. I know you resent that but you are the kid and we are the grownups. That's the way it is. Now unless you want to walk home with your suitcase, obey your mother and put your things in the car. Thank you."

I looked at Cait and raised one eyebrow in question. I knew I had just usurped her prerogative as Liam's mother. I hoped she'd back me. She did.

"You heard Mrs. K. Do it."

Liam broke into a pure age-fourteen snit and stomped off. We heard him go down the back stairs to the car and heard the car door slam. Twice.

"Maybe he'll actually ride home with me, but he'll probably take the railroad bridge or the Walnut Street bridge. Good. The walk will wear off some of that anger, but, Anna, he needs some other kind of help."

"We'll find it, Cait. Don't worry."

I told them just enough about my relationship with Ramon to satisfy them. No more than that. They don't know about Jorge and about Adelina's revelations to me.

They left, and I stood alone in my kitchen for the first time in what felt like years. It has actually been just less than one month since Clayton Foster tried to murder me and two months since Big John O'Keeffe shot me. At least I think that's how long it's been. Time feels so strange. It has passed and my mind can't measure it, even in days or weeks.

## Twelve

I've wandered through the house, remembering the years when Art was alive, the eight years since his death, his long years of secret betrayal of us, and all that happened leading to the attempts to murder me.

*Why is it still going on? Whatever have I done to get this kind of attention from someone? Why isn't it finished yet? Why would anyone be after me, threatening me? It doesn't make sense.*

I've been interrupted by my cell phone. Cory.

"Mom. Where are you? You haven't answered your phone. You were supposed to be home days ago."

"Hi to you too. I'm home and rested. You can come home now. Liam's gone."

He breathed out a long sigh.

"Finally! I want to fumigate his room and mine. I hope the house is all ours now."

"It is. Come and bring Marthe if she's available and I'll tell you both about my adventure getting home. I'll pull the sheets and blankets from your bed. I bet it hasn't been done all month."

"Mo-o-om! I changed them once."

I heard Marthe's voice in the background.

"Marthe says she's coming and we'll be right over."

I ran upstairs to start on Cory's room so he could feel there was some change and stopped in shock as I opened the door. The ripped pillow told its story. Liam's rage was written in the long slashes that shredded the material. His sickness hung in the air of the room.

I shoved the shreds into a garbage bag and found another pillow as a substitute, then changed all the bed coverings and quickly vacuumed the sea of small feathers.

I didn't want Cory to see that. I opened the windows to fresh June air and sunshine.

After they arrived and I made us tea, I told my story again and insisted again on having more bodyguards.

Cory argued against that.

"But, Mom, you were safe coming home. That was in Mexico. We're ok here."

"No. The danger is here, too, Cory. I don't know why but I'm the focus and I think the danger will extend to anyone around me."

Cory's guard, Harry, echoed my cautions.

"But why, Mom? I don't get it."

"Neither do I. I thought it might just be in Mexico, because I know about Jorge's efforts to organize the people there to fight cartels. But there's more. The threat in Cancun was directly at me. I think the explosion in Dallas was too. I don't know why. I just know I want you safe."

Harry added his two cents.

"I agree. Cory, the heckling at your gigs could turn really dangerous. She isn't the only target."

"Harry, show me the internet problems."

The harassment on Cory's phone and Facebook page was disgusting. Brutal, filthy and crude.

Harry showed me what he'd done about it.

"We've traced some of it to individuals and turned our findings over to police who have warned them. It's mostly a few classmates, Mrs. Kinnealy. But there are some nuts out there who've read the newspaper accounts of your late husband's involvement in drugs and are using that as a reason to harass Cory and Alex just because that's the kind of sickos they are. We check out Cory's gigs very carefully. All computers and cell phones too. So far everyone's cooperated with us."

"I'm glad to hear that. Keep up the good work. I'll be talking to your company tomorrow morning to find out about Melissa, if I can, and to set up further security."

Marthe had been rather quiet and I noticed she didn't look quite as perky as she had when I left for Mexico. I looked at her silently for about thirty seconds before she caved in and spoke.

"Anna, I'm not well. I have a strange illness that's leaving me so tired, with pain through my shoulders, neck and head. Even my scalp hurts. My doctor hasn't diagnosed it yet but I'm going to have to have someone living with me for a while, just until I feel better. I hope you don't mind."

"Mind? Of course not! I'll find someone right away. We'll call an agency, interview people. I'll get you a housekeeper too so you don't have to clean. Marthe, you're the mother I can talk to, my friend of years. I would never 'mind' caring for you."

"Well, you have MomKat and she requires care and..." her voice trailed off as every part of her sagged into her chair. It was obvious her condition was worse than she wanted to admit.

"Marthe, I don't really have MomKat anymore. She's alive but soon won't even recognize me at all. I need you well and alive. We'll get you to a doctor who can help you."

"Marthe, why don't you stay here for now?" Cory asked. "Harry and I can go and close up your house and bring your things."

"Yes. A very good idea," I said, standing up. "Let's do that."

It feels good to be with family in the house, to be doing just ordinary family things.

Tomorrow Greg picks my brain again for whatever I can remember about Ardith. There's so little. We never were close personal friends. Except for cooperating in planning his funeral, it was all business for Conrad.

## Thirteen

...one week later...

I've been on guard so long I've come to expect some sort of disaster. Nothing's happened for a week. Hypervigilance. Three nightmares. PTSD. I know the symptoms too well. I don't trust that this relative peace will last. If anyone is looking to find me, they know where I am now. I haven't curtailed my comings and goings.

I have a new bodyguard. Her name is Stacy Andre. I met a wall of polite obfuscation when I called to find out about Melissa. The secretary at the firm's office was all solicitous help and no information. Stacy reveals nothing as well. I think she knows more than she says.

Greg is disappointed. I can give him nothing more about Ardith. I try to picture her as head of a cartel and just can't see it.

Today is the day I meet about my finances. That's this morning. This afternoon, Cait, Caroline and I are going to scout the west side for a place to have our business. I look forward to that. It's a trip down memory lane whenever I walk those streets.

Rob's office occupies a freestanding red brick one-story building in Ashwaubenon on Cormier Street. In the lobby, autographed pictures of Donald Driver and Aaron Rodgers compete with a large portrait of Martin Luther King Jr. I had given him three of the African masks that had been in Conrad's office and they are also featured. The furniture is all black and chrome on a sumptuous white carpet. His receptionist, Adriana, sent me right to the conference room.

A huge mahogany round table dominates the room, saying more about the way Rob does business and about his life than any brochure could. No "power chair" here. As an African American, Rob has a strong aversion to human domination. I slid into one of the comfortable padded armchairs.

Abigail Woodman, my lawyer, has the voice of a ringmaster at a circus with no need for a microphone. I could hear everything she was saying long before she entered.

She swooped in, her voluminous skirt whirling around her, black high-heeled leather boots thumping on the floor. Like me, she is not a small woman. When I first met her she described herself as "the product of carbohydrate addiction and a mother whose experience of life included the Great Depression. We had to eat everything she could find because she always thought we'd never eat again."

Her hair, a mousy brown, nevertheless adds to her dominance by its abundance, all of it wound around her head in a huge swath with the intricacies of a Sikh turban.

She carried two café mochas and set one firmly in front of me.

"You're thinner. Have to fatten you up. It's about time you're home. Had your fill of sun and sex?"

Abigail always gets to any point quickly. She says judges love her for that.

"We have a lot to talk about, you and I." she continued. "I'm taking you to lunch when this is done, which of course will eventually be included in my bill to you. You need to be here for testimony at Foster's trial but it looks like that's a long way off. His lawyer is someone I don't know, from out of this area, and fighting it with all the lawyer tools he's got. Eventually we're going to sue them for all the money you have to spend on security and me. This will drag on. That's OK. Gives the police more time to make a case against him. How are you, by the way?"

"I'm physically healthy, having some nightmares, nervous and on guard because someone is still after me."

I gave her the account of my journey.

"What the hell! I would have thought that was over."

She sat back in her chair, thinking, shaking her head.

"Crap! That adds more fuel to this fire. Yes it does," she muttered, rapping a rat-a-tat-tat with her knuckles on the table. She might have continued but Rob walked in with two other men, obviously from the investment firm.

There must be some proper "look" men in the accounting field need to maintain, a look that is de rigeur—gray business suits, carefully pressed, with thick glasses, very short hair, physically thin in spite of the time they must spend sitting, and, of course, looking very prim. Rob is an exception, being large as a linebacker.

They were introduced but I can't for the life of me remember their names unless I consult the pile of information I received. One had a daring yellow tie and the other had a gray and black striped tie. Yellow Tie did most of the talking. Striped Tie wrote notes.

"We'll begin with mutual funds," Rob said as he dropped a pile of brochures and reports in front of me and handed copies to the others.

"Before we're done here today, you'll know every investment you own and the status. From this you can then make decisions about any changes in your investment strategies."

In two more hours, I actually knew what he was talking about, finding it surprisingly easy to comprehend as Rob and Yellow Tie explained it.

"Why would I keep so much money in bond funds, which earn very little interest, when there are other funds which have been steady in their earnings and earn a lot more?"

"Very good question, Anna," Yellow Tie said. His voice was slightly tinged with patient condescension and I found it annoying.

"This money was slowly transferred to bond funds over the year before Wentworth died. He seems to have been preparing for some financial uneasiness, maybe even a crisis. Bond funds are safer, less responsive to market fluctuations. We'll never know his real reasons but he was being cautious. You don't need to be that cautious at this time. You can invest in funds that have high interest earnings and monitor the trends, then change when a decline is forecast. You should check these holdings three or four times per year anyway."

Rob changed the subject. I think he thought I might snap at Yellow Tie.

"Now about the art you own. You already have some idea of how the art market works and you have Sotheby's to help you with that. With the art, you have a very long-term investment and don't have to worry about selling any of it unless you lose all the rest of your money. Then you would either borrow against them, using them as collateral or sell those works to gain more cash.

"Likewise for the gems and gold. You have your own bank, as it were. The only risky investments are the stocks in individual national and international companies. Those you must pay close attention to because of market changes."

"That's where we come in," Yellow Tie interrupted. "We'll watch those for you and be able to help you move around in the market, but you have so much money that you would be fine if you sold all of those risky stocks and invested the money in safer funds."

"What do I have in cash? I have to pay all of you plus expenses for my houses and my younger boys. Alex and Cory's education costs will increase, and AJ wants his clinic. Marthe is ill and needs a housekeeper and possibly a nurse. Last but not least, there's the security we all need."

After years of paying bills very slowly and worrying about money, I still can't imagine having enough for everything.

Rob laughed.

"You don't have to worry on that score, Anna. All these investments give you dividends and interest that provide cash flowing in, and there are several cash accounts that hold more than enough to cover all your present expenses.

Yellow Tie continued.

"We're advising that you make the clinic a non-profit. Contributions—meaning all money you spend on it—will then be tax-deductible. Likewise for the school in Mexico. I have the papers and information here. Think about getting other people to contribute to those entities too. You shouldn't fund it all. Eventually, or maybe even right away, you might think of hiring a person to do the fund-raising and keep tabs on this for you. We can do it for now but if successful, you'll need a full-time person."

"Rob, where did all this come from? How did Conrad get so much? Why do I need to go to Switzerland?"

"Other than your signature on papers there, I don't know, Anna. The man in Switzerland I spoke to said he has information for you on Conrad's life. Quite rightly, he won't tell me anything that isn't financial in nature. I'm as curious as you are. This kind of money isn't usually earned in a lifetime. It's usually inherited. I don't know a thing about Conrad's early life or his family. You'll have to wait and see."

I left the meeting with pictures of Conrad running through my head. His kindness to me at our first meeting. His laughter at parties. The many women he escorted to social gatherings. The erotic portrait that hung in his very sensual bedroom in Mexico—a young Conrad with a half-naked woman and a naked man, most certainly lovers. Who was he? Years of working for him and I scarcely knew him.

We had lunch at St. Brendan's Inn and Abigail listened as I told her some of my memories.

"Well, Anna, you'd better get to Switzerland soon. I want more of this story. Most lawyers are pretty dull. I want to know everything about this guy," she laughed, and then turned serious.

"You keep in close touch with me, Anna. This danger isn't over yet, not by a long shot. You keep that security firm on your payroll and I want written permission to talk to them if I need to do that. Here are the papers to sign for that." She shoved them across the table. "Those are the papers for your will too. Sign that as soon as possible. You definitely shouldn't be without it.

"I remind you that you are to give no interviews to any reporters. If they become too obnoxious, you call me. I'll make sure they back off."

"You needn't worry on that score. I don't want any contact with them at all."

"You may need a wall around you. I want you to consider living in a protected setting. That house of yours is fine but it's too easy to access, to see into, and to spy on all of you. So is the one in Allouez."

She saw the protesting look on my face.

"Think about it, Anna. Think hard. You're vulnerable and so are your kids. What are you willing to do to protect them?"

We finished our lunch and I went home overburdened with too much information and a decision I didn't want to face.

This house has been my safety and shelter for years. I can't leave here. Yet soon my kids will be grown. Then what?

I put off the meeting with Cait and Caroline.

# Fourteen

Violence broke out last night. We're all frightened and Cory and his band are terribly disappointed. The crowd demonstrating at the band's gig became completely out of control.

The gig was at a small club in Appleton and when they arrived there were a few protesters, heckling about Art's drug involvement, but it wasn't any more than usual.

Cory is so rattled he can hardly speak. Harry told me the whole story.

"Half-way through the evening, the sounds outside began to interfere with their playing. I went to the front door to investigate and was horrified to hear a huge ugly crowd chanting, not about Art and drugs, but chanting a direct attack on Cory. I've worked crowd control in other places and recognized one serious element.

"I've only seen it twice, Anna, but that was enough. These were professionals, practiced at manipulating a group, hired to incite malevolence. Club security locked the front door and called the police. When the officers got there, it became a fight. I got the band out the back first and then the patrons were led to safety. We still have to go back for their instruments."

"They were after me, Mom, chanting that I'm a druggie and a dealer, and I felt their hate. I was really scared. I didn't know what to do."

Cory slumped over, putting his head down on the kitchen table.

"I can't put my friends in danger any more, Mom," he said, his voice thick with tears. "I told the band I won't be back. They'll need a new lead singer. I hope they can find someone."

He slowly raised his head and the disappointment in his eyes broke my heart.

"Alex offered to get me a gig—a job—as a counselor at the camp. They lost one and need another. I think I'd like to do that until we leave for Ireland. And, Mom, I'm thinking about maybe changing schools for my senior year."

He got up and ran up the back stairs, his almost eighteen-year-old life falling apart around him.

My own fury filled the room.

# Fifteen

Cory is at Sitting Bear Lake Camp with Alex. I'm providing four security guards for the camp. I felt I had to tell the head counselor the whole story and he was grateful.

"If we have tight security, I don't see any problem. There's been no sign of any unusual activity with Alex here and I don't see that happening with Cory either. They're great guys. Your boys sure know their stuff when it comes to living outdoors and that's what we need here. Besides, the sheriff is a friend of mine. I ran it past him and he'll add his attention to anything out of the ordinary. Don't worry. He'll be fine."

I'm relieved. Now I can concentrate on other matters without feeling guilty. I want to visit MomKat more and get more help for Marthe. It turns out she has some rare rheumatoid disease called polymyalgia rheumatica, meaning she feels sore, tired, aching, has nagging headaches, pain across her shoulders and neck, and needs to be on prednisone. There is threat of a more serious form of the disease which can cause blindness but no sign of that. Yet. I'll have a nurse come in three times a week to check on her.

If I'm the focus of whoever is threatening us, I'm determined to smoke that person out and the only way is to be very visible. This has Stacy really annoyed with me, but she'll have to earn her money—my money—the hard way. This morning she ran the river path with me.

"If you're going running, I run with you. If you go anywhere, I go with you. You'll be training with me in hand-to-hand combat. You'll be doing PT with me. I'm determined you'll be in good shape and know how to fight. Just in case."

I'm fine with that. The added exercise keeps me from dwelling on the threat to us and my longing for Ramon. At least while I do it.

Today Cait and I, with Stacy trailing along protesting our vulnerability, took Caroline on a long walking tour of the streets of the West side, from the old railroad station at the mouth of the Fox River north beyond St. Pat's and west and then south to Fisk Park and farther south to the streets around S. Broadway and Ninth. We regaled both Stacy and Caroline with all the stories of our adventures, scrapes and scandals we could remember. Caroline was amazed.

"Really, I'm quite astonished. I had no idea someone could know a neighborhood this well. I grew up in a big home on acres of land in a wealthy suburb of Philadelphia. We didn't know our neighbors, or, if we did, it was because they had money my father wanted...all business, that was. So, this restaurant wasn't here then?"

We ended where we started, eating lunch in Titletown Restaurant, in the old railroad station.

"Nope." Cait laughed and looked around. "This sure brings back memories. I used to wait down on Broadway by our old house until an open freight car came by slow and hop in it and ride it up to here. They had to crawl through town back then. I was pretty good at that."

"You didn't!" I gasped. "You never told me that. My mother would have killed me if I'd done that."

"That's why I never taught you how. I thought your mother would psych it out somehow. She was known as the resident witch," she informed Caroline and Stacy, "a good witch but a witch nevertheless. I always thought she was really psychic."

Caroline laughed at the same time as she took a sip of her coffee and spluttered it all over, grabbing her napkin to wipe herself and the table off.

"Sorry about that! I hope you didn't get sprayed with coffee. You both certainly had a different life from mine. But let's get to business. I agree that the west side is the place for our office and storeroom. I called realtors and went online a week ago and I've narrowed it down to five buildings in this area. Can we go see them when we're done here?"

She laid out her notes on the table.

It took us all afternoon and we found our place just off Broadway on Howard Street—a free-standing three-story building with a generous space for storage of any furniture and accessories, a freight elevator (which is what sold us—no lugging stuff up and down stairs), a reception and sales area, and two offices. We finished at Kavarna with a great vegetarian meal and some tasty pastries and cheeses to take home.

In mid-afternoon the white-haired woman stood at the second-floor window of the Design Imports building overlooking Broadway.

The large man with deep ebony skin standing behind her drew himself up and peered over her shoulder. He hoped she would be impressed by his efficiency. She was paying him well and he wanted that money. He had debts.

"Those are the three women I want you to have followed. I want to know every move they make, everything you can find out about them. You already know Anna Kinnealy. The short redhead with gray in her hair is Caitlin Fitzgerald. The tall blonde is Caroline Bradley. That fourth woman is Kinnealy's bodyguard. Now, what is the report on the Kinnealy siblings?"

"The oldest is still in Guatemala at the Doctors Without Borders training," he reported. "The young nurse practitioner he lives with is there also. The situation is the same, unguarded for the most part. It is easy to have them watched.

70

"Our agitation of the crowd at the nightclub has resulted in Cory joining Alex at the camp in northern Wisconsin."

The woman smiled in satisfaction at that news.

"The camp is very well guarded by four security men in addition to the personal security guards for both boys. The sheriff shows a great interest in the place as well. He is rumored to be incorruptible. We are checking those rumors out.

"The daughter is still in Chicago. She goes out almost nightly to clubs but so far has not returned to drugs and alcohol. We have a man, a very sophisticated foreigner, attempting to become her lover. So far she has shown no interest in him but he is persuasive and persistent."

"And paid well."

"Yes."

"What of the aunt, Carrie Brennan?"

"She remains in Chicago but she seems to have no control over the daughter."

"Good! I want her watched as well. I want no information, no move by any of them missed. Do you understand? Are you monitoring cell phones and computers?"

"Yes, ma'am."

She waved a hand in dismissal.

He left the room, a look of relief on his face, tension leaving his body. He did not like being in her presence.

She was well aware of that and savored her power over him, over them all.

"Soon," she mused. "Soon I can make a move against them. Not all at once, not to end it, but to keep their tension and fear rising again and again, to confuse, to heighten stress, to torture them all slowly. She will know what it is like never to be..."

The phone rang and she answered. Immediately she focused all attention on her business. Shipments were due to arrive and depart. Money was to change hands. Far away, women and children were already in holding pens waiting to be sold. Now it was time to concentrate on moving the cache of stolen art to black market dealers and to find out where the art from Anna's home in Mexico had been stored.

Most important of all, the partnership with El Cocodrilo must be made firm, and the extent of his business investigated secretly but thoroughly.

## Sixteen

...journal...

Today, when I visited, MomKat didn't know me. She sang every word of the old songs with me but she didn't know me. In the middle of singing "My Wild Irish Rose" she stopped and asked me how I know these songs and what my name is. How can this disease be eating away at her so fast? I came away from her feeling an emptiness, a sense of loss, of eerie disconnection with my childhood life and her presence in it.

Stacy and I took the dogs for a run on the river path after supper. Cory called and he feels safer up north. Good.

I have my library back. Cait's boys moved out all C&C's business records for us. I spent several hours reclaiming it with my books and decorations.

Stacy patrols the house and yard several times a day. She has notes and pictures of all the traffic that passes by on the path—who repeats, who is occasional, who lives in the neighborhood as well as all who walk on our streets.

"If any one person or set of persons is watching you, we'll have photos of them. I've checked out the school across the street. There could have been someone watching from the windows but I've spoken to the staff and run security checks on them all and I'm satisfied they're legitimate. Police are running all license plates."

I have to admit to myself I'm eased by her vigilance. I've been able to concentrate on our plans.

Today I got our foreign travel finalized. We leave the last week of August, later than we first planned. Cait and three of her boys will go, including Liam. Caroline

and her twins will leave with us and be joined later by
Rob. Alex and Cory will go with me. Marnie refused
Ireland, saying she has photo shoots to do. She'll go
directly with Aunt Carrie to Paris.

Our itinerary: Ireland first, for three weeks, then
London to check out acting and music schools for Cory.
After that, Paris and Switzerland and Italy. Stacy is
grimly checking every destination. She has a new crew of
security at the house for the graveyard shift.

I have the absolute best surprise for Cory for his
birthday. If he can't finish high school here and would
have to go somewhere strange, then why not finish his
education overseas? The British have produced some of
the finest actors in the world. I think he'll be delighted to
be there. He can be tutored in high school subjects, even
go to an American school for the children of diplomats,
and live in a secure place. I can hardly wait to see the look
on his face. What a delight that will be! I have feelers out
for an apartment in London for him and Harry.

After settling him in, I'm going to meet Aunt
Carrie for the Paris couture shows, then we're off to
Switzerland and Lake Como. Alex will go to see AJ and
then to Belize to begin his first gap year placement.

Marthe will remain here in the house and I've
hired a housekeeper, a full-time nurse-companion, and a
person to care for the dogs. The library will be Marthe's
place to write.

I've been told her disease lasts from two to six
years. Thanks to Conrad's money, she'll have all the care
she needs. Security too.

We'll rent out the Allouez house and we can still
use it as one of our demo houses for C&C.

It's all planned out. I'm very pleased I got so much
done today. All seems calm.

Ramon is back in my head and body. I can feel
him. I've tried phoning. No answer. Not even voicemail.
That worries me.

Does he visit his wife at the institution, his children up in the mountains?

No. I know what he feels like when he goes there—his deep sadness at seeing her, his joy seeing his children, his fear for their safety.

He has to be with Jorge. What I feel is an ominous danger.

# Mexico

## Seventeen

The dirty beggar had been sitting outside the Santa Maria School in Puerto Juarez for several hours and had gained nothing much in the way of alms. It was not good to be a beggar in this town of poor people. His ragged clothing made him look even more impoverished than many of the people who noticed him but they themselves did not have much to give. Even so, some left him a few coins and some pieces of fruit. One woman left him a tortilla with meat wrapped in it. He was very grateful to her. Hunger had been gnawing its way through his stomach for hours.

At last he rose and followed a short woman with her blue-black hair pulled to the back of her head in a bun.

"Señora Sálazar Díaz, may I speak with you?" he said in a Mayan dialect.

She stopped and turned, curious, looking at him with caution, waiting.

In a very quiet voice that did not carry more than an inch on the air, he breathed, "I know Anna Kinnealy."

Without a word or any change in her face, she motioned him into the school first and followed, after taking a good look at the street to note who else might be lingering. She saw no one.

She led him into her office far down a narrow corridor. He was careful to note that the corridor ended, some way further, in a rear door. Adelina closed the door of the office.

"Speak now!" she commanded.

Mac relaxed and motioned her to sit.

"I am the one who left the note at your bank. I can trust the clerk who handles your account. Can you?"

"Sí. She is a safe person. She has a child at our school here. What is your name? How do you know Anna?"

"Not only do I know Anna, I know Ramon and Jorge."

He told her the story of the events at the dig.

As he spoke, Adelina mentally compared his story to what she had been told by Ramon and Jorge and decided she could trust him. For now.

Mac read both acceptance and reservation in her eyes. It was what he was feeling, what he would feel if he were in her situation. He decided he would disclose everything he knew, then changed his mind. Some things he was not sure of. He could not speak of those things yet.

"Members of your family have opposed certain persons in the cartels and there is a rumor that Jorge is trying to organize Mayans against the cartels."

In fact, Mac knew it was not just rumor. Jorge had said as much, albeit obliquely, while at the dig, and while searching for Anna in the jungle. Jorge had been the one to organize the Mayan men for that search and Mac had overheard much he was not meant to hear.

Adelina's face closed tightly, but she motioned him to continue.

"I am Native-American from Canada. I am a contractor and work for myself but my government has asked me, contracted with me, to help destroy the drug traffic from South America, through here, through the United States, to Canada. Anna lives in one of the cities where these shipments pass through and she is still in danger. I was the one who got her out of Cancun and back home, by kidnapping her. I am sorry Ramon and Jorge were left distressed and perhaps frightened for her but I had to do what I did. She made it home safely but not without what might have been attempts on her life."

Mac added a description of Anna's passage to Green Bay.

"You care for her. I know that, Señora. I know that Ramon and Jorge also care for her. Will you help me?"

Adelina looked at him for a long time, a searching and probing gaze which left him wanting to squirm like a schoolboy in front of a stern nun. Finally, she sighed, relaxed and nodded.

"Sí, Señor. What do you want of me?"

Mac smiled.

"Muchas gracias, Señora, I know I have made a very good ally today. I will not waste your time. Here is what I need."

And he told her.

# Eighteen

The beggar left Santa Maria School some time later looking satisfied, having forged another link in the long chain he was creating. He hitched a ride on an old wagon pulled by a dusty donkey which was headed for Cancun. He appeared to fall asleep.

In Cancun, in the market where the tourists were thickest, he awoke, thanked the old man who drove the cart and slipped away into the crowd.

Hours later, a well-dressed tourist sauntered into the bar of a luxury hotel in the Zona Hotelera. His cream-colored suit was hand-tailored and rode over his body as well as a silk dress skims the body of a wealthy woman. He moved easily, with a dancer's balanced carriage. A Panama hat was on his head, a green tie at his throat, and brown wingtip shoes completed his outfit. He tossed an American twenty on the bar and ordered a drink, then scanned the room casually. Pulling out a large Cuban cigar, he made much of the ritual of lighting it.

He was noticed, as he intended to be. After a short time, another patron, a man with a face pitted with the scars of chicken pox, casually slid onto a nearby barstool, ordered a tall cool drink, and began a conversation in Spanish. The well-dressed tourist responded in accented Spanish that clearly labeled him as Cuban.

"Why do you visit here, Señor?" asked the patron with polite interest.

"I have business here, Señor," the tourist said, carefully reserved. He blew a swirl of smoke into the air.

"Ah! You are more than a tourist, then."

There was a long pause.

The man with the pitted face took a long slow pull from his drink.

"¿Cómo se llama usted?" he asked.

"Just call me El Capitan."

"I have heard many things about you. I am very happy to meet you at last. What kind of business do you wish to do, Señor?" the pock-marked man murmured, voice low.

The tourist looked slowly around the bar, noting there were few other customers and they were at the other end of the room.

"My business is of a very lucrative kind. It draws unwanted attention from those who would like to be as rich as I am so I do not discuss it in an open place like this. Are you a *businessman* also?"

"Sí, Señor. Perhaps you would like to join me in a private place to discuss our *businesses* further?"

The tourist offered the patron a cigar and when it was lit, they both adjourned to that more private place, the tourist's room.

The tourist's drink was left untouched on the bar. The twenty went into the pocket of the bartender as he picked up a phone and made a call.

Some ways away, a beggar in a small old room, in a small ancient hotel staffed by yet another member of the Aguilar family, flipped a switch and began recording. Mac smiled in satisfaction. It was working perfectly. His smile disappeared when, quite some way into the conversation, one of the men mentioned the name of Anna Kinnealy and the name of another woman, a name he had heard briefly when Anna had been questioned by police, a name Anna had brought up again while he was getting her out of Mexico.

"This woman who now runs Los Serpientos cartel is obsessed with the Kinnealy woman. She seeks an alliance with me but she will ruin the business. She loses focus. She will lose me money. I want to ally with you against her. When the time is right, I will eliminate her. In the meantime, you can make much money."

Mac's first reaction was to rush to Anna's aid. But that would not be possible. This was just the beginning of the elaborate web he was weaving. He could not leave. He reviewed what he knew of the security she had around her.

"It has to be enough. It will be," he told himself. "She's smart."

He had checked out the security firm she'd hired. They had a great reputation. He reassured himself that she would be safe in their hands.

His commitment to gathering information on the cartels was now cast. He could not, dared not, leave.

## Wisconsin

## Nineteen

"Listen up, all you campers!" Big Bill, the head counselor, shouted. Slowly, excited voices subsided and, after a few "shhhh" and "Quiet!" commands made the rounds, attention focused on William Holworth, a burly man with pale blond thinning hair, broad shoulders, double chins and a jolly look. With clipboard in hand, he climbed on a small pile of rocks and took roll call. Breakfast over. All present and accounted for.

"OK. Parents' weekend comin' up. Are all cabins clean? Everything shipshape here?"

Murmurs and nods of assent came from children and camp counselors.

"Great job, all of you. Now remember, as your families arrive, the first thing is a tour of the whole camp. Then you can bring them to the workshops of your choice, show them what we make and how to do it and even have them do some crafts if they want. Box lunches at noon, swimming in the afternoon. For supper, we have a campfire and cookout. Be ready to show them what you learned about fire safety. After supper there's a sing-along and volleyball. There's canoeing for those who've made Wolf Level. Lights out will be at ten p.m.

"Ok, all kids to the waiting area at the parking lot. Camp counselors, I have your schedules here."

Cory and Alex shooed their charges off, picked up their assignments and followed the kids.

"What have you got?" Cory asked Alex. "I've got knot-tying. It's a good thing Mom taught us that when we were kids. Some of this I don't know anything about."

"It'll be OK. That's an easy one. There's a chart on the wall if you forget. I've got ceramics. Messy! See you later."

Ten p.m. came. Camp counselors counted heads. In the dark, Cory and Alex headed for Bill's office to report in for the day. Just outside the door, both froze dead still. An angry male voice issued from the door of the small log building.

"I don't want my children associated with those two boys. How do I know they aren't bringing drugs here? How do you know that? I want their belongings searched right now. I want this entire camp searched. I demand it!"

Bill's calm voice came through the darkness.

"I know both boys. They aren't druggies. I'm always on watch for that and I'd know. I'm trained to recognize signs of drug exchanges or drug abuse. We all are these days. Alex and Cory are fine young men. There's no reason for a search. I'm not going to disrupt the whole camp at this time of night, or even in the day, for a search. I don't even think that's legal."

"We'll see about that. I'm going to the sheriff of this county and report their presence here. I'm not letting this go. I'm taking Barry with us and he's not coming back here until a thorough search has been done and those boys are gone."

The screen door slammed open. Barry's father lurched out with Barry's arm clamped firmly in his meaty hand. Barry's mother, head bowed, followed meekly after.

Alex and Cory stayed in deep shadow.

"Damn! Even here. We can't get away from it anywhere. Alex, what am I going to do? You can escape it in Belize but where will I go? How can I go back to school in fall?"

Alex stood very still for several minutes. He felt as if someone had kicked him and he waited for the pain to subside.

"I don't know, Cory. I just don't know." He hesitated, then moved toward the door of the cabin. "Bill's fair. Let's talk to him."

They opened the door and went in.

Bill looked up, saw the boys' faces and knew they'd heard.

"Sorry, guys. Barry's dad is so hot under the collar I didn't even have a chance to tell him your mom's providing security for the camp. Actually, I'm not sure that would have helped. It probably would have made him crazier to know we even considered security. He'd want to know why. Matter of fact, I'm pretty sure he's been drinking. He may not even be capable of being rational about anything."

He watched their faces, thinking how another father, Art Kinnealy, screwed up his sons' lives as Barry's father was messing up Barry's.

Alex started to speak but Bill stopped him.

"Guys, this man is not the only parent who ever complained and I can handle this. It's my responsibility. What I need you both to do is do your jobs here."

He pointed a finger at them.

"Go back to your cabins and be sure all your kids are ok for the night and then turn in. We've got a long day tomorrow. I need you both to carry on. Ok?"

Cory nodded and Alex, after some hesitation, assented with a nod too.

Outside and away from Bill's cabin, Alex admitted, "I almost resigned. I'm so tired of the fallout from dad's shit. I just want to be off to Belize and..." his voice trailed off.

Cory remained silent. There was nowhere to go, nothing to say any more. With a light clap to his brother's shoulder, he headed off to check on his kids and get some sleep.

...journal...July 5...

I went up north to see Alex and Cory for the Fourth, Stacy riding shotgun, of course. On the way we caught a little parade in one town. I love little town parades and fireworks. It's so really American, right down to the fire truck, tractors and farm machinery.

All is not well. Bill told me about the complaint. Nothing came of it, but the poor boy was pulled out of camp. The family is no one we ever knew. I have to face the fact that more people are talking about us than I've wanted to admit.

Alex and Cory agreed to stay. The sheriff is alert. The guards are there. I don't know what more I can do, a helpless feeling. I almost told Cory about England but I so want to surprise him.

After I left them, I drove down through Crandon, to show Stacy where we used to go in summer. Now the lake where we rented cabins is surrounded by private homes. Our waitress at the restaurant where we stopped for supper was chatty, telling us there are more and more homes around the lakes. One lake is privately owned and she gossiped a bit about the huge house someone built there.

"It looks like the American idea of a log castle. It's still under construction, or I should say, under construction again. There's new construction machinery on site now. The home itself has been on the lake for years."

"Who owns it now?"

"No one knows. Somebody from Chicago is the rumor. Maybe it's a mobster, just like the old days when Al Capone and other gangsters came up to Eagle River and other points north to vacation."

"I think those days are long gone. Mobsters go to the Caribbean, or the Far East, or, I don't know what or..."

I was thinking more of Mexico but didn't say that.

# Twenty

Greg Klarkowski answered the call at his desk.

"Detective, I've got more information for you," the familiar voice said. "About the robberies."

"Can you talk safely?"

"Yeah, no problem. You're not going to love this. The robberies are supposedly being planned by one person. I overheard two guys talking last night in the King's X. It's all part of a scheme to keep police very busy, to keep all your attention on robbery and not on anything else. I think I know who were talking although I didn't get a good look at their faces. I didn't want to risk that, but what they said verifies that this isn't some random string of robberies. I'll give you the names. I'm keeping my ears open. This isn't much. Sorry."

"That's OK. I'll take anything I can get right now." He wrote down the names. His caller hung up.

Greg sighed at the ever-growing pile of files on his desk. Done in groups of five or more in a row, the robber (robbers?) never had netted more than a few thousand dollars in any one place, if that. Still, the money was always enough for a person to use for a drug buy.

This past Fourth of July weekend had seen seven more and not one clue left. Masked, voice disguised, police only knew the robber was male. Covered from head to foot, witnesses couldn't even tell what race or ethnicity with any accuracy, or even if the man was the same one each time.

He and Iron Mike had crawled over every crime scene hoping the perp had dropped something, anything, left a footprint, shed a hair...

"Damned nothing," Greg muttered. "It's planned through and through. This guy is trained. He sure is succeeding in keeping us busy. Most criminals are dumb. This one isn't. I hate smart criminals!"

Iron Mike, approaching his own desk, heard the last remark and laughed.

"You hate criminals who are smarter than you. You gotta be careful, man. That's a lot of hate."

Greg shot him a sour look.

"I just got a call from one of my informants. There's a rumor on the street that these robberies are to keep us busy so we don't have time to dig into drug cases. Planned that way. He's going to try to find out more information. We've got a meeting with the captain. I hope we can get more help on this stuff."

"Yeah, me too. Geez, if that's true, we can expect even more. Still, it's a long stretch to try linking these with drugs. It really could be some addict wants money to buy his stuff, but there's no evidence for that. I don't see any clear link to these crimes and the drug scene."

Both men headed for the captain's office.

Captain Arnold Schwartzkopf had endured no end of imitations of the more famous Arnold Schwarzenegger, in spite of the fact they looked nothing alike. Arnie was built like a hairpin, a large head and two thin prong-like halves to his long body. No one could possibly think of him as a bodybuilder, or that he had ever even seen the inside of a gym, much less played in a movie or become governor of a state. They would be correct, but it would be a vast underestimate of his abilities. Arnie, as a patrolman, had been quite calm and collected for the most part, but when annoyed, his prongs could disable even the toughest of the tough in whiplash action. He preferred, however, to outthink criminals, physical force being much too much of a bother. He preferred to use his whiplash mind.

Arnie was annoyed. He did not like to have the work calendar clogged with petty burglaries. He had a pedophile/murderer who should be in jail, but was instead living in his own home on a bracelet in a nervous neighborhood whose residents didn't want the taint of pedophilia near their children, whose major trial was being delayed by legal tap dancing, and whose personal life needed a vast amount of investigation. He had fifteen to twenty long years of the operations of two questionable law firms awaiting fine-tooth-comb investigation. He had a drug scene getting worse, and the dogged press could not resist chewing over and over on the Kinnealy bone. He smiled. He liked that metaphor.

His smile didn't last long.

"I want you all to report again everything you know and everything you've done on these cases, no matter how small, so we can all hear it," he ordered the assembled crew.

Every officer who had anything to do with the Kinnealy and Foster cases stood before him, as well as anyone handling drugs and those damned robberies.

He listened until they were all finished and then was silent for some time. The crew became restless, shuffling papers, shifting from one foot to another, clearing throats, taking deep breaths. Finally he barked out his thoughts.

"OK. Here's what your information and my gut tells me. Greg, I believe your informant is right. This is all related. I want you to push him to find out more. You and Iron Mike see if you can find that drug connection. Re-check anyone who was involved, was present, where they live, what they do, when and where they spit. Check out those geographic areas where they occurred and when they occurred against any other information we could have on drug cases. Bring in Foster for questioning again. Now he's denying any knowledge about the drug scene but maybe, just maybe he'll let something slip when pressured, or he'll remember something he wants to blame on someone else. Sleazy bastard!

"Patrol officers, I want you walking, not just riding, your territories and talking to anyone and everyone. I want you to find every addict and drug house in this city and know who is there and who comes and goes. I want to know if there is anything, anything at all, odd or unusual going down anywhere. We'll concentrate on the east, north and west sides nearest to the river but don't rule out any other area of the city, including the most affluent. I'll be informing all the other police departments, Ashwaubenon, Howard, Allouez, and De Pere, etc. Someone with brains and money is behind this. More than one someone if Foster is to be believed. We're looking at layers here. We want to know all the layers and all the players, bottom to top and top to bottom."

"Bennett and Klarkowski, stay. The rest of you can go."

After the shuffling and noise of leaving was finished, Arnie spoke.

"Bennett, you know the Kinnealys and you were in on the attempted murders and the arrest. I want you to consider becoming more involved in the case on the west side, going undercover. Here's what I'm thinking."

Arnie outlined his plan and dismissed Ben Bennett.

"You think hard about this, Ben. We need this." Arnie called after him.

"Greg, I need to know who your informant is. In fact, I think I know. It's one of the Fitzgerald boys."

Greg nodded.

"Good. Can you recruit one more?"

"Their mother will kill me, but yeah, I think so."

"Good. Do it. Recruit their mother too. From what I've heard, she's fearless, tough, smart, and knows more gossip than anyone else on the west side."

"Captain!"

89

Greg looked horrified and spread his hands out in what he hoped Arnie took for supplication, because it was.

"Do it. She'll love it." Arnie grinned.

Greg groaned and left.

Arnie's grin disappeared.

*That ought to spice up his life a bit. And mine. If they get hurt, my head will roll for involving three people of one family. I don't like ordering Greg to recruit them but we need a break here. We haven't gotten it so far and if it doesn't come from citizens, then where?*

Greg stomped down the hall.

*She'll do it but she'll kill me when she finds out two of her boys are working as confidential informants as well.*

## *Twenty-one*

Ben Bennett parked behind the Broadway buildings and got out his guitar case reluctantly. He was not in a good mood. He'd thought if he'd been offered a chance to go undercover, it would be great, a real plus for his career. Now he had it and it was anything but great. Going undercover meant his parents could not know and they thought he'd lost his mind.

"How could you want to do this after all these years as a policeman? How could you want to be just a musician in a band?"

His mother was in tears. She'd bragged for years about her policeman son and now he wanted to play in a band? In a bar on Broadway? Throw all that schooling and learning away? For nothing?

His father had looked so disappointed. Years spent in a mill had left him tired and worn. He'd wanted more for Ben.

'This is foolishness," he'd told Ben "You're just throwing away a better chance than I ever had."

Ben, in jeans and an old sweat shirt, dragged himself down the street to the string instrument workshop to see if they could repair a bad fret on his guitar. Did they even repair guitars? Where would there be a band he could join? What good would that do?

He watched the pedestrians cross in the middle of the block, fighting the urge to warn them against it. Cars slowed to parallel park, holding up other traffic. Cars drove at a snail's pace, their drivers searching for the store they wanted. People of every color and race sauntered, stood still, or hurried down the sidewalks.

*This is sure a different neighborhood. I grew up on the east side. I don't even know anyone over here. What good will it do to have me here?*

Twenty minutes later he came out, guitar still in hand. The man inside had made it clear they repaired violins, violas, and other *stringed* instruments. Ben's guitar was apparently beneath their level. The man had recommended a new place on Dousman Street where they repaired only guitars.

He turned to head in that direction and a flash of red hair hit his shoulder.

"Sorry," he said. "I wasn't looking where I was going."

He stepped back.

"Hey! I know you. You're Sean Fitzgerald."

"Yeah, that's right. Oh, I know you too. I forgot your name but you're that cop from when Mrs. K got hurt. Hey, I'm glad I ran into you, literally. Sorry. It was my fault. I was preoccupied. I'm trying to make a big decision. Maybe you can help me. Can I talk to you about being a cop? I want to know more about police work. You got some time?"

"Yeah, sure. Let's go get some of that Thai food."

Ben pointed to the Bangkok Garden Restaurant down on the corner.

He followed Sean across the street in the middle of the block, dodging cars.

Two hours later, after Sean had called his brother Mike, a band had been born, an old building to practice in had been found, and two gigs had been set up.

"And now," Mike announced with a grin, "we'll take you on the Fitz boys' tour of the lower west side and tell you the history of each place from the bar where Paul Hornung and Max Magee used to bring their call girls, to the gay/Lesbian/trans bar, to the restaurant where Martha's Coffee Club, a group of old Green Bay Packer fans, used to hang out..." and he continued with a list of the strange, the dirty, the fancy, and even a few of the mundane.

"Then we'll take you to talk with my mother. If we don't tell her what we're doing, she'll kill us all," Sean said, "and you'll need someone to cover your back if you get into trouble. She's a fund of information. She knows more of the history of this neighborhood than anyone. Oh, yeah, and she's in the sack with Greg Klarkowski. She thinks we don't pay attention to that kind of stuff, but we do. We're all for it. It improves her mood a lot. All of us except Liam are fine with it. Liam is creepy right now."

Sean's forehead crinkled into long horizontal lines.

"I'm worried about him. Damn Foster! He's one of the reasons I'd like to be a cop. To stop men like him."

"I appreciate what you guys are doing," Ben said. "I didn't have any idea how to get started on this, and no backing or contacts, and I don't even know if it will do any good, but..." he left the sentence unfinished.

"If there's any information to be found, we'll find it. Come on! We're going Broadway bar-hopping!"

"My sons are doing what? You've recruited my sons to be snitches? Are you all crazy?"

Cait glared at Greg.

"C'mon, Ma. It's our civic duty."

Cait turned narrowed eyes to her sons.

"You told us we have to cooperate with police since we were little. You do it. Why can't we? Besides, we're over eighteen. We're adults."

Sean and Mike drew themselves up to full height.

"We've recruited Father O'Doul so we've got God on our side. What can go wrong?"

Cait wheeled on Greg, her eyes sending lightning from the red-haired thundercloud that was her face.

"You! You just remember Andy and Seamus are under eighteen. I want them kept out of this. I've got enough trouble handling Liam. And now this."

Greg looked suitably contrite. He wasn't. He figured she'd help too, knew she couldn't keep herself out of it.

*She's too nosy. She'll want to know the whole operation. Not gonna happen.*

"Now, Cait. It's only information gathering. Nothing dangerous. Our police undercover guy will be the one in danger."

"It's just playing music in bars and listening to rumors, Mom, and you've had us listen to rumors now and then. Everyone knows we sit in with a good band when we feel like it. You're in more danger than we are. You're the one who works with Mrs. K."

Greg assessed Cait's face.

*She'll go for it but I won't be getting any loving from her for a while. Good. Maybe I'll get some sleep.*

## *Twenty-two*

The blonde woman lay across her large and comfortable bed as the young dark man stroked spots on her body that aroused her. On the phone at her ear she spoke one phrase. "Continue Phase One," and then directed his attentions to several parts of her body she wanted him to stimulate. She began stimulating her own imagination with pictures of the pain, confusion, and fear she was causing in Anna's life and the lives of Anna's friends. Orgasms came quickly, several times.

...Anna's journal...end of July...

Today has been a nightmare. All that was going well has fallen apart in the last few days. This morning we were all at C & C setting up the warehouse with the purchases we'd made for the Ashwaubenon hotel project when they called and cancelled our contract.

"They can't do that!" Caroline protested. "How can they do that? We have a clause in that contract..."

She never finished her sentence as, to our horror, a bleeding Jake and Jim stumbled in the front door, pursued by two KKK-hooded men who halted at the door, yelled racial epithets at the boys and then ran.

Jake was bleeding from a cut lip and a substantial cut across his forehead which I knew would require stitches. Jim was bent over holding his stomach and he fell to the floor as we watched. Both twins shook with fear. Caroline ran to Jim as Cait picked up a phone and dialed 911. I got Jake seated and ran out the door looking for their assailants. No one to be seen.

Within minutes the police and a rescue squad were there. After a call to Rob, Caroline left with the boys.

I am completely stunned. I know there's prejudice here. I've known it for years. But it's usually subtle, a frown on someone's white face, a condescending tone of voice when talking about "those people", a separation of white and color in certain neighborhoods that prevails even to this day. But this? I have never seen anything like this.

I need time to sort out what's happening.

I spent this afternoon at the hospital with Caroline and then at her house. Caroline has always been beyond calm and collected. Not today. She wants to be out of C & C. I tried to reassure her, and even Rob, though coldly angry, pointed out this may be a one-time episode. I can't call it an "incident" as he did. There is nothing "incidental" about it. But I fear we've lost her for the time being. The police are investigating. The assailants are unknown.

This is not random. I know that because, in addition to the cancellation of the contract, Cait has pointed out that people have come in enthusiastic about having their house renovated by us only to grow cool and even to cut off all further contact. Why?

Sean and Mike came later this afternoon and said they found out the two men who harmed the twins were hired to do it. They've called Greg.

Stacy has gone over our office building from front to back and found we are bugged. Someone is keeping tabs on who comes to us, on all our conversations. We've had a long discussion on whether or not to maintain the bugging as it is so we can feed false information. No decision. I've had my security firm there today, setting up cameras and alarms. It was dumb and very naïve of me not to have that done right from the start. It's part of the old me who always believed the best. Even now, a small part of me still wants to deny these things are happening.

I called Abigail and she'll look over the hotel contract and do some digging into the deal. She has one of her investigators looking for possible behind-the-scenes libel or slander or bribes or...what?

It's hot and muggy tonight and I'd like to float in air-conditioning but that too went out and the repairman didn't show up this afternoon. Is he part of it? Did someone get to him? Was someone in our house? No. That's too paranoid. I don't have any sense of intrusion here.

My skin is sticky with a fine sweat as I write this.

I know something's wrong down in Mexico but I can't leave here.

Greg said Mac called him and might be coming here. I hope not. His desire for me just adds another burden.

I'm so depressed right now. I just want all this to stop. I want to back away from conflict, like I used to do.

I'm not who I used to be, but I don't know who or what I am now either. How far will I go to protect my children, my friends? How far can I go until my courage fails me?

## Twenty-three

Ben's father had disowned him and ordered him out of the house. His mother had cried uncontrollably.

His hair was in Goth style. He had a nose piercing and multiple earrings in both ears. He now wore a small goatee and a thin mustache. His arms bore some badass tattoos.

It was the end of the first week of the gig and two in the morning. He had been watched all evening by a middle-aged man in a dark brown suit who sat at the bar and drank very little. An unnerving experience.

As he put his guitar in its case, the man approached.

"You're a fine guitar player. I enjoyed watching you play. Been playing long?"

*He's making chit-chat. Is this what I've been waiting for?*

"Thanks. I've been playing since I was a little kid." Ben continued to fuss with his equipment, stalling, trying to look like a pro musician, which he clearly knew he was not.

"Make much money at it?"

"Sometimes it's good, sometimes not."

"Hungry? Can I buy you some food after a long night's work?"

Ben hesitated, looking around the bar.

"Uh, yeah, I guess. I usually go out for food. I was hoping for my buddies to come with me but it looks like they've gone, so OK."

*Don't seem too eager.*

"My car is in the back parking lot. I can drive." Ben said. "I have to take a piss before we go."

"No. No. I'll do the driving."

A knife-edge in the man's voice told Ben this was a command.

"After we're finished, I'll drive you back here to pick up your car."

"Uh, well, OK. Be right back."

Ben left his guitar case on the edge of the stage and headed for the john. Once there, he stood, took several deep breaths, and scrutinized his own strange face in the mirror. Danger hung in the air like smog.

*Where did Sean and Mike go to? I'm taking a chance going off without backup. But what's the choice? I have to take this. I'm so nervous I really do have to pee.*

He finished at the urinal, washed his hands, dried them, and walked out.

The man stood outside the bathroom door with Ben's guitar case in one hand. His other hand was in his coat pocket and Ben felt fear crawl through his abs.

*What am I getting into?*

They left the bar. Ben got into the man's car and they drove away.

"Got the number of the license plate?" Sean asked Mike.

"Got it. Let's go."

They followed in their own car at a careful distance.

The man found his way to Ashland Avenue and from there to Ashwaubenon. Ben was relieved when they pulled up at the I-Hop.

*At least it's a public place. Not much nasty can happen here. I hope.*

Sean and Mike were equally happy. They could be just another pair from the bar crowd wanting to chow down after a night of drinking. They were even lucky enough to be shown to a booth where they could keep Ben and the man in clear view.

99

"So, you're new at this music business, aren't you?" the man stated after they had ordered food. "What did you do before this?"

"Well, nothing much. Construction jobs, waiting tables once, stuff like that."

"Like money?"

"Well, sure, everyone does. Makes the world go round and all that."

Ben grinned a bit, hoping he sounded casual but interested.

"Yes it does. Indeed. How much do you make at a gig like this? A couple hundred a night?"

Ben laughed outright.

"Not really. Sometimes, in some bars, but not in the one tonight. I play for the experience a lot, just so I can get the experience."

*God, I'm repeating myself. Calm down, man!*

"You got ambitions of making more?"

"Oh yeah. I'd like to make a lot more."

"Good. I may be able to help you in that, if I like you."

"Are you an agent or something like that?"

It was the man's turn to laugh.

"No, not that kind of agent, but I may be able to send some money your way if I can come to trust you."

"I don't understand."

"You don't have to. You just eat this good food and I'll be contacting you again. As I said, *if* I can come to trust you."

Ben, having seen Sean and Mike, became a little bolder.

"Is what you have in mind illegal?"

Ben tried out what he hoped was a semi-conspiratorial look.

The muscles in the man's jaw stiffened slowly, just a trifle.

"We'd best leave that discussion for another time."

"There'll be another time?"

"Oh, yes. There will be another time. Now eat your food. It's time I got you back to your car."

Which is what he did.

Sean and Mike had parked their car two blocks from the back of the bar and were in the shadows as Ben drove away. His cell phone rang.

"Hi. We spotted him watching you. We'd have waited to go eat with you but we wanted to see what he'd do. We've got your back, man," Sean said.

"Thanks. I saw that. He's into something illegal but wouldn't discuss it. He's going to be very cautious. I hope my cover will hold."

"I'm glad we set you up in the old apartment on Ninth Street. He's following you. Stay on guard. We'll make contact tomorrow."

"Got it."

# Twenty-four

...journal...

I awoke from dozing in my bedroom chair choking on smoke. A thin haze filled my room. Jumping up, I opened my door and a thicker haze billowed into the room pulled by the draft from open door to open window.

"Marthe!"

I yelled her name once, then again, coughing from inhalation. The dogs began a howling and barking din. From upstairs, where Stacy was sleeping I heard a thump, then feet running. She was awake and coming. I dashed into Marthe's room. She was out but had a pulse. The night security crew made no response at all.

"Call 911!" I yelled to Stacy as I picked up Marthe in a fireman's carry and went down the front stairs. She was right behind me and on her cell phone. The dogs were right behind her, barking and jumping wildly.

Of course, the front door was locked and I started to lay Marthe on the long pew in the hall but Stacy got it open and we burst out onto the porch into fresh air. Smoke began to drift out after us. Stacy shut the door hoping to prevent fire from following although we couldn't see any flames.

It wasn't long before police and fire and rescue were there.

Stacy stayed to help them find the night crew and I left with Marthe for the hospital.

...late morning...next day...

"It was arson, in the basement," the chief told me. "We'll be doing a thorough investigation but it's clear it was deliberately set. Someone cut the glass in a basement window, climbed in, piled up rags, doused it with gasoline and lit it, then piled debris on to make it smoky. You were lucky. It was set so that you would have died of smoke inhalation before the fire got to you. Your security crew will survive, but barely. They were out when we found them, one in the living room and one in the kitchen. They're in the hospital."

Two other night security people, stationed at outer corners of the yard, never heard it, never saw anyone. The person knew our setup well.

Stacy and I are still having coughing fits. Marthe is worse. Her doctor is keeping her at the hospital and she's been on oxygen since we got her there.

"Is there any way of discovering who did this?"

"Not unless that person was careless and dropped something or left some clue. We'll sift through everything and hope we find a lead but I don't think we'll be that lucky. Whoever did it knew what he was doing. I'm sorry about that."

He left.

A fire in a house leaves it smelling like the entrance to hell—stale, rancid, irritating to our eyes and nose. Like it or not, I'm facing having to leave my sanctuary, my space, at least until I can have it cleaned. Everything will have to be cleaned. Everything.

I took the dogs to my vet and I'm having her board them until she can be sure their lungs aren't seriously affected.

"Don't worry. I think they'll be fine. I just want to observe them for a couple of days," she said, trying to sound soothing.

That's when my furious stubborn streak kicked in. Abigail was advocating a gated property somewhere. Stacy too. Fire, bad smell or whatever, I became even more determined not to leave.

Now I've been through the house, opened all the windows and doors and I'm refusing even to close and lock them at night. Fans suck in the day and night air and blow it out again. I pulled all the drapes, curtains, and bedding out and sent them to a laundry. I scrubbed down the woodwork with Murphy's Oil Soap and I'm having the carpeting cleaned.

"No one, no one, is going to get me out of my house. I won't let them!" I yelled to no one in particular.

There are new guards at night and then another to add to outside security for day. If I knew who was behind this, I'd be up in his or her face using every multi-syllable, triple-pronged word I know to rip them up one side and down the other.

Ramon called. He'd felt my fury. I'd like to say we had a wonderful call but I can hear distance in his voice and feel it. He has been pulled, or walked willingly, into danger. He would not discuss it. He's deeply hurt that I left. I'm deeply hurt that he won't trust me enough to tell me what he's doing.

I told him what Adelina had said, that I would be coming back, but I don't think he believes it.

My room stinks. I've moved bedding and an air mattress to the front porch and I sit here in the dark wondering why. A guard stands in the shadows behind me.

What next?

## Twenty-five

Alex is missing! He went into the woods for firewood this morning with three boys. They came running back to camp saying Alex had been kidnapped, taken by force by two men. The men wore disguises, hoodies over masks, and the boys were unable to give a description of their faces.

"You have to get up here fast, Mom," Cory insisted. "You have to see if you can feel where he is."

Stacy and I left for the camp immediately. Bill Holworth had the sheriff there within a half hour and they are searching. They found signs of a struggle.

I called everyone. Aunt Carrie is coming. Marnie is not. AJ and Sheila, his lover, are coming. They have bad news too.

They've been living part time in the small town in southern Yucatan State where the clinic is to be set up and they were attacked. Sheila is injured. Jorge and Ramon and the men got them out but they're coming home to recoup.

"It was bad, Mom. They killed some of the villagers who supported us and almost killed Sheila. Jorge has organized more men. When he heard—and I don't know how he heard, but he did—he came and got us out. Mac was with him. They've been running some sort of sting operation to go after sex slavers. It's been partially successful and at least one of the cartels retaliated. It will most certainly get nastier."

His voice broke, which really worried me, because AJ almost never falls apart emotionally.

"I hate to see this dream die, Mom. I can't let it, but I have to rethink it all, especially after what they did to Sheila. Now don't worry. We'll find Alex. He might even get himself out on his own. He's smart, Mom, and resourceful. See you soon."

At the camp, a very worried Bill greeted me with relief. Behind him stood the sheriff and a deputy. Three boys sat on a log across the small clearing from the office.

"Any news?" I looked back and forth among the three men.

"No, Anna, I'm sorry." Bill replied. "We haven't found him yet. We have a search going over this whole area. This here is Rich Wolcott, our sheriff. Rich, this is Anna Kinnealy, the boy's mother."

A tall, dark-haired deeply tanned man stepped forward. Grey hair lightened his temples and eyebrows. A beard shadow covered his lower face. His voice was low, commanding, and firm.

"I'm sorry to meet you under these circumstances, Anna. I wish I had good news for you but we have very little. Those boys over there," he nodded to the three huddled on the log, "are the ones who saw his kidnapping. We've questioned them but they haven't been able to tell us much. We only know he was dragged in a general westerly direction."

I looked at the frightened faces of the boys.

"May I talk to them, please? I want to reassure them it's not their fault."

"Of course, and then I'd like to talk to you too. The more we know about Alex, the better."

I sat down on the log and introduced myself to the boys. It didn't take long to find out they felt guilty. Kids almost always think what happens is their fault. But they had no clue to who might have taken Alex. He had shouted at them to run and they did. They had been able to lead deputies to the scene but that was it. I spent some time reassuring them. They seemed a bit less frightened when I was through.

Parents arrived and left with sons and daughters. The camp became deserted except for Bill and a few staff.

I moved into a cabin with Stacy. Harry and Alex's bodyguard, Pete, who was beating himself up for not stopping the kidnappers, took cabins near us. When it happened, Pete had been hanging back in the woods because he had to pee.

I insisted on being taken to the scene. We all hunted for any little clue, any sign, but the place was a mess of trampled plants. If there were clues, I was not the person who could find them.

The next day one tracker found a trail. Dogs were brought and given a sniff of Alex's clothing. The trail ended at a barely used old logging road where tire tracks were found, but those ended when they reached a paved road. The searchers concluded Alex was not in these woods any longer.

I can't sleep. I have a migraine. I'm waiting for a call from someone wanting money.

## *Twenty-six*

One tense and frightening week later, after endless speculation on what happened, another search of the woods for miles around the camp, and days of waiting for the ransom demand which the FBI said would come and which never came, Alex walked out of the woods on his own into the town of Star Lake and into the nearest bar, asking them to call police.

Unshaven, dirty, wrinkled, smelling like he pooped his pants and bathed in skunk sweat, he looked like a bum and someone thought he was one of the mountain people who live back in the wilds of Wisconsin, the ones who have come up from Kentucky and Virginia. Except, they would never talk to the law.

We stood some distance from him as he gobbled down a hamburger, fries, and a large root beer.

When he finished the sheriff took over.

"Ok, son, let's hear it. The boys you were with have been pretty scared. They said you were kidnapped."

"I was. I've been in the basement of a big log home. They held me for three days before I escaped."

"Who are 'they'?"

"One was called Black, or something 'black'. I heard it through the floor when the woman screamed at him, but she was so mad she hardly made sense. She was really crazy. She was mad at them because she said they botched the job. She sent them after Cory, not me. She thought Cory would make a better target."

He looked at Cory.

"I don't know why they thought I was you. We don't even have the same color hair, but anyway..."

"How many were there?" the sheriff cut Alex short.

"There were two who grabbed me in the woods, another driving, three more men and the woman at the house where they took me."

"Can you pinpoint the location of the house?"

"No. I can't show you on a map..."

"Damn! We need to find that place."

"...but I can take you there."

"If you were lost, how come you can take us there?"

"Because when I left, I marked my trail. I didn't know where I was but Mom taught us to blaze a trail when I was ten. I can lead you there but it's a long way. I walked for hours and hours before I got to Star Lake. I didn't even know the name of the town. I had to ask where I was.

The sheriff looked skeptical, the FBI man looked amused, Cory high-fived Alex, and I looked smug.

"That's my kid."

Big Bill, who had rushed to the sheriff's office when called, grinned.

"That's our boy!"

"What did they do to you? How did they treat you?" Bill asked.

"Um, not too good."

Alex stood and took off his dirty shirt, then turned around. His back was streaked with welts.

We all sucked in breath, a collective hiss.

I was horrified. Then fury took over.

Cory looked sick and turned away, then went to Alex and hooked a hand around his neck, careful to avoid the red streaks.

"Sorry, bro. I'm really sorry."

Alex hugged him.

"I'm ok, man, I'm ok."

"We have to get him to a doctor. I want him checked out. Now!" I snapped.

The sheriff signaled to one of his men and a phone call was made.

Alex continued.

"One of the men beat me. The woman stood by watching him. Another man stopped them. She didn't like that but she got a phone call and ordered them to put me in the basement for later, only there was no later. I don't know why.

"I know I was there for three, maybe four days. I'm kind of confused on that. At first one of them fed me and then she ordered them not to 'waste good food' and I think she would have left me there to die. After I didn't hear anything for a long time, I began to search for a way out. There was an old storage bin, like a coal bin with an opening where stuff had been dropped into the basement. It was a tight fit but I wiggled out. It was dark and I had to wait in the woods until morning began and then I could see. During the night I crept far enough from the house that I couldn't see it through the trees but when first light came I sneaked back and I can identify it.

"So then, I began to find my way out of the woods. I don't think I went in circles. I knew the directions and went east toward the light of the morning, to an old dirt road, then went south for a while, and then east again and then, when it started getting dark, I went north toward the lights of a town. Pretty simple, really, except it seemed like a long way, walking that is, like, all day."

"It's too late now to head into the woods. We'll get you to the nearest medical clinic and let a doc check you over and then you can get some sleep," the sheriff said and issued orders for a car to take us to the clinic.

"We'll be up early in the morning and you'll need to show us that trail. Meanwhile, we'll mark off a 25-mile wide area and set up roadblocks."

"To catch them? That might not work," Alex said. "I heard the chop of a helicopter on the third day. They might be gone."

"Crap! I hope not, but we still have to find that house."

Later, at a motel where we were given rooms, Cory, Stacy, Pete and I sat with Alex. I had gotten AJ and Sheila on speakerphone and we talked.

"Alex," AJ asked. "Did you get a good look at the woman?"

"Yes and no. She had on this really weird gray wig and dark glasses but I think she could have been Conrad's secretary, except I really never saw Conrad's secretary that much, maybe once when I went there with mom, but that was years ago and I remember her as kind and blonde and...I don't know."

Pete paced, rubbing his arms, unhappy. "I'm sorry, Alex, that I didn't get to you in time. I'll never take a pee in the woods again."

"It isn't your fault. You asked me to wait and I didn't. I was in a hurry to get more wood. I forgot to ask, are the boys all right? Did they get scared or hurt?"

"No, they're ok," I said. "I talked with them and told them it isn't their fault. I'll fix it so you can see them and reassure them.

"I'm so furious that she had you beaten. I can't imagine why she would do that. Maybe this isn't Ardith after all. This woman sounds sadistic."

"I know. She was a real weirdo. She paced and yelled. One of the men tried to calm her but she turned on him and threatened him. One of the other men turned away and if I read his face right, he didn't like being there. He was a black man and he's the only one I really got a good look at.

"Mom, I've got to get some rest. If we have to go through the woods tomorrow, it will take all day. Can we end this?"

Cory cut AJ off during his medical lecture on how to care for Alex's back.

We fell into our beds.

## Twenty-seven

The phone rang very early, dawn just barely breaking.

"Mrs. Kinnealy," a deep voice said. "I'm sorry to awaken you but this is the sheriff. We think we've pinpointed some houses where Alex might have been held. We've got one or two old-timers who know this area pretty well and they have some ideas about where Alex wandered. We might be able to cut the time spent searching if we get a very early start. Can you get him up? I tried and couldn't wake him."

My heart skipped a beat.

*Oh, god, is something wrong again?*

"I'm awake and I'll go to his room right away. I'll call you back."

I took my key and hurried down the hall to the boys' motel room.

*Why aren't they waking up? Are they that tired? Are they still in danger? No one thought to post guard. We all thought it was over.*

I knocked on the door. No answer. I pounded on the door and called their names. No answer.

"Um, ma'am? Ma'am? They're gone."

I turned to see a motel employee standing there.

"Gone?"

"Ma'am, they're eating breakfast across the street in the restaurant.

I could have kissed him.

*Eating. Eating. Of course.*

I thanked him and would have run out of the motel except I realized I was still in my robe and pajamas.

I returned to my room and stood there shaking. All the adrenaline of the past week drained out of my system, leaving me feeling sick.

We met the sheriff within the hour, dressed for trekking in the woods. He had Alex begin at the bar. We walked down the road, while Alex pointed out his marks in the shrubbery at the edge, searching for the place where he came out of the woods. One car followed us slowly, and the sheriff walked with us.

"We've got three possible places where Alex could have been held and we'll cut this short if his path leads us in any of the three directions," he informed us later as we made our way through the forest of leafy greens.

Two hours later, the sheriff stopped us.

"If this is the direction you went in, Alex, I think we can pinpoint the house. There are two old roads we can use to get to this area. I'm betting it's in this neck of the woods. One of those roads is just east of here. Let's go check the maps. I ordered a car there."

Within fifteen minutes he had spread a map on the hood of the vehicle waiting for us and circled a space not far from where we stood.

After another cautious hour of approaching a large log cabin from the safety of the thick woods, Alex identified it as the place he had been held.

"That's the one. The opening I crawled out of is on the west side.

"Are you sure?" I asked.

"Yeah. See that red mark on the back porch post? I remember seeing that and wondering why anyone would mark it."

"All right. You folks need to go back, now," the sheriff ordered. "We'll take it from here. This is a crime scene and we don't know who might be in there.

As we were being herded back the way we came, we heard shots. Pete tackled Alex and they hit the ground. Harry took Cory down and I went down on my own. Stacy remained standing, listening from behind a tree, her gun in her hands.

After a long silence, she ordered, "Get them back to town."

Town, the sheriff's office, is where we've been, waiting to find out what happened.

We've waited all day.

We were in the restaurant eating supper when the sheriff called.

"We need Alex to see if he can identify a man. I'm sending a deputy to get you all and bring you to the office."

The man Alex had to identify is dead. He recognized him as one of the men he saw briefly.

The sheriff explained.

"He was the only one we found and he pulled a gun, fired, and my deputy shot him. We think he was left to guard the place.

"I sure was hoping we could get someone alive. We've found traces of heroin in a storage room, a white wig, a bottle of White Shoulders perfume, evidence that a number of people were there, ate there, used the beds, and they fled quickly, leaving clothing, etc. We'll be able to get DNA and prints and hope that will lead us somewhere. There's a clearing about a quarter mile away where a helicopter landed so you were right about what you heard, Alex. However, we don't know for sure that it's this gang that used it. We're tracing property ownership and plane registrations now."

# Twenty-eight

The elegant blond woman paced the second floor of Design Imports fuming in vicious rage, fueled by the adrenalin of hate.

"One million dollars! It has cost me one million dollars! Bitch!"

She spat a long string of profanity from her mouth. It slimed the ears of her dark companion.

He stood with his clenched fists held tightly to his sides, his face a black stone mask, his eyes focused into deep space.

*It has cost me my brother, bitch!*

He didn't dare remind her of that. She had made it clear from the beginning that he and anyone else who worked for her were expendable. He and all her contractors were paid very well to be expendable. His brother was now dead, killed by a deputy while guarding her property. His brother's family would live fatherless but in comfort. However, a crack in his idea of loyalty opened in his mind.

"She'll pay dearly for this! She'll beg for mercy for her sons and daughter before I'm through."

He breathed a sigh of relief as she turned to leave, then froze as she turned back to him.

"Double the number of burglaries and robberies. Get all the drugs we have here onto the street. Triple the number of addicts! I want this hick town destroyed."


...mid-August...

Alex is home and doing well. His bruises are almost gone. Cory is home too. I'm sending them both to a counselor who is an expert in trauma. Harry, Stacy, and Pete patrol the house in shifts.

Greg believes that Ardith is really involved, that she was the woman up north who ordered the kidnapping. He thinks she's probably in charge of the drug trade up here.

He's pacing my library floor.

"I can't fathom what her motive would be. We're started combing records of that firm again but from what we've seen, she carried out her job title of executive assistant and never left a clue about any other activity. Not one clue. We had to find out where she lived through the IRS. When she disappeared, she took with her everything that identified her in any way. But she had to file taxes and that's how we've found out some things. Now we've been through the duplex she lived in south of De Pere near The Ledge but it's as clean as can be. Of course, we're circulating all the information and our artist has created a good picture of her from your and other people's descriptions. It's eerie. We can't even find pictures of her at legal gatherings in the newspaper morgue. That's the one thing that raises my suspicions. It seems she was extremely careful to avoid any publicity for a very long time.

"At the same time, I don't believe she's the only one. There have to be more, higher up, middle, and lower. We're getting a good idea of the lower. An increased number of addicts are showing up at the hospitals overdosed. We've identified a number of drug houses we hadn't known about before. Still, it's been frustrating. Burglaries have escalated and yet we still don't have absolutely clear connections from burglaries to drug ring.

"You really have to take care, Anna. It looks like she's got it in for you for some reason. Maybe she thought Conrad should have been in love with her. Hell, I don't know what was in her head!

"You take care!" he repeated as he left.

## *Twenty-nine*

AJ and Sheila came and have departed for Mexico again. We have their non-profit corporation in place and they'll use the house north of Cancun as a base for now, and begin fundraising. They will choose a new town in which to build the clinic, one that seems safer. But are any towns in Mexico safe?

At least I've had a chance to meet Sheila. She's something else. Full of life and delightful to know. She can really hold her own with AJ. He can't pull even the slightest Dr. God act on her at all. AJ is lucky and I told him so.

"I already know that, Mom. Prepare for a wedding late next year."

My time with them was just too short.

The camp's reputation suffered and Big Bill reluctantly told me it would be best if Alex and Cory didn't return at all. Some parents pulled their kids out and others cancelled.

Cory plays his guitar almost constantly.

"If I don't, Mom, I just get angrier at the man who was my father for getting us into this in the first place. Would you be offended if I changed my name?"

"Oh, Cory! Not everyone is judging you by what your father did. You do have friends. Look ahead. You and Alex get out the maps of Ireland and decide where you want to go. That's not far off, you know."

But I understand how he feels. One of our neighbors made a nasty remark yesterday as he passed by. I was chatting outside with the staff of Hazelwood. They were embarrassed. So was I.

Ramon has withdrawn himself from me totally. I can feel it. He refused to call me when AJ asked him to and refused to discuss why, but I know why. He's deeply enmeshed in Jorge's group.

I was so foolish to hope, even slightly, that he and I could continue our relationship. We're from two very different worlds. I think Adelina was wrong when she told me I was matched to him. I believe it was her wishful thinking. I'm better off undistracted by my longing for him. Still, the prospect of living without our deep connection makes my life seem bleak.

Adelina and I have been in touch. The school is off to a good start. Many parents have become supporters and it looks like the community will rally behind the teachers and keep it going. Good. It should be their school, not mine.

Our big concern right now is how to help Liam. Cait was weeping softly as she told me.

"He's out of control, obeying no one, not even his older brothers. He disappears from our house anytime he wants, day and night, and roams wherever he wants. He found out where Clayton lives and he's been seen standing outside that house for hours, until police chase him away. I have no control over him at all, Annie. All his beautiful innocence, his sweetness, is gone."

Stacy says he watches our house too at times, perhaps still thinking he can have some kind of relationship with Cory. If I go outside, he runs.

Cory is appalled.

Cory finally sat me down and told me he's gay. I've known it, of course, but he's always seemed to handle it well so I've never brought it up.

I told him that.

"It's never made any difference to me, Cory. I was prepared to help you through adolescence if necessary because I know it's so very difficult for some kids, even for grownups, but you always seemed to take it as natural."

"I did and I didn't, Mom. The guys in the band know, and two girls I know and dated—you remember Gracie and Terri—they both know. But I'd be scared to tell the world, you know? I know a few other guys like me and one girl who's Lesbian. None of us want a lot of fuss and publicity. God knows I've had enough with dad's drug involvement."

He leaned back into the chair, clasped both hands behind his head, and frowned, looking thoughtful.

"You know what, Mom, I don't think Liam is like me. I think he's twisted, that Foster twisted his sexuality somehow and he's really messed up. I don't feel twisted like that. I feel clear about what I am and clean with it. Do you understand?"

"I do. I feel that when I'm near him too—that sickness that Clayton forced on him, into him. Do your brothers know you're gay? Well, silly me! Of course they do."

I was remembering their attitudes, little things they had done, words said, and I realized that they had protected him.

"Oh sure they do. Since we were little. After Dad died, AJ made us discuss sex with him so he could be sure we didn't get into trouble. He practically made us study anatomy and medicine with him." He rolled his eyes. "I could give a lecture on it."

I laughed.

"You mean in addition to what I made you learn and what school taught? Wow! You had sex education in spades. You never even told me that. Why didn't you? Never mind. Just don't lecture. I've heard enough of that from AJ too. Dr. Be Sure To Know It All. I should have known he'd be on it. So, do you have a boyfriend? Anyone I know?"

"No. Not yet. No Mr. Right, even no Mr. Wrong."

119

"We women have a saying we use when we get discouraged about searching for a man. 'All the good ones are gay.' I bet there will be quite a few girls who apply that to you. You're a good one, Cory Kinnealy, a very good one."

Cait and I have been looking for therapy for Liam, but he'll come with us to Ireland before Cait places him somewhere.

It's almost 11 p.m. I turned off the lights and checked the security in the yard. All four are at posts in each direction.

Then I spotted Liam standing just beyond the lilac bushes near the river. How did he get past our security? I texted Stacy. She notified the guards. He ran and escaped into the night. I called Greg and Cait.

## Thirty

The band finished its gig at two a.m and Ben unplugged his guitar and fitted it into its case. He looked up to find the man. Calling himself Mr. Black, the man had approached him twice more since that first night. Both times there had been no attempt to further recruit Ben for anything. Just an early-morning visit to I-Hop and mention of the possibility of more money. Sean and Mike had slowly eased into the man's consciousness as Ben's friends, as fellow musicians. The man was very suspicious still but tonight his energy was sinister, tense with a dark edge. Sean and Mike left early and Ben knew they were in place watching for him. Did the man know that too? It was hard to tell.

"Breakfast?" the man asked.

"Sure. Why not? Same place?"

"No. We're going to your apartment over on Ninth. I have some food in my car. You can take your car and I'll follow you."

He had emphasized "Ninth", making sure Ben knew he'd been checked out.

"Well, OK, I guess. I don't have anything to drink."

"I know that. I've got it covered. Go ahead. I'll follow you closely, just so I don't get lost."

A small cynical smile appeared on the man's face.

*He's been in my apartment. Has he made me? Does he know I'm a cop? I've left nothing to give him a clue there.*

Sean and Mike were nowhere to be seen. Neither was any car that might hold them, or any other surveillance. Ben drove to his apartment house and let them both in. True to his word, the man had breakfast for

121

them. Bagels, cream cheese, milk, sweet rolls and butter, and bacon, egg and cheese croissants.

Ben ate silently, wondering what was coming.

When they were finished, the man told him.

"Beginning now, you are to recruit eight people to distribute drugs, free, to at least eight more people until they are addicted. Then they will begin paying for more and you will get a cut of the price. You are to continue this until you have sixty-four under you. After that you will be able to move up. This is how you prove loyalty in our organization. The long term result is you'll be paid..." and he named an astonishing amount of money.

"And if I don't agree? If I don't want to make people addicted?"

"You won't see your next birthday. Your parents won't see you alive. I do know who your parents are and what you were. You were a cop. But as I see it, you woke up and realized you're not cop material. Most artists aren't. True artists aren't cut out for that rigid thinking. Besides, I checked very thoroughly and the word is the police force doesn't want you either. You didn't fit in, didn't do your job very well. I repeat, we have checked that out *very* thoroughly."

Ben, his gut frozen, watched the man's face, the threat hanging like thick fog in the air between them.

"I have very good connections. You will break off any friendship with those Fitzgerald boys. They're snitches. They will be dead soon. If you want to live and want your family to live, you will do as I say. Yes or no?"

Ben, seeing his parents in his mind, did not hesitate.

"Yes."

The next morning Ben's parents got a phone call from a young man who said he'd heard they might have a room to rent. Could he come and see it? They were puzzled but, now that Ben was no longer contributing to the household, they knew they needed extra money for medicines. They said yes. He was charming and moved in the next day.

The hurt they'd felt when Ben left was eased a bit by the willingness of the young man to listen to the terrible turn their son had taken in his life.

Sean and Mike stood in the shadows of St. Patrick's sacristy door, watching the line at the confessional. When Ben walked in and was not followed, Mike moved into the light in the sanctuary, came down the steps, genuflected, and walked through a door across the church. After a time, Ben entered the confessional and reported his "sins" from a list Sean had made him memorize. The good priest reminded him to say a rosary as penance and sent him on his way. Ben didn't know what a rosary was.

He crossed the church and left through the door Mike had used. Once again, he reported his "sins", detailing what he'd been blackmailed into doing.

Mike spoke.

"Sean won't be going to Ireland. He'll stay here. It will look bad if I don't go. Mom will become really suspicious. She knows what we do but we avoid giving her details. Well, actually she's suspicious already, but Sean told her he has to work his regular job or lose it, no excuses and she'll accept that. He'll pass on any info you have to Klarkowski. Father O'Doul is totally trustworthy. He's worried about the people here and the increase in drugs.

"If you can't meet with anyone and need to leave a message, light a candle in front of the Blessed Virgin's statue and drop the message into the coin box. By the way, you have to look more Catholic. You forgot to genuflect when you went into the pew and came out of it. Remember, always genuflect on your right knee and cross yourself with your right hand and let's hope your contact doesn't suspect you weren't raised Catholic."

"I made up a story to cover that—that I converted and kept that from my parents. I think he'll buy it. Catholic or not, I just feel sick about addicting people though."

"Don't worry. Klarkowski's got that covered too. He says just play your part. Reluctant, feeling guilty, but not wanting your parents killed. No matter what you hear from anyone, don't believe it until Sean confirms it. Don't worry about us getting killed. We have nine lives. Of course, we probably used up five or six already but...I'm joking, man. Ease up."

Ben leaned into his hands spread against the wall and looked down at the floor.

"This is scary, Mike. I can hardly sleep and I feel like throwing up a lot. I'm feeling so bad about my parents. Black is a killer. But I want to know who's ordering him around too. That's what keeps me at this. I want these guys."

"We all do, Ben. You're not alone in this. The drug scene here is awful. You're doing this whole community a great service.

"Time to go. You've been here too long already. Go out the side door just down the hall. I'll make sure you're clear, that we haven't been seen. Sean will find a way to meet with you. You're watched, so look worried, look frightened."

Ben left, playing the part of a man in trouble, head down, hands jammed in his pockets, shoulders hunched. He headed for Ashland and walked south, then east on School Place and south again on Broadway, heading for Ninth. Getting his guitar from his apartment, he ducked into an alley and walked back to St. Pat's. Checking for watchers first and seeing none, he got in his car and headed for band rehearsal at the empty warehouse.

Mike waited in the room behind a half-closed door. Fifteen minutes passed. A large black man appeared in the hall. Mike glided into the back of the closet that held the long cassocks and waited as the man entered the room, looked around it and left. Mike listened to the sound of footsteps fading and to his own breathing.

Eventually Father O'Doul came in, took off his cassock, hung it up, and very softly began to hum "Johnny I Hardly Knew Ye".

Mike grinned, stepped out of the closet, gave a quick salute to the good father and left, a description of the man burned into his brain.

*Progress. Not perfection but definitely progress.*

## *Thirty-one*

Anna stood in the library of the house listening to the boys' voices coming down from the second floor. Cory and Alex were packing for the fifth time for Ireland. Alex was insisting Cory take more clothes and Cory was insisting he didn't need more. Anna had told Alex about her plans to surprise Cory.

Cait called and reported that now Sean and Mike were staying home and Liam, Seamus and Andrew would be going.

The phone rang again. Ramon's voice was cool and distant, and he announced he had made the call for Adelina, who then came on the line.

"¿Cómo está, Anna? You are well. ¿Si? Bueno. I am reporting to you about the school."

Her voice was loud and she seemed to believe she must shout for Anna to hear. She gave a lengthy and detailed report.

Then her voice lowered.

"He has left. Now I can talk. He is well. He is still loving you but he must find his own way and help his brother and you still have more to do with your family. It is not time yet for you to be here. You will know when that time comes. For now, be very careful. Los cocodrilos lie in wait for you. I will take good care of AJ and Sheila, like my own children."

There was a pause. Adelina's breath shook. The memory of the kidnapping of her youngest son flashed through her mind.

"Even better."

"Adelina, ..." Anna heard the guilt and pain.

"It is good. I am good. Someday perhaps I will find him. But for now, I am helping many children. Adiós.

She hung up. Anna stood with the silent phone in her hand until the muted sound of the dial tone began and she turned it off.

The sound of someone in the kitchen brought her out of the library. It was Caroline, pouring herself coffee.

"Hi. I need a break. Our entire home is filled with maps of Ireland and Africa. I've got weeks of school assignments the boys need to complete while we're on the road. I'm being outvoted on everything I'd like to do. Rob wants to add in Switzerland because he wants to go with you to find out more about Conrad. Jake and Jim want to see every country in Africa. I want a romantic villa in the Dordogne in France. I fell in love with it on my 'grand tour' after high school with my grandmother. She was such a romantic. You would have loved her. I'll be surprised if we all survive this and I'm not talking about any threats. I'm talking pure exhaustion following around my husband and twins."

She got cream and sugar out and heaped them into her cup, her hands shaking slightly.

"You don't drink that stuff."

"I do today. I have to talk to you. There are threats. We're getting threatening phone calls. Racist. I'll be very glad to get my kids out of here, and yes, I did report that to Klarkowski. Our phone is monitored. It could be the cranks calling but we can't be sure. We're all going to leave early, including Rob, and fly to New York for three days and then join you when you finally reach Dromoland Castle. Rob has security set up for the house, just in case."

"Oh, Caroline! I'm so sorry! This is because of me, because you've helped me and are my friend"

"Yes, it is, but you know, I'm ok with that. I don't want you to feel it's your fault. It's not. The blame lies with those who are doing it. I just want you to know you need to keep alert. Don't let your guard down."

"I won't."

Caitlin checked over the rules for carry-ons and read them aloud to three boys as they checked off the items. Two bags stood in front of each young man, the larger one to be checked and the smaller to be carried.

"Ma, I can't get my camera into my carryon."

"Take that food out. We *will* be able to find food along the way. This is not an expedition to Mt. Everest. You will not starve and your cell phone has a camera."

"How come you have three bags and we only have two?"

"This is my purse, which is big enough to be a third bag and legal. Should I get you all purses?"

Silence.

"Who's going to watch the house while we're gone? Do we really have to take school assignments?"

"Sean and Mike. Yes, you do have to do schoolwork."

"I don't want to go! I want to stay here." Liam crossed his arms over his chest, spread his legs, and glared.

"You don't have a choice."

Seamus stood over him.

"Give it a rest, Liam. Any other kid your age would be out of his head with glee at flying to a foreign country at the beginning of the school year. You're spoiling your own life."

Andrew, usually quiet and uncritical of his brother, added to that.

"Liam, lighten up! You're going to Ireland, man, the original home of elves and fairies. You'll fit right in." Sarcasm dripped from his voice.

Cait's face turned red with anger.

"Andrew, that's cruel! Apologize right now!"

"I'm sick of his crap, Mom. Yes, he was sexually abused. Yes, it's terrible. But he doesn't have to make everyone else's life miserable because of it. He's not facing it. He's done nothing to face it. Counseling isn't helping because he won't face it. Not can't. Won't.

'All right. All right. I'm sorry," he added when Cait continued to glare at him.

Liam turned on him.

"You shut up! You don't know what you're talking about. I'm gay! I like it, what he did to me. I liked it. Do you get that?"

"No you're not. I remember even when you were little you liked girls. You're not gay. You're sexually messed up from what he did, confused. I looked it up on the internet."

"Boys! That's enough! This can't be solved right now and there is still a lot to do before we go. Liam, stop the pouting and posturing. You're going and if you want to sulk about it, sulk on your own time. And you two! You are not counselors and until you are, stay out of this. I do agree, Liam, that you are spoiling your own life right now. Your choice is go and have fun or go and hate the whole trip and yourself along with it. You choose."

Cait walked outside to cool herself down.

"Crap!" she muttered. "If I live through this..."


...11:30 p.m...journal

My cell phone rang while I was in the bathtub a half hour ago.

"Bitch! Your interference cost us a million dollars. You'll be dead before you reach Ireland."

A rough rasping voice. Sounding drunk.

"Who is this? What interference are you talking about?"

The line went dead.


"Greg, I just got a threatening call, a male voice. I couldn't keep the person on the line and the phone number was blocked."

I repeated the threat.

"Anna, I want you to consider leaving early and by a flight not planned ahead of time. Go to Chicago or New York or wherever. Call your travel agency and have them change your plans. I'm having Cait's trip changed too and I'll call Rob and Caroline. Marthe will be under 24/7 guard and so will your mother. Get out of here."

# Part Two

## Thirty-two

...journal...travelling now, written in bits and pieces...

When I made a visit to MomKat and told her where we were going, a strange thing happened. She became very agitated and frightened and kept repeating, "Tell the boys to stay away. Tell the boys to stay away. I don't want to visit them in prison."

It took two hours to calm her down and then she dissolved into sobbing, crying about losing her sons. She didn't know who I was.

She hasn't mentioned my brothers in years. They left so long ago. I don't even remember what they looked like. I don't know where they went. MomKat would never talk about them. I only know their first names, Jamie and Pat. I'm going to see if I can find them in Ireland.

...Chicago...

I left Green Bay with great reluctance, worried about Marthe and MomKat, but I've provided as much security as I can and they're watched carefully.

Chicago is humid and hot today. Instead of flying, I decided to drive and we got away very early this morning, while it was still dark. I didn't make any reservations ahead of time. There are numerous hotels near O'Hare and we've found rooms in one. Hopefully our movements are untraceable because they're unplanned.

Stacy, Pete, and Harry think we managed that. They followed us in a second car watching for anything suspicious. Our travel agency got our flights changed. I send thanks to Conrad's spirit for all the money! Airlines charge a lot for changes for so many people.

Caroline and Rob flew to New York and then took off on an unplanned flight too.

Of all of us, Cait hasn't left yet. I'll feel relieved when she and the boys are out of there but then, will any of us be safe anywhere?

I got us all prepaid cell phones. Less chance of tracing our calls. Maybe. I don't know for sure. I'm guessing, hoping. No emails or internet surfing in case our computers are hacked. Harry says that hasn't happened but he's checking them all again.

Aunt Carrie is going with us. After we got settled here in Chicago, I went to see her and Marnie. Marnie was rude and sarcastic. I almost lit into her but decided to pick my battleground and her apartment wasn't it. Aunt Carrie had no problem telling her what she thought.

"You've become one nasty person, my girl. I've flown in higher circles than you have and believe me, you aren't close to being the high-falutin' gift to the world you act like. When you fall, it's going to be a long way down and with your attitude, you will fall."

She walked into her own bedroom and came out with her suitcase.

"I've been packed for two weeks. Let's go."

Marnie looked astonished, a little hurt, and then put on her stubborn look and closed us both out.

I faced my pouting daughter.

"If you want to talk with me about this, I'm open to listening, Marnie, but when you shut us all out you only hurt yourself. Please think about what you're doing."

She stalked to her room and slammed the door.

Aunt Carrie and I left.

I can't help but feel I've failed her in some way. Letting go is hard. What I said wasn't the whole truth. Shutting us out hurts us too.

I love O'Hare. It's the perfect people-watching venue. I can't forget Marnie's resentful face, but being here is lifting my mood.

Alex and Cory are so excited, scarcely keeping still. We're waiting at the Air Lingus departure area and all around us the lilt of Irish fills the air.

"Mom, it's so cool. They're already talking different. There's a lot of Irish tourists here!"

"Not really, Cory. Many are Americans who still keep their ties with Ireland close. There's a huge population of Irish in Chicago. Families visit all the time, back and forth."

He was delighted when an old man came up to us and asked what county in Ireland we came from.

"You look like a Mayo girl," he said to me.

"That's partly true, but also Dublin and Cork if the stories I was told are true."

"Ahh! Yer a Duke's mixture, ye are."


Years ago Art and I had gone to Ireland. I had become enchanted before we ever landed as I watched from the window of the plane while the impossible multiple shades of that green land grew closer and larger. It happened again as we dropped down over the dark blue ocean and landed in Galway in that sea of greens.

It was early morning here. After all those hours in the air, I was just about frozen into a seated position and struggled my way out of my seat and along the aisle, stiff and achy. I thawed out my muscles by walking around the airport while we waited for Aunt Carrie's plane. She had made her own reservations and was due two hours after us. Harry, Pete and Stacy were delighted, less tense, although they made a point of introducing themselves to the gardai at the Irish police desk.

By afternoon we were settled at Castleview House just outside of Adare. Carrie and I slept off jet lag. Everyone else went walking.

135

I woke up early this morning and caught up on this journal.

...second day...short notes...

Caroline and her family are here. They arrived this morning, earlier than they planned. We're waiting for Cait and the boys.

We began sightseeing at Adare Manor.

I called RTE Radio 1, gave them my brothers' names and asked that they put out an announcement to see if they could be found. I expect nothing. It's been years and years and I don't even know if they really came here. I think this is a strong hunch though after watching MomKat's reaction.

...third day...

I called Greg. We haven't heard from Cait.

"Bad news, Anna. I was going to call you shortly. Liam has disappeared, run away. Cait is still here, waiting for news of him. She's beside herself with worry. I don't think this is related to your situation. This is Liam rebelling. Mike and Sean are prowling the streets, checking his haunts and I've got police out looking too. I think you and Caroline ought to begin your business on your own. I'm going to urge Cait to go anyway but if he doesn't turn up, I don't think she will."

He swore and then apologized.

"Frankly, I'd like to turn him over my knee and spank him but that wouldn't do anything but make him worse. If he gets in any trouble, I'm going to see if I can get him into detention. Well, maybe not. I'm really so pissed at him right now I can't make up my mind what I want and it's really Cait's call anyway. I'll have Cait phone you if there's any news."

...still the third day...

Greg is jubilant.

136

"We found Liam at Clayton's inside the house, inside, mind you, a total violation of Clayton's release conditions. I have happily hauled Foster's ass into jail. What a relief he's off the streets!

"Cait, Liam, Seamus and Andy are on their way. I don't know what happened in Foster's house but Liam agreed to go with Cait without a whimper of protest. He won't talk, but whatever it was, it changed his attitude."

...fourth day...

Now begins the business we came for. Cait and family are here. Liam is eerily silent but cooperative. Cait, Caroline and I begin our tour of everything decorative and the others will go see the sights.

God help Ireland! Our list is long. Their list is endless. We meet in five days at Dromoland Castle.

## Thirty-three

"I need at least seven people now!" the exasperated man reported.

"That's impossible, ridiculous. Why would you need that many?"

The blonde woman was annoyed. He was interrupting an important negotiation. The large patio of her island home held an important arms dealer, a Colombian drug dealer and a Russian pimp of young Serbian girls.

"Where are they now? Report to me at once."

"Yes, Ma'am. Anna Kinnealy is somewhere in Dublin photographing architectural details and front yard gardens. The Bradley woman is on Grafton Street buying linens and home furnishings. The Fitzgerald woman is taking tea with an antiques dealer in Galway. The rest of the Bradley family is at the Giant's Causeway in Northern Ireland. Cory and Alex and their bodyguards are touring the Dingle peninsula. Seamus, Andy and Liam Fitzgerald are on the cliffs of Moher. There is another group, a mother and daughter named Jennifer and Mary O'Keeffe, friends who are also from Green Bay and are currently touring an old abbey in Sligo and have plans to join the others.

"That's just today. I only know that because I heard Alex tell someone this morning. I have no idea what they'll do tomorrow. It's like keeping track of a field of mice. There is one bit of news I found out. Anna Kinnealy had two brothers a lot older than she is and she sent out an announcement on the country's radio station asking if anyone knew of them and I have the phone number she gave. I don't know where the Brennan woman is. She was singing in a pub in Cork last night."

There was a very long silence. He thought she had left the phone.

"Find out all you can about the brothers. Drop the attempts to keep track of everyone right now and focus on Anna. I'll send two more men. Please do not make any excuses. A field of mice can be managed with traps. And bait. Use some imagination!"

## Thirty-four

"Forty-two years it's been. Forty-two years and I haven't seen her. Why am I going there now? She don't know me and I don't know her."

The old man, his thick shock of white hair tossing in the stiff breeze, continued to mutter to himself as he walked the final mile of the road to the Castle.

"Dromoland. I don't belong here. How is it she belongs here? Where did she get the money to visit here? Did my mother make money? How could she? No one in our family ever had any brains or luck for that. Maybe Anna married money. That must be it. She married money."

His clothing was gray, worn and rumpled, even though he'd put on his best suit, his only suit. Cars drove by him on the way to the entrance.

"They won't even let me set foot in the door here."

He worried they'd send him away before he could ask for her. A neighbor had made the call, without even telling him, to the phone number mentioned on the radio. The invitation was given to that nosy old woman and passed on to him. All his neighbors had insisted he go.

"Naggin' me, that's what. Pure naggin'."

His arthritic legs and feet hurt as he walked and he wanted to sit down but there was nothing to sit on.

"By the saints and Jesus, if I sit on the ground, they'll have to bury me right here."

He trod on, the pain showing in the set of his jaw and determination of his lips, thin and drawn. The wrinkles around his eyes were tightly bunched against the creeping ache from his shoulders and the back of his neck. Once he stopped, thinking he'd never make it, but the aching became a bit less and he began again, slowly.

Finally he came to the foot of the grand portico and the flight of stairs that sheltered the front doors.

"I'll not make it up the stairs," he whispered, nervously rubbing his face with his left hand and tugging at a tuft of hair that fell at his ear.

At that moment a red-haired young man descended, paused, and asked, "May I escort you to the other door, sir? There are no stairs there. It's just around the corner."

Patrick scanned him up and down and decided not to be proud. He nodded a thank you and took the arm the smiling young man offered.

"Dromoland Castle. Sure and I never thought I'd be standing here," he said to make conversation as they walked. It was all he could manage. His breathing was coming slow and hard.

"Neither did I," replied the young man. "My name is Cory Kinnealy. We've been waiting for you. I'm your nephew. Mom's waiting inside."

The old man tugged again at his hair with his left hand and ducked his head to hide tears beginning in his eyes. Emotions he'd forgotten to feel for years welled up from deep in his chest. He could feel his heart beating fast. Too fast.

Inside, Anna, holding her hand over her mouth, said through her fingers to the others, "He's done that, tugged his hair and hung his head just exactly like that since first I remember him. He did it whenever he was embarrassed or scared. I wouldn't have recognized him otherwise. He was just seventeen when he left."

She watched as Cory had the old man sit on a bench halfway to the door. Cory looked up at the window where she stood and, unseen by the man, tapped his chest over his heart. She left the window and headed quickly for the door. By the time she got there, they were again walking in her direction. When they neared the door, Cory stopped, tapped his uncle on the arm and pointed.

As Anna left the door, the old man crumpled and Cory caught him. Anna ran and put her arms around him and lifted him up.

"Ahh, by the saints, girl, you're a beauty!"

Tears fell.


...journal...

I've persuaded Pat to stay here tonight. He didn't walk the whole road to the castle. He had enough money for a cab for part of the way and he walked a mile and a half, too proud to borrow enough for the whole way.

Pat has lived in near poverty his whole life but has "good-hearted neighbors" who have always helped him out. They paid most of his way here. He lives in a tiny village in County Mayo and earned his living as a thatcher. He's never married and has no children. I can't get over the sadness of his life. So barren it seems to me. So lonely.

Pat says he doesn't know where Jamie is but that's a lie. He did his hair-tugging while he told me. I know Jamie has to be still alive or Pat would have said he's dead, said where he's buried. He's covering up something and I'm deep in remembering my life before eleven, when my father died. Looked at through an adult lens I see something was wrong. This lens is magnifying little things, like the silences when I walked into a room and the forced conversations, the nervous laughter over nothing. It didn't happen often, but I am remembering...

...Pat and Jamie and Dad together and the lightning of anger in the air...

...Mom's voice descending into quiet or nervously ascending higher in pitch...

...being quickly set at some task outside that just had to be done right then and there...

...being hustled off to someone's house on an errand...

142

...Jamie shoving yet another glass of beer at Da.
Can I get him to tell me? I don't know.


...next day...

I persuaded him to stay over yet another night and
we've talked. He wanted to know of my life and I held
nothing back when I told him. Then he began.

"You've become strong, Annie, so I'm goin' to tell
you what happened. You can take it now. We was
protectin' you, Annie, from your own father. Did Ma tell
you he's not our Da? Did she tell you about our Da, her
first husband? Jimmy O'Reilly. He was a bad one too, like
your father. He died in a brawl in a bar on Broadway. We
was glad he died because he was mean. You're Da was a
bad one in a different way. We had to protect you."

He saw the protest in my face and raised his hand
to silence me.

"Annie, your father was a bad one," he repeated
again, "but we protected you from him, from what he
wanted to do to you. We caught him when you was two,
undressin' you when he wasn't supposed to, and we saw
the looks he gave you. We was only boys ourselves but we
knew. We told Ma but she didn't do anythin' so we told
the priest and he said we was to keep him away from you.
We did, for a while. But we was only boys and then he
started in again, like flirtin' with you, makin' comments
about your body. We'd get you away but he was gettin'
worse, talkin' about you even when you wasn't there. His
drinkin' got worse and his mind got dirtier."

As he spoke, memories of my father's teasing
remarks about my small budding breasts or his flirtatious
manner with me came flooding back. So did memories of
the hurt and confusion on my mother's face, the shaming
blush on my own face.

"Annie, Jamie isn't here to visit because he's afraid
he'll be sent to prison. He made sure your Da died. He
poured the drink into him until he died. They said it was
the alcohol that killed him and they're mostly right but it

was Jamie who made sure he drank it day after day, as much as he could get down the man's throat. There was suspicion but nothin' could be proved. We were on the run when we left. Ma knew. She watched. She sent us away because she thought Jamie would go to prison and she sent me with him because she didn't want him to be without family.

"Where is Jamie now?"

"In a safe place. He's atoned for his sin, Annie. He's in a monastery, has been since he was twenty-five.

"We never wanted you to suffer that abuse, Annie, and it sounds like you never did, from Da anyway. Yer husband sounds like he was a gobshite though. But yer stronger for it, and you met a man who loved you. I'm talkin' about yer lawyer. He loved you, Annie. Really loved you, he did. Maybe this other man in Mexico does too. That story don't sound like it's got an ending yet.

"Our story, Jamie's and mine, it's almost over. We're old, Annie, and we know it and that's fine with us. We think we did the right thing. Yer Da beat up on yer Ma before you was born. We stopped him from doin' that too."

He nodded several times with satisfaction.

"We've lived a peaceful life here, a good life, in a beautiful land. We learned all the Irish songs, heard the poems and legends, spent our nights at ceilidhs with friends, drank our share of Guinness and paid for it in the morning. What more could we ask?

He paused, then continued shyly.

"Well, and there was one thing more and now I've done it. We wanted to see you. I brought me a camera and I want a picture of you for Jamie. He's in a cloistered order now but..."

He paused and his mouth spread into a slow and slightly wicked grin.

"...I'll sneak a picture in when I see him next time."

We took many pictures and he has a gift for Jamie from me. For many years I've had a small flat rock that fits in the center of my hand when I pray. It's from the mouth of a stream on Chambers Island in Green Bay, where I had gone for a retreat. Chambers Island is a holy place, an ancient sacred site for Native Americans even before the Catholic Church built its retreat center there. I sent the rock with Pat for Jamie with the story of how I found it, a gift from the Holy Spirit just after my little girl died.

I've set up a trust fund for the two of them and they will have enough for food, housing and a good wake at their funerals, although Jamie's will be a quiet wake. The brothers at the monastery don't put up with the crazy Irish send-offs.

I still don't know where he is. Maybe when Jamie dies, Pat will tell me, if Pat doesn't go first.

## *Thirty-five*

Our business in Ireland is done. We have enough ideas for years, enough materials, connections, and even some great furniture to last us through any business that comes our way. This morning I saw the others off at Shannon Airport. Caroline is ecstatic, fully committed to the business once again.

"We can do months and months of design and we've made connections that will allow us to furnish any high end homes we do."

She looked like a cat who had eaten an entire bowl of whipped cream.

"I've just loved being here. This was a great idea. With all the pictures you took we can do gardens forever, and we have to recreate some of those Georgian doors."

"Wait until she sees Egypt and Africa," Rob said. "She'll go nuts over the designs there too. If it weren't for northern Wisconsin winters, you might end up with African huts on the lower West side of Green Bay. Don't worry. I'll rein her in."

He grinned affectionately at her as she raised indignant eyebrows at him.

"Rein me in? Ha! That'll be the day!"

They're off to Egypt and the rest of Africa. Rob secretly told me he'll be sending the boys to some friends later and taking Caroline on that second honeymoon to the Dordogne, just as she wanted.

As they bantered, I turned my attention to Cait and her boys. Liam is frighteningly depressed. We became aware of it when he told his brothers as he stood on the Cliffs of Moher that he wanted to jump over, that he's been thinking of suicide. Apparently, though he

146

won't tell Cait, Clayton Foster brutally rejected him, telling him he was "too old" to be attractive to him anymore and other harsher comments.

"Greg has a list of treatment facilities for traumatized adolescents and I hope to get him in one of them. God, Annie, I just hope we can get him home without any more trouble. We've got that long layover in New York and another in Chicago. I'm afraid he'll run again."

Cait looked exhausted.

"Don't worry, Ma," said Seamus, who was standing with us. "Andy and I will watch him like hawks and actually, I think he knows now that he needs help."

I haven't yet heard if they all made it safely.

Today, our last day here, we got bad news for Alex. Someone informed the agency who arranged his gap year that he was involved in drugs. They have suspended his time there until they have further information. He's crushed.

However, it leaves me breathing a sigh of relief. I bit my tongue while we were planning this because Belize is so close to the cartel activity. He, of course, thought it all perfectly safe. Then, too, I've been having second thoughts about leaving Cory alone in London, even with Harry as his bodyguard and so I got on the phone and changed arrangements. We now have a London apartment where all of them can live and where I'll stay when I travel. I don't give a damn what it costs right now. Money does wonders opening doors. I'll arrange for Alex to go to school or take an internship studying finance.

*Thank you, Conrad.*

...London...

"You mean, this is ours? Where we can live?"

Aunt Carrie, Cory, Alex, Pete, Harry and Stacy stood or wandered through the apartment. I had to admit it was fantastic. Long windows that let in lots of light,

Furnished in comfortable chairs and sofas, English artwork on the walls. A small, but well-equipped kitchen. Five bedrooms. Huge. All that money could buy and worth every penny if they'll be safe.

Pete and Harry spent an hour checking security and approved it all with minor changes. Stacy is concerned about Paris and on the phone checking out our hotel there, pretending to be my "secretary."

"Cory, Alex, I'd like you to read this literature, please. It concerns you."

Silence while they read became wild enthusiasm.

"Oh! My! God! Mom! I can study acting, singing, dancing, everything!" Cory jumped up and grabbed me off my feet and whirled me around and around.

"I can go to school here studying finance and business. In London! This is so cool!" Alex said. "I had my heart so set on Belize but this is awesome, Mom, or, as the British say, brilliant."

When they finally set me down, I continued.

"When I come next I'll expect you to be able to take me on a tour of London as well as introducing me to your new friends and...and...well, I like the idea of you being together. Cory, you still have your senior year to finish but you can get that at the American school here, and you can return to attend the graduation back home at the end of the year. So, happy birthday!"

"Thanks, Mom! Wow! Thanks, Mom!"

Aunt Carrie and I left four days later, after I had checked out all arrangements for the boys in person and treated them all, sons and bodyguards, to a long list of Mother's Lectures.

Now we are in Paris. I am to be taken on the rounds of certain couturiers and shops for a wardrobe makeover. Aunt Carrie has become a dictator.

"We begin with Chanel, an oldie but goodie for suits. You will need at least four. I shall have to check out who is best now for day dresses. Then a dinner-into-evening dress, no, two, one black and one in a color that flatters you. Accessories, yes. Shoes, yes. Undergarments, yes. But there's no sense going overboard because you'll only be living back in the USA. We'll get high-end slacks, blouses, and jackets off the rack here. Give me your credit card. You won't want to look at the total."

I winced. I had just looked at the total from the trip so far.

"Just remember, she said, seeing my eyebrows rise, "you don't want to walk into Marnie's show looking like a dowdy American housewife, or into the bank in Geneva like that either.

"And a makeover too" she continued as she unpacked her suitcase in the Pension les Marroniers.

"And hair. Drat! We should have done that in London. Maybe we can run over at the last minute and have you done at Vidal Sassoon. At least you chose this place near the Luxemburg Gardens. Not five star, but adequate and what a delightful hostess we have."

"Carrie, I want to see Paris—the Louvre, Notre Dame, the Eiffel Tower..."

"We will, but first to business. You do realize that you are a businesswoman now. You are the owner of a decorating business, the owner of real estate and vast, well, not actually vast, but huge financial holdings, and you need to become that woman. Jeans and chinos and American casual are fine but you have to look the part here or you won't get the respect you need. I know about this. I made this mistake when I was young. You need to look like you belong."

"The world has changed since then, Carrie. A lot."

She gave me her indignant look.

"Besides, I don't believe I belong here."

I was feeling queasy-scared thinking of this strange world I now move in.

"You will. Remember another Alanon saying, 'Fake it 'til you make it.' I read your Alanon book. One day at a time and all that jazz."

149

So began days of shopping and nights at first class restaurants as pupil in Aunt Carrie's crash course in how to order in French, and an actual class at a cooking school about wines, and when I finally lost all patience for this stuff, a long afternoon in the Louvre.

...journal...

I did not disgrace Marnie at her show. Her jaw dropped when she saw me in a Chanel suit. But she refused to speak to me for more than an hour afterward, then made a few remarks about her part in the show. She refused to speak to Carrie at all.

An older Frenchman who reminded me of Ari Onassis (eeeww!) showed up to escort her to a late dinner. He paid polite lip service to me, also ignored Carrie, and slithered his way through the young girls at the party we were attending to celebrate the success of the show.

Marnie is drinking. There is nothing I can do except hope that I, or someone who loves her, will be with her when she falls.

Earlier today, I called the number Rob had given me and a car is to be sent tomorrow to take us to the airport. I was informed all arrangements are made.

Stacy prowled her way through today, suspicious, not able to check out who is coming or where we are going in the thorough way she wants to.

I can't get Marnie out of my mind. She's not happy.

## Thirty-six

"Wear the blue suit for travel. The red is too ostentatious for a trip but will be great in any business meeting. The grey is elegant but ever so slightly too much so. Save that for something special. Your hairdresser will be here in fifteen minutes, from London, from Vidal's salon. Thank heavens you have the kind of hair that will take a very elegant cut."

Aunt Carrie is out of control. I've wrestled the credit card from her.

I do need the haircut. After all this travel, my hair is also out of control, but "Vidal's"? Oh, please!

I was informed this morning that our limousine will be here to take us to the airport at 2.p.m. with "my staff". My staff?

Stacy, who had her own room, is now checked out and waits with us. Aunt Carrie insisted on outfitting her too. She looks quite smart in a navy blue pantsuit with white trim. It hides her gun well.

At 1:45 Marie, the owner of our pension, bustled in and chided me in shocked tones.

"Madame, you did not inform me you require much better service. You are a personage of importance, of, of...money! Are you packed? How can I be of further assistance? Surely, there is more I can do."

I was reassuring her I needed no more assistance when a young blonde woman in a smart gray suit and incredibly high pale pink platform heels with a matching pink briefcase entered, followed by a uniformed young man who waited respectfully just inside the door.

"Madame Kinnealy," she said to Aunt Carrie, who shook her head no and pointed to me.

"Oh! I am so sorry, Madame."

She held out her perfectly manicured hand to me.

"I was not given any picture of you. Please pardon me for this terrible mistake. I should have known you would be younger. Are you ready?"

She spoke English with a very charming French accent. If Alex had been here, he would have been drooling. Cory too. He adores French accents.

I was swept off, followed by my "entourage" of five: the young woman whose name was Gabrielle de Launay, the nameless young man who piled our bags on a cart and followed, Marie, Aunt Carrie and Stacy. One more joined us at the car—our driver, Henri. Marie waved goodbye with multiple invitations to come again, grasping my generous tip.

"Even though we are not in Switzerland yet, I wish to welcome you," said Gabrielle, seated facing us in the limo, and she pulled out a small shelf, opened a small cupboard in the door, and made us tea.

"Monsieur De La Vergne will be so happy to see you at last. He is most eager to entertain you. We have drawn up an itinerary for you, pending your approval. Today, we go to the Tiffany Hotel in Genève and there is a small dinner for you in a private room which Monsieur will attend to introduce himself and his wife. We know you love art and the Tiffany's décor is Art Nouveau. We hope this is satisfactory.

"Tomorrow he has arranged for your business meeting at eleven with lunch to follow at Auberge du Lion D'Or. One of the owners is an Irishman, a chef, and we thought you would enjoy that. Tomorrow evening you are invited to a dinner at Monsieur's home in the Cologny district. It is formal and I will help you find clothing if you need to...no? Good. I notice you wear no jewelry. I have a jeweler who loans us her pieces when needed. I will have her bring some pieces to the hotel from which you may choose what you wish to wear.

"Monsieur and his wife have a beautiful home and you will meet friends, I assure you. The following day you will be flown to Italy to Lake Como to see your home there and to examine your art collection. It has been moved there for your convenience. It was stored in an underground archival room at the bank but viewing it down there is most unpleasant. C'est impossible!

"I have arranged then for a week of rest. I hope that is satisfying to you."

She handed me papers with details.

"Yes. That's fine."

It was all I could manage to say.

Aunt Carrie face was smug with self-satisfaction. She didn't say a word but I heard her thought.

*You can thank me later.*


A private plane flew us to Switzerland. Gabrielle was a gracious hostess and travel guide extraordinaire. We were entertained with slides of the best of Swiss sights and fed more tea, cheeses and fruits.

We are now at the Tiffany Hotel Geneva, and I am writing at a beautiful little desk, definitely Art Nouveau, and looking down to the Rhone River a few blocks away awaiting dinner with Monsieur De La Vergne and his wife.

I love this hotel. It's not one of the huge five star immense places. It has only four stars! Tsk! Tsk! But the décor is all wonderful and colorful, one of my favorite periods of art, and it all reminds me of the Hercule Poirot series on television, although those sets were Art Deco, if I remember correctly. I have a white orchid on this desk, a real one. I would love to leave here and just walk. Who could possibly know where I am? I feel safe for now, the first time in weeks.

At eight I was escorted to an intimate room on the fourth floor and seated at a table next to a broad window overlooking the lights of the city and the boats on the Rhone. I wore my late-day-into-evening black dress with a low cut back and, on Carrie's insistence, the "on loan" emerald earrings, bracelet and necklace.

Monsieur and Madame De La Vergne arrived within minutes. She was loaded with diamonds.

He is tall, slim, with a rim of white hair around his head and a small white goatee, looking anywhere from sixty-five to eighty in age. She is at least thirty years younger and looks like an aging, but still gorgeous blonde trophy wife, which, as it turns out, she is.

I thought I would be in for a very stuffy time. Not the case. They are such fun. Her name is Yvette-Louise "but you can call me Louie," she said.

"And if you call me, call me loudly because my hearing isn't what it used to be," he joked. His name is Robert, pronounced "ro-BARE", the French way.

The meal was perfect. Louie proved to be accomplished at putting me at ease. It wasn't long before we were laughing at stories of travel glitches, strange characters we'd met, a hilarious story of how they met, and they were most impressed that I had found a suitable apartment in London so quickly for the boys.

I expected they would leave as soon as the meal was over, but we were finished with dinner and having an aperitif when Robert's face suddenly became solemn.

"And now, my dear Anna, I will tell you about Conrad." He paused. "Where to begin? It is difficult to know. Perhaps...no, you must know it all."

He took a deep breath and slowly released it, settling himself into his chair.

"Conrad was born into a very wealthy Jewish family in 1934. The family had homes in Paris, Bonn, here in Geneva and the chalet on Lake Como. His father was a banker and his grandfather an industrialist and they did business all over Europe, England, and the

Middle East. Do you know when it was Hitler became president of Germany? No? It was that very year, 1934, a very bad year for Jews, and gypsies, and the developmentally delayed, and the mentally ill, and for all those who were labeled enemies of the Third Reich. But very few could possibly imagine what was yet to come. The wealthy thought their money and influence would protect them. Never did it occur to them that they were vulnerable until, suddenly, they were.

"Conrad's parents, Auguste and Marie, had four children. Two boys and two girls. They were in Bonn, at their apartment, when the Gestapo pounded on the door and pushed their way in.

"Terrified, Marie had little time. She shoved Conrad into the arms of her maid, who fled out the back door. Auguste and the other children were in the front rooms of the building and as far as the maid knew, they were all carried off. No one ever saw them again.

"The maid, Gertruda, was childless. She and her husband had wanted children and so they kept Conrad, eventually escaped Germany to England, and told everyone he was theirs. He was blonde, like them, and with blue eyes. He looked the part. They took the name Wentworth."

Robert paused, drew out a pipe. "Do you mind if I smoke this? It's my only bad habit I have left."

Louie rolled her eyes and shook her head in amusement.

I shook my head in shock. I was still at the first sentence of this story. *Conrad was German and Jewish?* Other bits from the story lay scattered on the floor of my mind. *The Gestapo? Oh god! Two sisters and a brother?*

Robert scarcely noticed my shock and went on with the story.

"The Wentworth's did well after the war. Conrad was their only child, brilliant, talented. They gave him everything money could buy, spoiled him really. He became something of a playboy, playing quite a lot, in

155

fact, with both boys and girls, and he got into a few minor scandals, which was when his parents decided to enlighten him about his heritage. He fell back to this earth with quite a thud. They took him to Germany, got in touch with Elie Wiesel. Do you know who that is, what he did?"

"I've read of him. I think he spent much time searching for those of the Jews who disappeared into Hitler's camps."

"Yes, much more than that he was, but yes. Conrad became obsessed with finding out what happened to his family of origin. That is where I come in. I was also searching for my relatives. My father, a Lutheran minister, opposed Hitler and he too ended up in a camp, as slave labor. He died there, and my mother died in the firebombing of Dresden. Do you know of that?"

"Yes, I know of that, and I'm sorry. I know it was the Allies who firebombed Dresden and that many civilians died in that holocaust."

"Yes."

Robert was quiet for some time as he gazed out at the lights. His mind was far away. I could only imagine what painful scenes he was remembering. Finally, with a deep sigh, he came back.

"I became a banker and I was given the task of tracing money which had been lost in the war, or misplaced, or stolen, or was sitting somewhere unknown. That is when I became aware of Conrad's family fortune.

"We made our acquaintance at a meeting where I was helping Jewish families trace their art works and money. We became friends.

"To make this story of many years shorter, I found his family's money and art and the deeds to their properties. The property in Bonn was destroyed. But the Paris apartment was not, nor was the chalet on Lake Como. Nor were the family jewels, stocks, bonds, et cetera. Somehow, the Nazis didn't get any of it. A great miracle.

"Some of the stocks and bonds were worthless, others quite valuable. Conrad became very wealthy and very depressed. He tried for years to trace his family, to find any mention of them in records. He could not. He did find that his father was supposed to have been sent to Auschwitz in Poland. He assumed his mother, sisters and brother were too. Finally, he gave up.

"In the process of all this, he became a lawyer. He should have been a concert pianist or an artist. He could have been anything he wanted. He was so intelligent, so talented."

Robert sighed.

"I never knew why he chose to bury himself in such a remote town as Green Bay, Wisconsin. His excuse was that he just got tired of all the trappings of wealth. He asked me to look after his fortune, sold the apartment in Paris, and he left Europe for good. He did visit to buy art, to enjoy the museums, but he had no heart for living here.

"And now, here you are, his heiress. His love. He loved you. Did he tell you?"

Robert gazed at me silently, waiting.

I was close to tears and could only nod at first.

"He left me a letter in which he told me. He never told me while he was alive. But he was my support, my benefactor, my guide and mentor. He was trying to find out who wanted me dead when he was murdered. He was investigating a drug cartel, art sold on the black market, and sex trafficking. He was in great danger—much more danger, I know now, than we ever imagined."

My tears spilled over then, uncontrollable. I began to sob. Louie helped me up and took me to the bathroom, just letting me cry until my grief subsided. She bathed my face with cool water and dried me off.

"Robert and I are very happy to know you at last. If Conrad loved you, then we will love you too, for you must be a very good person."

"Thank you, Louie."

She led me back to the table.

"We must go," she said, "and I will not blame you if you are not up to our dinner tomorrow night. This has been difficult for you to hear, I know."

"Oh, no! I want to come. I want to be there. I'm so happy to know you. I want to know you better."

Robert rose.

"Good! A car will come for you tomorrow morning for the meeting and luncheon and again in the evening at seven for the dinner. If you want to walk, the gallery section of the city is close by. The concierge will help you find your way wherever you wish to go."

They left. A moment later Carrie walked in and sat down. Her face told me more of the story.

"You knew this, didn't you?" I asked.

"Yes. I was one of his "scandals" before he became aware of his family of origin. We had a very good time. We fell in and out of love quickly though. He loved you much more than he ever did any man or woman. Real love, not just passion. I've envied you.

"But he came to Green Bay for me. Two aging friends who didn't want to be left quite alone."

She stood up, snatched a roll that was sitting in a basket on the nearby tray and left.

"Well, I'm going to bed. Good night, Anna dear."

I sat for a long time at the window, watching the lights on the river, lights distorted by the tears forming in my eyes and dropping slowly onto the emerald necklace.

Before I leave Europe, I will go to Auschwitz and lay a stone there. It's the least I can do.

## Thirty-seven

It has seemed like a whirlwind.

The meeting at the bank was not long. I was shown the jewels and gold and given the codes and keys, and read and signed many papers.

The food at the luncheon was amazing and the Irish owner a delight. I'm being treated as if I'm a princess.

Best of all, after I returned to my hotel, Aunt Carrie and I walked the art district and I have bought a painting! It is small, and done by a French artist who now lives in Paris. I'll be able to visit her studio.

Last night's formal dinner was pleasant. Well, actually, I felt tension in the presence of one man there. I don't remember his name, but I felt such dark energy coming from him. However, he was not seated near me, nor did I speak to him after dinner. I can't help but wonder why Louie and Robert invited him. All the others seemed so pleasant, kind and open.

I have now flown in a seaplane! We—Gabrielle, Stacy, Aunt Carrie and I—went by limousine again from Geneva to Lausanne on Lake Lausanne, and then were flown to Lake Como in a seaplane, which taxied right up to a dock below the chalet.

My chalet. My incredibly perfect chalet. Of the three houses Conrad has willed me, I love this one the most. This one I can call mine without hesitation.

It's small compared to the neighboring chalets I saw as we floated over the lake but still, it has five bedrooms, a dining hall, a library, a large sitting room, and a smaller sitting room and of course, a kitchen and baths and storage areas. What makes it so beautiful are the hand-painted walls. What looks like wallpaper in delicate pastel floral motifs is actually completely hand-painted. Tall windows pour light into the rooms and outside there is a beautiful garden all the way down to the lake. I feel that I'm living in a garden indoors and out.

Gabrielle explained.

"There is a garden indoors because it makes winter much more tolerable. The winters are long and the springs often see floods here at the southern end. You do not have to be concerned about floods. As you see by our walk uphill from the lake, you are far above that."

She turned to Aunt Carrie, who was still breathing heavily and bore a very flushed pink face.

"I am so terribly sorry I did not arrange for transportation for you uphill. There is a small motorized cart and also a neighbor has a donkey cart."

Carrie gave her a too-little-too-late look as she plopped into a comfortable chair.

"I'll want to know where to phone to have the cart here. I'm staying a while, if that's ok with you. I love this place. Always have. The portrait of us you saw in Mexico was painted right here in the master bedroom."

She lapsed into an exhausted reverie, gone back in time to her younger days.

*Carrie? That's Carrie in the portrait!*

The picture in my brain of my elderly aunt young and half nude sent my mind into a standstill for quite a while.

Gabrielle left this afternoon.

...chalet...second day...

I've examined all the pieces of art and can hardly breathe when I think of them. It's a major collection; mostly paintings, some ceramic vases, three small statues. Stacy tells me either we have a secure room built here under the house or it must go back to the bank's vault. I've kept a few vases, three less costly paintings, and the statues here. The rest I sent back to the bank for now.

I've also gotten to know our staff: a cook, two housekeepers, a gardener and a chauffeur. The neighbor with the donkey cart is a jolly German man named Gottfried, who gave me a ride and a tour of my garden.

I feel safe here. Stacy is happy with the setting and the villa but she wants to explore the whole neighborhood and is out walking right now.

My mood has gone from delighted to sad. It feels safe to grieve once again. Knowing what Conrad and his family endured makes this day heavy with sadness. I try to imagine his family living here and all the children's laughter but...

There were so many who suffered, so many children whose lives ended in horror. What has it done to those who lived, who still remember?

...chalet...third day...early morning...

My quiet day became a delight. Mac called my cell phone. He's in Geneva. He just missed us.

"Anna, I have to see you. There's news—a message from someone we both know. I've just met with De La Vergne, who told me where you are and I'm coming to Lake Como right away."

...late afternoon...

A small yacht pulled up to our dock and Mac, large duffel bag over his shoulder, hopped off, waved to the crew, and made his way up the hill.

"God, this is a beautiful building! Look at the arches! The tiling! And the view!"

He turned around and around, taking in the lake, the mountains.

"It is. Can you believe this drawing room? No less than six double doors under these arches, which I can open to the air, all looking out over the lake. Then the large patio and terrace outside and that patio roof with more wide arches and supported by marble columns. I love this house."

"Come here with me to the other side." I pulled him along with me. "Look at the mountain view! Spectacular! Sometimes I think I'm going to wake up from a dream."

As we paused in one of the arched doors, I suddenly felt his desire. It poured off him and I knew he barely had control of it. He wasn't looking at the mountains. He stood gazing at me, his heart in his eyes.

"Anna, I can't, won't stay away from you anymore. My contract is over. I connected the dots for law enforcement from Mexico to Canada and I'm out of it for now. I want to be with you. I have to be with you. I'm so tired of denying myself any love and I'm so tired of denying my love for you. I won't push you or beg you or attempt to persuade you but can we just try? Can we just be together for a while to see if it works, if we fit together at all?"

He turned away, then back, running his hand through his long loose hair.

"I know you've been with Ramon, have a deep connection with him, but..." His voice trailed off and he turned to look out over the lake.

"Mac, things have changed. Ramon...he's withdrawn from me. He broke the connection and so did I, in a way. Our lives are so different and we seem to be going in opposite directions. I've lost contact with him and...I don't know what 'and' there is. I don't know what I want. He's joined Jorge and I know they've organized other Mayans to oppose the cartels in the Yucatan. Well, I'm not totally sure about that. I asked him but he refused to talk to me about it."

I stopped talking.

*I'm babbling. How can I tell him that I accepted Jorge as my lover too on that last night there? What will he think of me?*

162

I felt myself blush from embarrassment.

He misread my expression.

"Anna, part of me is glad to hear that but I can see it's still a source of grief for you. All I ask is that you give us some time together, some time to get to know each other without threat of harm, without one or the other of us involved in some craziness. Will you? Can you?"

*Can I? Yes. Maybe Mac is my contact with some sanity, some ordinary love.*

"Yes. I think I can. Stay here for a while. Let's see what happens. I'm open to that."

"Oh, excellent!"

A smile spread over his face.

"That reminds me of why I came. I have an invitation for you from Matthew Simoneska. I ran into him in London. He was on his way to the island of Malta. He's been supervising a dig on one of the goddess sites there and said if I saw you to invite you there. Want to go? Malta and its sister island of Gojo are very interesting places."

"Simoneska? Oh, I'd like that. It would be so nice to see him again. I can go too. Alex and Cory are safely in school in London, AJ and Sheila are at the house in Mexico working on plans for the clinic in southern Yucatan, and Marnie is in France. Aunt Carrie is staying here and all my business here is done. I'm free, believe it or not.

"Oh, rats! There's my bodyguard, Stacy. I'll have to bring her along."

"No, you won't. I'm enough of a bodyguard for anyone. Let's just make it a vacation for the two of us. We both can use it."

Mac put his arms around me and leaned his forehead against mine.

"No pressure, Anna. Let's just ease our way into this. I can wait a bit longer, knowing it's a possibility."

"Done." I smiled. "And for tonight, let's take a boat to Argegno and wander the town for a while and eat there. I'd like to see it before we leave."

We did.

But now, in the deep of night, I know I'll have to tell him about Jorge, about what happens to me when I'm in Mexico. How will I make him understand? Should I take him to Adelina and have her tell him what she told me? Will he believe me if I tell him? What will he think of me when he hears what happened? In the days I've been here in Europe, when I've finally relaxed, I've been having more and more desire for a man inside me. I've dreamed of sex with both Ramon and Jorge several times.

Even now, at this moment, my thought is, why not have all three inside me. I have to be crazy. This can't be healthy. Is this some sort of sex addiction?

## Caribbean Sea

### Thirty-eight

One would think that the lovely Caribbean breezes, the sunshine, the beautiful azure sea, and the bright tropical birds would create human creatures who are peaceful, gentle, and laid back. That would be true of many. Unfortunately, there are others who respond to the climate as if nature and their fellow humans are an enemy to be annihilated.

The tall man, clad in a black silk shirt and loose black cotton pants, had long ago chosen to be one of the latter. It was not entirely the relentless heat and stifling humidity of the climate which shaped his character, however. Maybe it was the chicken pox that left his dark thin face pitted. The beatings and the cigarette burns he endured as a child might have had something to do with it. The starvation might have created the obscene hunger he now had for more and more.

But the delight he felt when he could be cruel, when he watched someone suffer at the torture he ordered, that was probably there to begin with. As a baby he bit his mother's breast when she tried to feed him. Many creatures died at his hands when he was a child. Many humans had died at his hands and on his orders as a man, as a police officer, as a member of a cartel, and now as head of his own cartel.

The blonde woman who stood at his side was an enigma to him and even partly, to herself. For many years she had told people her name was Ardith Seacrest, had worked under that name, had actually attended church under that name, and traveled under that name. She did not know her real name, the one she was born with. She knew what she had been called in the European orphanage. She knew what three sets of foster parents had called her. Bitch! Brat! The c... word! *How I hate that word!*

She knew the man beside her would use all those words and more to describe her in his harsh staccato Spanish. Which is why she would never tell him who she believed she was, nor would she ever trust him.

But the cruelty, that she could understand. They recognized and mirrored each other. They knew the addiction to power, control and evil and loved it.

"What will you do now?" he asked. His voice had a rasp to it.

*He would have made a great blues singer*, she thought, *except he has no soul.*

"I have a business plan I follow based on the knowledge I picked up in my years in the law office. I've accomplished Phase One. I've met my financial goals even though the woman cost me that property in the search for her son. My attention to business was diverted. I had to leave a perfectly good distribution center there in the woods. I won't allow that to happen again. I'm expanding now into Phase Two."

He remained silent. He was quite sure Phase Two would be profitable for him as well. Trading in women and children had already brought him many millions. Allied with her, he would have more sources of income—drugs and black market products such as art and the animal trade. Together they would control a vast market. If she proved intractable at any time, he planned to eliminate her.

She planned the same for him, intractable or not.

On her cell phone, she gave the order. "Report."

The man on the other end began.

"Anna Kinnealy is at the villa on Lake Como with Carrie Brennan and her bodyguard. When she was in Ireland, only one of Anna's brothers showed up, an old man. There is no information on the other and he was older so he may be dead. The one who did show up was with her for a few days and then returned to his home. Cory and Alex are in London. Cory is attending a school for the arts. Alex will be in a banking and finance apprenticeship. Marnie is in Paris. She is definitely drinking and we think she is using drugs. She may be mistress to Fournier, a politician in Paris."

The blonde woman smiled at that news.

He continued.

"AJ and his lover are at the home in Mexico planning their medical clinic for southern Yucatan. We will find out what town they have chosen and will inform you as soon as we know.

"The Bradley family is still in Africa. The Fitzgerald woman and her sons are back in Green Bay. Son Liam has attempted suicide and is now hospitalized. Jenny and Mary O'Keeffe, the other Green Bay people traveling in Ireland, seem to be out of the picture. They met only once for a meal. They don't seem to be close at all. At this moment, all is quiet."

"Continue to execute Phase Two."

She snapped the phone shut.

"You are wasting time on the Kinnealy woman. Why not get rid of her quickly and concentrate your efforts on making more money? She is a distraction."

"Anna Kinnealy has millions of what should have been mine. I will enjoy making her suffer, watching her fall apart. I want her to live in misery."

Her voice was nearly as harsh as his as she said this. "I will eventually have her wealth as well."

He looked at the woman with lust. Perhaps she would agree to satisfy his delight in cruelty before he killed her.

*Yes, I will include that in my "business" plan for you, my dear.*

It would not be tonight. He preferred very young boys and one would be brought to him. He smiled at the thought that the child would be dead by morning.

## *Thirty-nine*

Mac has come with me to Auschwitz. We rented a car and drove. I told him Conrad's story as we made our way there.

He was silent for a long time after. Finally he spoke, his voice hard with anger and a bitter pain I'd never heard come from him before.

"Then I want to pay my own tribute. I know what my ancestors lived through as a conquered people, what they are still living with—the incursions today of the oil companies on our land, the refusal of governments to acknowledge what they did and still do, the removal of children from our reservations and placement in the homes of whites. It has gone on for generations."

All the way to Poland I could not get out of my mind the picture of a family with children in a cattle car for hours and hours with no food, water, toilet, and little hope. Then death by gas.

I tried to make myself face it all, take the "tour", look at all the pictures, read all the words.

I broke down when I saw the ghosts, the spirits who haven't left, even now, and heard their cries. Their silent screams shred the air.

"What is it?" Mac asked, seeing my eyes wide with horror.

"I'm seeing the spirits who still wander here. They're weeping."

"I visited Wounded Knee once, and other Native sites in the US and Canada where my people were slaughtered. It's the same."

We drove to Berlin and took a plane to Malta, both of us silent, solemn, lost in shock, feeling the abomination of the cruelties of humans toward other humans.

...Malta...

The sun of Malta lifts our spirits again. I look out of the plane window as we drop down onto the island near the city of Valletta and I am amazed.

"Look, Mac. I've never seen so many boats and such an extensive harbor. There must be thousands of sail boats and yachts and fishing boats too."

When we were finally on land, I kept taking deep gulps of the salty air, with its pungent smell of fish and seaweed, its tang.

An enthusiastic Simoneska met us at the airport, his dark face even darker now that he'd been in the Mediterranean sun for some time. He was grinning from ear to ear and gave me a big hug that took me right off my feet.

"You sure look a lot better than you did when I saw you last, struggling for your life in that hospital bed. I'm glad to see you so alive."

He pushed me from him with his big hands on my upper arms and held me at arms' length.

"Yes. You definitely look a lot better now."

He shook hands with Mac.

"I have a car and a room for you at the Hilton Malta, right on the waterfront about fifteen minutes north of Valletta. Wait until you see it! It's breathtakingly beautiful, with wide arches, pools in terraces down to the sea and even a check-in desk at the waterfront for tourists who arrive by boat.

"Your hotel is where we'll eat tonight," he explained. "Tomorrow I'll pick you up and we'll tour the archaeological sites. You're in for a real treat here. Five to seven thousand years of history with temples from approximately 3600 B.C.E. on at least two of the four

169

islands. One island is small and not inhabited and another, Comino, only has one hotel and not much else, but the sites, the digs, oh, man, wait until you see those!"

During the fifteen-minute drive he never stopped talking. He was there to learn everything he could about the first cultures found on the islands, and then was to begin a search for more of those early sites in the Mediterranean countries, especially seaside and island sites, "where early men and women were worshippers of the Mother Goddess."

I felt my skin tingle when he said that but put it down to the coming evening coolness. He pointed out the open-air restaurant where we would be eating under a pavilion with many beautiful arches, and then accompanied us up to our rooms.

To my relief, Mac and I have a suite with separate rooms that adjoin a common sitting room. Our balcony overlooks the harbor. I changed quickly into a loose turquoise cotton dress and a chain of beads, brushed my hair into its well-behaved cut, and slipped on jeweled sandals. Just as I finished, Mac knocked on the door to my room.

"I'm ready to eat," I said as I opened the door. Simoneska grinned his appreciation of the way I looked and Mac took my hand, mouthed "Wow!" and whispered in my ear, "You look good enough to eat."

We took much time over our food and I felt so relaxed I almost slipped off my chair. I had a quick realization of the immense tension and stresses I'd endured for the past year and thanked the goddess for the relief I now felt.

Simoneska gave us a site-by-site summary of all the archaeological periods and sites on the island and as he left us, he said, teasingly, "Anna, I have a great surprise for you tomorrow. You're going to love it! No hints now. You get some sleep. I'll pick you up at 9:30am and we'll be off."

With that he waved goodbye and Mac and I stood alone in the shadow of an arch, looking out toward the glittering lights on the boats and shore.

Mac took my hand and led me, not to our room, as I expected, but along the shore, slowly, quietly. We reached another darkened arched shelter and he put his arm around my waist and pulled me to him.

"Tonight?" he whispered.

I was floating in the darkness and the moment, but I hesitated. He felt it and backed away.

"Why, Anna? Why the hesitation?"

I took a deep breath.

*I have to tell him now, before this goes any further.*

"Because I feel unworthy of you. Because what is between Ramon and I was never finished, but just cut off, ended without any real ending. Because something happened to me in Mexico I can hardly explain to myself let alone explain it to you. I'm embarrassed to even speak of it. I don't quite know how."

I could feel my face red with shame.

"Will you try?"

I thought about that.

*I have to try. I have to be honest with this man. He deserves to know the truth about me.*

So I told him the whole story—the long years of no intimacy with any man, the gallery, the night in front of the mirror, the first time Ramon and I came together. Our first separation, and the events in Green Bay, then my recuperation in Mexico where our relationship became so intense I lost my ability to control my sexuality. I told him all Adelina had told me and then, taking a deep breath, I told him about Jorge.

At that he turned and walked away into the darkness down the beach. I waited and waited, but he never returned.

Finally I left, tears of shame staining my dress.

171

# Forty

...after one a.m...

The hotel lobby was alight and small groups of guests lingered, sitting and sipping drinks. I only wanted to get to my room without being noticed. I was passing an alcove when I heard a soft, "Mrs. K! Mrs. K!"

I looked around and, standing partially behind a screen, was a thin-faced Lindy Stewart. I was shocked, my mouth hanging open. She was the last person I'd expected to see. She and her archaeologist father, Ian, had been flown out of Mexico before I was even fully conscious, while I was still in the hospital. I'd had no news of her at all. Her belongings were still stored in my attic in Green Bay.

"Lindy! What are you doing here? Is your father on a dig here?"

I would have asked her more questions but she reached out and pulled me behind the screen as her eyes darted back and forth, wide with fear.

"Please, I need to talk to you. Where can we go that's private? I'm afraid to be seen! Please, let's get out of here!"

"Lindy, calm down. I have a room here where we can talk in private. Come on. We can take the stairs."

I led her to the nearby stairwell door and to my room on the second floor. Opening the door, I realized Mac would be coming back to sleep in his room and that we couldn't talk in the sitting room. Without explaining to Lindy, I led her to my bedroom, where I finally took a good look at her.

She's horribly thin and looks exhausted. Her eyes have bags under them and there's a sadness in them that tells of grievous disillusionment. She's frightened too. She's finally sleeping now and I can write down everything she told me.

"Mrs. K. I knew you'd come here. I'm the one who asked Simoneska to invite you. I was supposed to wait until tomorrow to see you. He doesn't know why I'm here and he wanted to surprise you. He thinks it's just a visit. I've been with my mother in Paris for months, and I saw you there by accident but I couldn't reach you. I found out about Marnie modeling there and hoped to contact you through her but she's changed a lot and she didn't even want to talk to me."

She broke into tears at that and curled into a ball on my bed, sobbing. I could only wonder where the bright confident healthy girl had gone, the one who'd led the search of the archaeological site for clues when her father, Ian, was a prisoner at the cartel's river camp. My questions about their whereabouts after my kidnapping had been deflected by everyone. Ian and Lindy had been swiftly removed from the scene. Why?

When she regained control of herself she told me, through hiccupping and small sobs, that she has come to mistrust her father.

"I never thought I'd think like this. He was my rock, the one I could really trust, even my hero. You know all this—how far away I've always felt from my mother and how close I've been to Dad. Now..." another round of tears took over.

"Now, I think, oh, this is so bad. I think he might be involved with the Mexican cartels. I thought he opposed them and he did, at least that's the behavior I used to see, but now I think he's given in to them. Mrs. K, I saw him drinking with a cartel dealer in the town of Felipe Carrillo Puerto and I saw him with one of the girls they sold and he wasn't...he was...he...she was...he was feeling her up!"

Disgust and anger made her voice thick. She almost choked on the words.

My mouth hung open. It was the last thing I expected her to say. I know her well enough to know that she is aware of and resigned to her mother's long succession of men. Her mother has provided that example many times. But her father has not, at least not that she's ever mentioned. To see him with a young girl who'd been sold for sex has obviously been horrible for her. What is just as frightening is his implied involvement and approval of this activity of the cartel. Because she saw that, Lindy thinks the cartel has her followed. She's been devoured by fear.

I'm on edge again, knowing this. *Was Ian a victim or a participant in the cartel's activities when we were prisoners in their camp? Was the beating he got faked? No. He was brutally beaten. He seemed a victim. When did he succumb to them? Has he really begun to cooperate with them?*

Lindy finally sat up. "I had to find you. I can't go back to my mother. I can't go to my father. I..."

"Wait! Where is he right now? Someone told me he would be sent to another country, not Mexico. Is he back there?"

"Yes! He's right back on the dig where we were! He hangs out with members of the cartel. Smuggling goes on right around him and the cartel leaves him alone.

"I saw that Mac was with you. I know he and Dad had a big argument but I'm not sure about what. One of Dad's workers told me about it but he doesn't understand English very well and couldn't follow their rapid speech. I left after only a week and told Dad I was going to take a summer school class and then I went to Paris when I found out from Marthe that you were traveling there.

"Please, can I come back to live with you? I'll get a job and pay my way and go back to school. Please? I don't feel safe on my own. Your house is where I can feel safe, and wanted."

174

"Oh, yes, you are certainly wanted, but, Lindy, I don't know about safe. Someone has been trying to hurt me, to hurt those around me, and drugs are involved in it somehow. I can't promise safe. I can promise we'll have security. I can provide a bodyguard."

"It's safer than Mexico and watching my dad with a prostitute or in Paris watching my mother run through a bunch of gigolos. You're not like her."

A wave of shame washed through me.

*At least in Green Bay I'm not.*

I agreed to have her come home with me and she feels safe enough with Simoneska so we'll stay for the visit already planned and then leave.

I don't know what Mac will do, if he'll even talk to me or want to stay.

Morning will be painful for us both.

When Lindy walked into the sitting room where he was reading a morning paper, Mac's jaw dropped just as low as mine had last night. Some of her old bubbly self emerged as she threw her arms around his neck and told him how glad she was to see him. I called and got her a taxi as she poured out her story and asked him about the disagreement.

Mac's explanation was, "We didn't agree on how to deal with the cartel's activities. I had to leave and I don't know what he decided, how he decided to handle their activities. I just know he was very determined to continue his work. I'm sorry, Lindy, that I can't tell you more."

She seemed disappointed but didn't continue questioning him about it.

"I'm going back to my hotel. I don't want to disappoint Simoneska's surprise. Please, please act surprised to see me later today."

She was off and gone.

Mac has been polite to me all day, with no sign of anger but he has definitely withdrawn emotionally from me.

The old archaeological sites we saw today, Hagar Qim and Mnajdra, are amazing. Even though they are thousands of years old, they are powerful sites of the Mother Goddess worship. I could feel the energies and thanked Her that She didn't take over. I'd love to spend time describing them but we are to have dinner and then Simoneska will take us on a moonlight visit to the Hypogeum, an underground site.

Our surprised act went well when Simoneska brought Lindy to lunch. She will not be with us tonight.

The goddess took over my body again.

I stood underground where the ceremonies had been held and felt Her essence explode in me. She was ecstatic at being able to exist through me in this time and place, exultant, exuberant, and delighted to be with two males. Both of them felt Her. I tried to turn away or walk behind them and I completely avoided eye contact. It was all I could do to control that. She is so powerful here.

Simoneska's skepticism was a barrier to feeling Her as he focused on his lecture to us.

"There are still groups of women who come here, those New Age crazies, who hold ceremonies. I suppose women might like that. I don't believe in any god or goddess. I think we make them up because we're in need of some sort of justification for our existence and behavior. I just don't want those worshippers to harm these sites."

He talked and talked on even as I was leaning against a wall and forcing myself to take deep breaths. Her thoughts and mine fought for attention in my head...

I wish he'd stop so we could get out of here.

*I want him! I want a man now! Fill me! Fulfill me!*

This is not me. I'm not like this. I'm ordinary.

*I am the Goddess! I am the Female! I give life! Create life in me now!*

Breathe. Breathe. Walk through this. It will go.

Mac saw it happening in me. He felt Her. If we'd been alone, we'd have been locked in sexual intercourse. Finally, he turned and left the place and waited outside for us.

As soon as we left the site, to my great relief I felt Her leave.

# Forty-one

Chaos has shattered our lives.

The phone call from Green Bay...

"Anna, it's Greg. I'm so sorry to have to give you this news over the phone but your mother was found dead an hour ago in her bed. We'll need to have you here as soon as possible. There will have to be an autopsy. How soon can you be here?"

I couldn't speak and sank into a nearby chair. Mac, seeing my face, took the phone from my hand and finished the call, promising he'd have me on a plane within hours. Lindy, with us this morning for breakfast, put her arms around me and just held me.

Mac was on the hotel phone making travel plans when my cell phone rang. London. Alex was near panic. His voice shook as he spoke.

"Mom, Cory's missing. Harry was found unconscious in an alley. Police don't know what happened. You have to come. We have to do something. Pete's called in our security firm but please, you have to come."

"How did this happen? What happened?"

"Mom, I don't know. No one knows yet. They went off to classes this morning and police just called after finding Harry. He had this phone number and my cell number programmed into his phone. That's how they knew to call here. I was almost out the door and wasn't going to answer the phone. Please come, Mom. I don't know what to do."

I told him the other bad news and promised to come.

We were packing an hour later and almost ready to leave when Greg called again.

"Anna, I don't have time to be tactful. I've been assigned to investigate your mother's death. It's suspicious."

"Greg, that's not all. I learned an hour ago that Cory's missing and Harry is in a hospital. I'm in Malta with Mac and Lindy Stewart. We're getting ready to leave. I have to go to London first. I'm going to send Aunt Carrie to Green Bay to stand in for me until I can get there."

"Anna, I have no proof but my gut tells me all this is not accidental. Where is your bodyguard?"

"Mac has been taking that role and Stacy's still at the villa at Lake Como supervising security installations there. I'll have her meet us in London. She can travel with Aunt Carrie. I don't want Carrie alone all that way."

"You're right. Absolutely not. She can't travel by herself. I'm calling your security firm. I know the woman who heads it up in this region. Let me make those arrangements. OK? I'll keep in touch. Let me talk to Mac."

I handed the phone to Mac and buried my head in my hands. Fear for Cory poured through me, almost blotting out my grief for my mother. I could barely breathe.

Mac was grim.

"We're getting out of here on a private plane flown by people I know. I'll be on the phone for a while getting that together. Anna, call Alex and tell him not to leave that apartment for any reason whatsoever. Talk to Pete. Tell him I said that. Tell him to ask Pete to have guards at the hospital watching over Harry. Tell him we'll be in touch every hour."

For three hours Mac paced and swore under his breath as delay after delay kept us from leaving.

"If this had been North America, I'd have had the contacts within an hour, but here..."

179

Six hours later we finally left Malta. For the last three hours we haven't been able to reach Alex or Pete.

We landed at a private hangar at Heathrow this evening. Mac had a car waiting. Stacy waited with it. Aunt Carrie has gone to Paris to get Marnie. Stacy has called Gabrielle who arranged security for her. When we got to our apartment, Alex and Pete were gone. A note was there.

*Mom, Police called from a small town south of London. This was a kidnap attempt. Cory got free and went to the police there. We're going to pick him up.*

No time told us when the call came in. No town. No phone number.

"Mac, this isn't Alex's handwriting."

Mac swore and called police. Within an hour we knew Alex and Pete were also missing.

"Someone breached your security here," Mac insisted.

Stacy received a call from the head of my security firm.

"He's flying in. When one of our own is killed or injured, we pull out all the stops to find out who and why. You'll have more help, Anna."

She put a comforting hand on my shoulder.

"This will go beyond what you hired from us. The firm picks up this cost. We take care of our own."

Sometime later Lindy and Stacy went to bed just after two other guards arrived to remain alert all night.

I sat on the sofa in silent and sleepless shock and pain until Mac finally lifted me up, took me in my room, laid me on my bed and covered me up with a light blanket. I was shivering.

"You're in shock."

He settled himself down beside me, kissed me lightly on my cheek and stayed there.

I must have fallen asleep. I came to consciousness because the London police arrived with the man who was the CEO of the security firm I'd hired.

I don't feel like I slept. I feel drawn and dried out. I can't eat. My stomach won't stop shaking from fear for my sons. An image of Harry bloody and looking dead in a dirty alley stays in my mind. I see my dead mother. Questions reel through my mind endlessly.

*Are my sons alive? Is Pete? Did someone kill my mother? Why? Why?*

Time is dragging. Seconds, minutes and hours are endless.

## Forty-two

Vincent Grant is just over six feet tall, with dark brown hair, a sharply angled jaw, a long narrow face and a suit tailored to fit his very lean frame. I don't know one men's designer from another but I think *Armani. Grey.* With a paisley-patterned tie which apparently echoes the convolutions of his complicated mind and his complicated business.

His security firm, he informs me with offensive pomp, is prominent in all of North America and six countries of Europe. I have only dealt with his northeast Wisconsin branch, an apparently minor section of his American Midwest division. He is personally taking over my account.

Without any preliminary explanations or even condolences, he dictates to me what I will be doing, which is nothing except remaining where he places me.

That is more than I can take. Anger hits me like a slap in my face and I come alive.

"No. You're fired. I will be placing myself wherever I can best help those I love.

I have entered a wildly angry stage of grief, my mind sizzling with fury.

"I would appreciate it if, after you find out who harmed Harry, and what has happened to Pete, you would let me and the police know. You will not dictate to me how I live. Thank you for coming and for your interest. Good-bye."

I don't rise. I just wait in screaming silence, fists balled tightly so I don't hit someone, eyes focused on a blank wall, until he leaves. Mac is appalled but I scarcely hear his protest. Blood hammers through me. I begin shaking.

Lindy watches, wide-eyed. Stacy stands still for a long while and then says quietly, "I'm staying with you, Anna."

"Stacy, don't shoot yourself in the foot. You have a good job. Go with him."

"No, Anna. I have a better job with you. I didn't receive one single word of comfort either. Harry is my cousin. Vincent Grant has always been an arrogant asshole."

This breaks me out of my rage.

"Stacy! I didn't know. I'm so sorry!"

"I'm sorry about your sons too, Anna."

So I hire her and give her a raise and put her in charge of our security. She immediately connects with Aunt Carrie's guard and Gabrielle, issuing terse instructions, and then leaves for the hospital to see Harry.

Mac mutters a curse under his breath, turns and follows Grant out. I'm sure he's shocked at what I've done but I won't be controlled. I won't!

Two London police officers have been here through all that, watching and waiting with patience and discretion and carefully controlled interest. I finally notice them and some sanity eases its way into my brain. I invite them to sit and ask my housekeeper to bring tea.

"Mrs. Kinnealy, would you be so kind as to fill us in on anything you think might have a bearing on the events we're investigating?"

The man speaking has introduced himself as Inspector Dalton and his assistant as William Wordsmith. Wordsmith, true to his name, takes notes.

Mac has returned and stands in the windows, waiting. He does not look at me. I can see he is very unhappy with what I've done.

Something is happening in my mind. I am here but not here. A part of me functions. Another part watches.

It was a long session. I filled the inspector in on everything that had occurred, even going back to Art's death. I gave him names and phone numbers of everyone involved, and photos of Alex and Cory which I carried in my wallet. Talking through this calmed me down a bit more but I could feel rage waiting to be unleashed.

"I have more recent photos which we took in Ireland but they're still on the card in the camera."

Inspector Dalton smiled.

"We can have those pictures very quickly. William, can you get the computer from the car? We'll put them on a flash drive. Or perhaps you have a computer here we can use."

"Yes, if Alex's is here, we can use his."

"Hold it, Inspector," Max interrupted. "Would you be so kind as to inform Anna that you want to examine her sons' computers instead of going at this sideways? Direct honesty is always much more clear and above board."

"And you are...?" the inspector asked.

"He's a good friend of our family and also an investigator in his own right, Inspector," I said. My defenses rose again.

"I hope you're going to be more open with me than it appears so far." I raised my eyebrows and waited.

"I'm sorry, Mrs. Kinnealy. I seem to have gotten on the wrong track here. I was actually trying to go at this with tact." He shot Mac a cold look. "Yes, we would like to examine your sons' computers. We'll work with your security team in every possible way. We also want you to be aware that because you have money, we expect a request for ransom. I hope you aren't leaving here anytime soon."

"Inspector, my mother was just found dead, possibly murdered, back in Wisconsin. I have to go home and bury her."

Dalton and Wordsmith looked shocked.

"I'm so sorry, Mrs. Kinnealy," Dalton said.

"I'll be remaining here to work with you, Inspector," Mac said, stepping forward.

"Anna, Stacy can go with you and Lindy. We can keep in touch constantly and you can return whenever we find out where the boys are. They may not even be in England any longer."

Mac looked at me. I knew what he was thinking.

Could I feel them near? Could I feel their distress?

I shook my head in a very slight no.

"Why would you think that, sir?"

"Because the persons who want to hurt Anna don't live here, Inspector. They're either in the USA or Mexico. The person or persons want to lure her back."

I was startled and horrified when I heard "Mexico". In my confusion and fear of the last two days, I had never even called AJ and Sheila to let them know what was happening. I stood up quickly.

"I have to end this. I have to call my oldest son. He still doesn't know about his brothers or his grandmother. Excuse me, Inspector. Mac, will you finish this business?"

He nodded.

I hurried to my bedroom and called AJ's cell. I got voicemail. I left an urgent message.

Marnie. I tried calling her. No answer. I know Aunt Carrie has seen her by now. I've received no call in return. She's removed herself from us completely. Aunt Carrie is due here from Italy within hours. Maybe she has news.

My brothers. Will they want to attend MomKat's funeral?

Where are Cory and Alex? Why can't I feel them? Are they dead?

I sat, dry-eyed, on the edge of my bed, wanting to cry, not wanting to cry, wanting to scream, and yet silent.

I know my behavior is erratic, that maybe I'm making mistakes, decisions that aren't right. What is right? A sick panic sits in my chest. I can feel my heart fluttering.

Mac came into my room quietly. He sat next to me on the bed.

"They're gone, Anna. I've arranged to work with them and they'll be able to check out my credentials with some very highly placed Canadian officials so I know I'll have every bit of information they have. Stacy said to tell you she'll contact your brother for you and arrange for passage to the US if he wants. Ditto for your brother in the monastery."

"Why can't I feel the boys, Mac?"

"Because they're not here. I'm really positive luring you back there is the objective, besides torturing you with their loss and the possibility of their deaths. Did you get AJ?"

"No. Just his voice mail. I left a very urgent message. No call from Marnie. Mac, our lives are a mess and I'm so emotionally upset I'm not receiving any sense of where or how the boys are because of that. Or of AJ. Or of Marnie."

"That's understandable. But your sense of them always comes back. Why don't you take some time and take a long hot bath and see if you can't get your balance back? I'm sending out for food and I'll get Carrie settled with tea, chocolate and maybe a stiff whiskey if she gets too annoying. Sorry, she's a bit much at times."

"You aren't the first to think that. She won't drink whiskey. She'll want Bailey's Irish Cream. And you're right. I have to find my balance. Mac, thank you so much."

I looked at his eyes and they had tears in them. I was so moved.

"Mac..."

He put his arms around me and held me.

"Anna, I want you to know this. Whether or not you ever can love me, I love you. No strings, no expectations, nothing you have to give in return. I love you."

That's when my heart opened to him and with genuine feeling my arms went around him and I held him to me and he held me to him. I felt his love surrounding me and I opened my heart to him. I cried in his arms.

"Better now?" he asked when I was calmer.

I touched his face and found he was crying with me. No man has ever cried with me before. I thought *I can love this man* and shame was not part of it *but I must find my children before I do anything for myself, for us.*

"Mac. Cory feels so far away. Alex might be here. My sense of him is so muted though, like he's unconscious. I don't know."

It was dark in the room but I could feel his smile.

"Then let's find them."

# Part Three

## *Forty-three*

It took Carrie Brennan a tense nine hours to find Marnie at the chateau of the French politician just outside Paris. It took her less than ten minutes to see that Marnie, very drunk, was in no condition to make any decisions. It took her a blistering seventeen minutes to rake the French politician over the coals for his corruption of a woman less than half his age, another five hours for she and Gabrielle to get Marnie into a clinic in Switzerland, two hours to find someone who put out scandalous information about the politician on the French internet, and then she hired a limousine to get to London through the tunnel. Stacy, on the phone, had been opposed to her leaving without a guard.

"I am quite capable of taking care of myself, dear. You belong in London helping Anna. Louie de la Vergne and Gabrielle have been a great help."

Louie and Gabrielle had been excellent help.

Finally alone, Carrie cried during most of her journey. Marnie had always been her favorite, her girl, her lovely beauty.

*It is just so painful to watch beauty self-destruct and that fat old fart to enable it to happen. One more thing to break Anna's heart. And mine.*

Twenty-four hours later she was on her way to Green Bay to bury her cousin, another woman whose heart had been broken.

An unseasonal September rain beat down on the streets of Green Bay as Greg Klarkowski ran from his car into the police station using his suit coat as an umbrella.

The feeling in his gut was fiery, not just because he had a stress-induced acid burn there, but because he knew hell had just broken loose in the lives of the Kinnealy family and there was more stress to come.

When he got to Arnie Schwartzkopf's office he elaborated on that.

"Every time something happens to Anna and her family, the ripples spread to us all around her. She's a magnet for trouble."

"What now?"

Greg ran through what he knew.

"Both her sons have disappeared into a British nowhere land with one of their bodyguards unconscious in a London hospital and the other bodyguard missing. Her daughter is involved with some dirty old Frenchman, and no one's been able to get hold of AJ.

"Cait, worried about Liam, has completely lost it and is now pissed as hell yet again because we're using two of her sons to dig up dirt on a possible drug connection that is somehow entangled in the web around Anna. It's also now clear that Anna's mother was murdered by asphyxiation. Smothered. Even with her mind gone that's a god-awful death. Anna's on her way here but her plane is stuck in Chicago by bad weather.

"We're monitoring phones at the Bradley home. They're still gone but Rob Bradley has security there. The phone calls are racially nasty—vicious harassment, and we'll follow up on where those calls come from.

"Macpherson is working with the London police on the disappearances of Alex and Cory.

"Anna's brothers are coming with her. Oh, and that's another story. They were suspected over forty years ago of involvement in the death of her father. Nothing was ever proven. They left town and the investigation was dropped, a long ago cold case. I don't even want to go there."

"I don't either. We've got too much on our plates right now. I want to know what we're hearing from Cait's boys and Ben."

"Between them and our other eyes and ears on the streets, we've got six businesses pinpointed as suspicious, mostly because of erratic activity observed, such as—one, sudden flurries of shipments in and out, two, accompanied by periods of inactivity and, three, most of them have no apparent real commerce.

"Four of them are small buildings, freestanding, that look like they're used as warehouses. The buildings are rented by firms with generic names that don't say what they do. Here's the list and names of the people who rent and those who own the properties."

He laid papers on Arnie's desk.

"I've talked to the owners by phone and they all say they just rent the buildings and don't have anything to do with what goes on there. That may or may not be true. We're digging deeper.

"A fifth building is a two story with a small tobacco store on the first floor in front and an empty space in back. It seems innocuous enough. However, the second floor is getting a lot of crate and box traffic.

"Locations don't seem to be relevant. Two buildings are on the northeast side near University Avenue. A third is just inside the city border with Ashwaubenon. Two more are on the northwest side.

"The sixth and last is a store on Broadway named Design Imports, Inc., and they have a small boutique style store on the main floor selling Central and South American arts and crafts. It's a perfect cover for shipping contraband from those countries but it seems legitimate enough. The store is staffed by three women, two part timers and a manager. All three are from here and say they were hired by a man who is the 'buyer' who apparently travels and ships the merchandise from the other countries. The staff all check out as doing only what they were hired for and that is to run the shop. None have

193

met anyone involved in the business besides the buyer. He calls himself Mr. Jones. His generic last name is really the only suspicious aspect of that setup.

"Ben is walking a thin line. His 'handler' is hardcore, vicious, and the hold he's using is a threat to Ben's parents. The handler, who calls himself Mr. Black, another blah name, found out Ben is an ex-cop. He reminds Ben of that every time they meet. He's using that as a threat as well to demand that Ben push more drugs to prove his loyalty. Ben wants out. If there is any connection at all, Jones and Black could be one and the same, but right now we see them as two different people.

"And that points to another problem. How did this guy find out that Ben is an ex-cop? Have we got a leak in the department?"

That remark brought Arnie's head up out of the papers he was reading.

"Crap! That's serious. We have to follow up on that. Well, but wait a minute. It's always possible with digging to find that out because police officers are public employees. Oh, hell, what a case this is."

He rubbed the side of his face, worry lines wrinkling his forehead and eyes.

"Go on."

"Our biggest problem is that we have absolutely nothing to allow us to enter these buildings and do a search. I sure would love to just waltz in and turn those places inside out."

Arnie continued to stroke his long face with his thumb. Greg knew from playing poker many times with him that this was a "tell". Arnie was more nervous that he appeared to be.

"Well, let's see," he said. "The fire chief owes me a favor. Maybe all those businesses have a fire safety inspection due. Of course, that still won't get us into any containers. Just eyes inside. Nah! Not enough. Tell your guys to let Ben know I've got eyes on his parents. Have had since he went undercover. When is Anna due home?"

"Today. The funeral is set for St. Pat's for next week Monday. The wake is Sunday evening. That's if AJ can make it. They might put it off if he's delayed. Arrangements haven't been published yet at all and I advised her not to do that. Too much potential for more mayhem."

Iron Mike stuck his head in the door.

"Greg, there's a call for you from MacPherson, urgent. I'll patch it through to you here."

The phone rang moments later. Greg picked it up and hit the speaker button.

"Greg here. What's up?"

"About Anna's boys, some very vague but maybe hopeful news. I have, quite possibly, tracked Cory to North America, via an airfreight shipment. British police discovered an airport worker who saw a bloke with red hair, supposedly drunk, being loaded onto a plane at a small local airport in the west of Britain. No proof it was him but the plane was headed for Canada. I've got people working on it. No sign of Alex yet but I have a hunch they're together. About drug investigations down your way, I've got a line on three possible drug connections to your city." He named three businesses as Greg wrote quickly on a nearby pad of paper.

"Can you check out those to see if there are any connections to Montreal or anywhere in Canada? I'll be in Green Bay tomorrow. I've got to run now. See you then."

Arnie began stroking his face again.

"More to check out. I hate this investigation. The longer it drags on, the more worried I become. What have we got on Ardith Seacrest so far?"

"Not a damn thing more than we had at first. We've gone back years. She rented an apartment just before she got the job at Wentworth and Foster. We lucked into that. She moved to better places as her salary rose but never lived beyond a modest middle class income. We checked bank statements, taxes, anything. She seemed to be a creature of careful and very consistent habit. To all appearances, she lived a low-key life for years while she was his executive secretary. After Wentworth left her all that money, she gave two weeks' notice and disappeared. Literally disappeared. I remember she fell apart at the reading of the will, broke into tears and left the room suddenly. Something really upset her. We all thought it was grief but I don't think so now.

"We still can't trace her money since Wentworth's death. Her bank accounts dead end one week after the reading of the will. The money she inherited from him was all converted into cash and stashed somewhere else. We have her fingerprints from the office, but she was in no system we could find. We've interviewed anyone who met her and no one can imagine her doing anything to harm a flea. We've gotten absolutely nowhere."

Greg picked up the papers again.

"I have to make copies of these for you. Then I'll see what I can find out about the businesses."

Arnie picked up the phone and made a call.

"Anyone approach Ben's parents' at all?" he asked the person on the other end, after hitting the speaker button again.

Greg paused at the door, listening.

"No sir," came the answer.

"Good. Double the surveillance. There may be an attempt soon. Tell our man inside their house to keep a close watch."

Greg left.


Ben and the band finished the gig at 1:30am. Patrons were still drinking, most too far-gone to appreciate music. Depression dragged at him.

*I'm getting nowhere. I don't know any more now than I did before.*

He felt himself being pulled deeper and deeper into the drug scene, a long slow whirlpool sucking him down.

*If I don't get a break soon, I have to back out of this. I'm so tired, so sick of seeing addicts destroy themselves buying this shit and Black wants more and more sold. It's like he wants the whole town drugged on coke and heroin. Vicious!*

Ben's mind saw his parents, felt the threat over their lives even more than his own.

He looked up. Black stood at the rear door of the bar, watching him. A shiver went up Ben's spine. He managed a quick casual wave, his face set in a stone mask to cover his feelings.

Black swaggered slowly to the stage where Ben was reeling in electric cords.

"I have some work I need help with tonight. How soon will you have that done?" He pointed to the tangle of electric cords.

"Not long. The other guys will do their own equipment. I just have to pack up my stuff."

"Well, hurry it up! I have a deadline for getting a truck loaded. My regular help isn't here. You'll have to do. Leave your car here. We'll walk. I'll wait in back."

Half an hour later Ben accompanied Black south through the alley to the rear of a store that fronted on Broadway. Ben looked for the name of the place but no name was on the back door or building wall. Trundling dollies from the rental truck, they took the freight elevator to the second floor.

"I need all these cardboard and wooden boxes on the U-Haul in the next hour."

The lights were dim. No labels identified the boxes. Ben was given no opportunity to move anywhere but from second floor to truck and back. Once he lost his grip on a slippery cardboard box while setting it on the dolly and its edge scraped painfully down his shin. He swore and dropped it. Black was on him instantly.

"What do you think you're doing? Watch it! Be careful!"

"I'm tired, man!"

"Just keep going. These have to be on their way tonight."

When they were finished Black escorted Ben back to his car.

"Just remember your parents."

He smiled to himself as Ben drove away.

Ben was also smiling. The longest blade on his jackknife had just 'slipped' deeply through cardboard into one of the lighter boxes and he hoped to have some residue of whatever was in there on it. A slim hope, but still...

As he drove down Broadway toward Ninth, he also figured out what store they had been at. Confession would feel extra good this week.

*I bet no Catholic likes confession as much as I do. In fact, I'd better do that tomorrow. Wouldn't want to go to hell now.*

# Forty-four

...journal...Green Bay...

I'm home. I'm exhausted and sick physically and emotionally. I have diarrhea and cramps, not from any bug I picked up but just because I'm so frightened for my sons. Grief for my mother has piled rocks on my spirit.

My concentration is poor. I've had very little sleep. My nightmares are back. The one where all my children die by drowning in a sea of white powder is the worst. It comes frequently.

Mac phoned and is here in town. There is no real news of Cory or Alex although he's pretty sure they're both gone from England. I haven't been able to contact AJ, or Ramon, or anyone in Mexico. No word about Pete. I am way beyond worried.

Carrie's news of Marnie is horrible but at least she's in a clinic. Louie called me and she and Robert will be sure to watch over her. Carrie herself is near exhaustion. I always have to remind myself that while she's a lively one, she's old.

Lindy is very depressed.

The House, always my place of refuge and security, now mocks me with memories of the times when life was so peaceful. The House itself has become a worry. We're not really secure here at all but then it's obvious we're not secure anywhere anymore.

MomKat's funeral is arranged but where is AJ? He won't be able to get here in time if I don't let him know today.

Carrie is putting my brothers up at her place. I haven't seen them yet.

I've tried over and over to relax, to connect with my sons, to feel out where they are. I can't. I only know they're alive.

*Who is doing this to us? What have we ever done to deserve this? Who have we hurt? How? And why? Why?*

As Mac got in the unmarked police car, Greg handed him a paper.

"How is Anna?" Mac asked.

"Not good. Sick. Grief-stricken. Very worried. Unable to feel where the boys are and she's heard nothing from AJ. Marnie is in a rehab place in Switzerland, thanks to Aunt Carrie and Anna's new friends there. Do you need to see her?"

"No, not right now. This is more important. Before I see her I want to eliminate any possibility those boys are stashed here right under our noses. What's this?" He held up the paper.

"It's our list of businesses we've pinpointed as suspicious. Yours weren't on it. We've got a man checking your list out and we'll talk to him later. On this list, we'll do the east side first, then the one near Ashwaubenon and then end on the near west side. You can follow on the map. I want you to meet one of our undercover people. For that we'll have to go to church. If we have time, we'll visit Cait Fitzgerald and her sons, who are informants."

"Church? Really? Interesting."

Three hours later Mac knew as much as Greg did.

He checked off two names on the list.

"My money's on two places—the Ashwaubenon place and Design Imports. Want me to see if I can make a buy? No one knows me here and I can act and look like a drug addict if I have to."

An hour later Mac sidled into Design Imports. Ashwaubenon had proven to be entirely legitimate. He had not even had to pretend to be anything but a guy looking for parts for a small engine, which was what the store sold.

However, at Design Imports his radar went off all over the place as he examined the imported arts and crafts from "all the states of Mexico and the countries of Guatemala and Costa Rica" which the store brochure advertised.

Mac made a small buy of a handcrafted doll and made his way to the Thai restaurant a few blocks away. Greg was in a booth in the back.

He grinned at Greg.

"I have a bit of good news for you. Design Imports would have seemed totally legitimate if I didn't have an encyclopedic knowledge of the arts and crafts made in every state in Mexico. Some of those products were labeled wrong, like this one."

He set the doll on the table.

"Each state has their own artisans in small towns and villages and their own special arts they sell. Design Imports has mislabeled the sources of no less than thirteen products that I could count in the time I was there. The sales clerks don't know that. Are they in on it? I don't think so, but whoever the buyer is, he ought to know. You mentioned your undercover man stuck a knife in a box? Did that yield anything?"

"Nothing." Greg looked disgusted. "It's been so damn frustrating. But this gives us a great lead. We'll follow up on it by having our informants watch the place. Now it's time for you to meet our undercover cop. Actually, you're going in alone to meet him. The church could be watched and if I show up, you'd be made. Even now, just our being together could create a problem. Here's what you do."

He gave detailed instructions.

Leaving the Thai restaurant, Mac ambled in a leisurely manner through the streets of west Green Bay, a tour brochure in his hands, until he came to St. Patrick's Church. He tried the main door and it was locked but a side door opened to him. Casually looking around, and glancing at his brochure as if to check where he was, he went inside.

Making sure the church was empty, he moved through a door that took him to the sacristy and introduced himself to Ben.

A half hour later, Mac was seen by a man, who had just come in, to move out of a pew, genuflect, make the sign of the cross and leave the church. Mac was no longer on the street when the man left. He was watching from inside the rectory, where Father O'Doul had treated him to shelter and a mug of strong coffee.

He phoned Greg.

"You were right. I was followed or at least seen. I think the guy was watching the church when I went in but I didn't see him then. My guess is he lives nearby and is probably ordered to check out any unusual visits.

"I don't think the boys are stashed here in Green Bay. No evidence one way or the other really. We can't rule that out but it just doesn't feel right, although it would be something this Ardith person might gloat about if she is behind all this. I need to talk to Anna about it. I hope she can make that emotional connection with them she does with her kids.

"It's almost dark. I'll wait until I can slip into Anna's house under cover of darkness and I'll be gone tomorrow. I'm really worried about AJ and Sheila. I have to go down to Mexico to check that out. Good luck."

"Same to you. Watch your back."

"Always."

## Forty-five

Mac came after ten tonight, with Sean and Mike. I was still up, still sick although I've finally been able to keep down a bit of medicine to calm my insides. We sat in dimmed light at the dining room table, shades pulled, I with a soothing tea and they with strong coffee.

"I'm sorry to hear about Cory and Alex, Mrs. K. We're really sad to hear about your mom's death too. I wish we could do more," Mike said.

"Mom is praying for you but she's really focused on Liam right now. He's not doing so well, still suicidal, hospitalized and still, well, a mess," Sean added. "When is the funeral? We've been watching the paper and the news but haven't seen the announcement."

"I haven't been able to get through to AJ in Mexico. It's supposed to be Monday. I've been told I can wait and have her body kept until a later time. In truth, my mind is a mess too. I can't seem to make any decisions. I'm so..."

*I have no words to describe my state. Panic? Fear? Even terror doesn't touch it. If, in my mind, I see either of my boys, I begin to shake inside until I feel I'll collapse. Add to that the intense misery I now feel from Marnie and I can barely function. I feel nothing from AJ. Blank. All connection gone. I still have the feeling I'm two people, one acting and one watching.*

Mac sat next to me holding my hand. He gave it a small squeeze.

Sean stood up.

"We have to get back home. Me, Mike and Andrew have set up a watch over our own house. We take shifts. Thanks for the coffee. I'll be able to keep my eyes open.

Mac, it's been great to meet you. Thanks for your help. We'll be watching Design Imports like hawks."

They shook hands.

"You boys be careful. These people are very dangerous. Whoever runs this seems to have many contacts set up to monitor this town. Be careful who you trust. Stay in close contact with Greg and don't take any chances."

"We will. Take care, Mrs. K."

"Tell your mom I love her."

They left by the back door and melted into the blackness along the river as I watched them through a darkened window.

The night is slightly chilly with only a hint of autumn.

I've been barely aware of weather or my surroundings. Every bit of energy I have I use to try to get connected to the boys. Frustrating. So faint. Is it useless? Maybe they are dead and I'm just not feeling that. I don't want to feel that. There has been no ransom demand, no word, no anything. Why? Why not?

Mac is pacing my bedroom as I write. He's been on and off the phone since getting here, making contact with every possible connection he has, keeping in touch with London.

Marthe is safely asleep and watched by a nurse, thank heaven. Lindy is still tearful, angry, and worried but sleeping right now too. Stacy has hired two more watchers for the house, working shifts. No news of Pete.

"Anna, you need to get some sleep. Leave that and let me give you a good massage. You're so tense. No sex, just soothing. No pressure. Just let me help you."

"Ok, I'll try but I'll probably dissolve into tears. I hate this feeling of helplessness."

"There's an elder in my tribe who says tears are the Creator's gift to cleanse our spirits."

"I'm thankful for that gift. When I can't cry, I feel like I'm losing my mind, what's left of it."

Much later, Mac watched Anna as she tossed in restless sleep. The sound of a wind-driven September rain splattered against the windows and sides of the house in a black moonless night. He allowed his mind to consider the worst—that all three of Anna's sons were now dead—and recoiled from the thought.

*Not yet. Not yet. Too soon to think that but I have to go to Mexico. Something's wrong down there. AJ should have called by now.*

Mac lay down on the bed next to Anna and pulled a blanket over himself. Sleep overtook him as he was planning contacts he could make.

# Forty-six

*Dream...*

*I stand in the waters of the jungle swamp, listening, listening, listening. A fish jumps, a hiss sears its way through the air, a snap cracks as jaws slam shut, a soft rustle whispers of a crocodile's long body as she slides into the dark water. It is blackest night. The smell of mud, musty and wet, rises from below me.*

*When the call comes—the long wailing cry of "Mo-o-o-m! Mo-o-o-m!"—I shatter inside. Where are they? My children. Gone. I dissolve into despair.*

*A low growl comes out of the night behind me. I hear rasping breath, smell feline musk, smell wet fur, feel wet fur rub against my leg. I look down and yellow eyes glow as jaguar circles around me. Her eyes rivet me to the spot, then grow larger and larger. I fall through yellow space into water as the jaguar slides her body into mine.*

*Suddenly my senses grow so strong I almost lose consciousness. Then water covers my whole body. I come awake. I jump. My arms shoot up and out and splash and my sleek body swims through the water to a hummock of land where I crawl up and shake off the water from my fur. I prowl back and forth, sniffing the quiet breeze. Yes! Faint but clear. The scent I've been waiting for, my children. Excitement races through my body as I leap in the direction of the scent. I race through the night, long leaps of movement, floating, flying...*

"Anna, Anna, what is it?"

I wake to find Mac next to me, his long body wound around mine, holding me. Inside me, She feels his body and desire races through my legs into my vagina, and up through me, pouring out around me. Hunger for him devours me and I open my mouth and clamp it over his, sucking, probing with my tongue. I feel his quick response and wrap my legs around his body, taking him inside me.

We dissolve into each other again and again.

The phone screams out of the night next to my bed dragging me out of sleep. Stacy, who had flown to London to see about further help for Harry, reports in a staccato voice that ticks off items one by one.

"Marnie has left the clinic. She was last seen on a security camera at Orly Airport in France in the company of a man with a Mexican passport. She boarded a plane with him bound for Mexico. I'm having them traced. Still no news of Pete. London police thinks he's dead. They are in contact with Interpol.

"I'm leaving here within the hour. Harry's conscious but won't be released for another week. My uncle will take over his care for me. I'll be in Green Bay in two days at the most. I've added even more security at your house. They'll arrive today."

I can't feel any of them now. What's happening? I can't feel.

As I try to eat some breakfast, Mac gets a call and puts it on speaker. It's Greg.

"It's been a hell of a night but we've finally got a break. We had three overdoses at St. V's ER, four at St. Mary's and more at Aspirus, and one major drug raid. One of the ODs talked to Sean and he and Mike *accidentally*—put that last word in italics—ran their car into a delivery truck in the Design Imports parking lot, a crate *accidentally* broke open, and lo and behold, a powdery substance spilled out all over. We've raided the store and found enough to close it down. Mr. "Black", not his name of course, was there and an African-American man who apparently was another of her henchmen. Black clammed up but not the other one. He isn't loyal to her any more. It seems it was his brother who was killed in the raid up north and he's singing like a tenor in an Italian opera because she refused to pay his brother's family the money the man had earned. Unfortunately, he doesn't have any idea where she is. Her name isn't Ardith, but he has no clue to her real identity. He's giving us a lot of information on the towns and businesses in this drug network. We've got police involved all the way into the Upper Peninsula.

"Anna, 'Ardith' is very dangerous. This guy reports she has it in for you big time. She's had all of you watched for at least three years that he knows of. Obsession is the word he used. This is in no way over, so double your guards and your watchfulness."

"But why, Greg, why? I've wracked my brain and I can't find anything I might have done to her."

"He doesn't know. Until she's in custody, we won't know.

Mac spoke.

"Does he say anything about what she might do next, where she might be?"

"He said he heard her refer to an island off the Mexican coast as her headquarters but he never heard where that is. As to her plans, she's been harassing Anna in what she calls 'phases' of her 'business plan' but he was never told ahead of time what those consist of. He knows part of Phase One was to establish the store here and the long string of robberies to tie up police. Kidnapping Alex up north may have been part of that but he said apparently something about it was botched. Of course, we know they wanted Cory, not Alex.

"Phase Two includes flooding Green Bay with drugs. I think the kidnapping of Cory and Alex is probably part of that second phase. Please, please be careful. She flies into extreme rages when things go wrong."

"Oh god, Greg! Marnie may be part of her plans too. We got a call from Stacy telling us that Marnie left the Swiss clinic and was seen in Orly airport with a man with a Mexican passport and they were headed for Mexico. I still haven't been able to get AJ on the phone and Ramon's phone isn't answered by voice mail or by him."

"Just a wild guess, Anna, but I think you'll have to look for your children in Mexico this time. Whatever you do, I think you should put off your mother's funeral. That could become a lightning rod for more retaliation from her and even harassment from whoever inflamed the crowd when Cory did his gig. Ardith could even have been responsible for that. God only knows what Phase Three will be about."

"Greg, you have to protect Cait and her boys. Caroline and her family too, when they get home. Anyone who knows me could be her victims."

"I'm on it, Anna. Law enforcement in the whole region is on intense alert. Where is Stacy?"

"She flew back to London to work with police there and see Harry but is on her way here right now. She's got two more security people here in the house watching us. When she gets back, I'll have her coordinate our plans with you."

"Good! Keep in touch!"

The phone went silent.

Mac and I looked at each other.

"We have to go to Mexico, Mac. I've gone numb again. I don't think they're here."

I cancelled my mother's funeral. What a terrible death. I shake with fury and horror if I think about it. No one can hurt her anymore but that is very small comfort.

# Mexico

## Forty-seven

Stacy arrived the next day and I left her in charge of security for Marthe and Lindy and for Aunt Carrie and my brothers. She'll join me when she's through. She and Greg will meet to exchange information and she'll keep me informed.

We used a private plane to Dallas, one of Mac's many contacts. In the air we set our plans. Or rather I did. I'm to be the bait. Mac is adamantly opposed but it must be this way. It has to look like I'm abandoning all protection to find my children and rushing headlong into the trap, if there is one. The only other alternative I can think of is that she (or they) won't 'trap' me but they will torture me by keeping me in the dark, not contacting me at all.

"Can you think of anything else they might do?" I asked Mac.

"Yes. I think this woman definitely wants your money and will blackmail you into it at some point and then kill all of you. I don't want you to disappear too. I want to know where you are at all times."

"But if you're with me then she'll know about you and will attack you somehow too. She doesn't know you, doesn't know what you're capable of, the connections you have. You're my ace in the hole, Mac, my only backup plan.

"Think about it! What if she's not the only one? What if there are others involved? How will we know unless someone watches the persons who watch me? That has to be you, Mac. Who else can we trust? I have to look like I'm all alone in this, like I'm totally upset, helpless, and have no place else to turn."

He didn't like it but neither could he come up with a better plan.

So I've taken a plane from Dallas to Cancun and walked into the airport, seemingly alone, and hired a taxi to take me to my house in the north. I just hope the taxi driver isn't part of this whole thing.

The market in Cancun is crowded and we're stalled in traffic.

Where is Mac?

Mac glided his motorcycle to the edge of the dusty side road and watched, waiting for the traffic jam to clear. Suddenly, he saw the door of the cab open and Anna darted into the crowded street and moved quickly around people in her way, heading across the road the cab was on. Mac looked further in that direction. At a far table he saw a blonde woman rise and walk quickly to a limousine nearby. She disappeared into the interior and it moved away, honking its way through traffic.

"No, Anna, no!" he muttered. His eyes returned to Anna as she stood still, watching the limo disappear. His stomach tightened as a tall slim man with a pitted face took Anna's elbow and moved her smoothly to a black SUV, shoved her inside, crawled in behind her and the car moved off north along the main road.

"Damn! Did you see that? I think that might have been the Seacrest woman but who was the man?"

The reply came over the microphone in Mac's ear.

"That was El Cocodrilo. A very sadistic man. He runs his own cartel. He will not kill her but he will torture her. Do not lose them. We have to find out where he is taking her."

"Got it."

Mac, happy he'd opted for a motorcycle, wove through traffic and followed them onto the main highway.

To his great surprise, just over an hour later the SUV pulled into the driveway of Anna's home. He had been forced to stay some way behind but another car, driven by his contact, had changed places with him several times. It drove on ahead, gave him the location of the SUV and appeared to drive on to another destination. Mac passed the road to the house, rendezvoused with his contact a quarter-mile beyond, and they made quick plans, hid the vehicles and raced back to the house as darkness came.

To Mac's even greater surprise, they arrived just as El Cocodrilo, commanding three cars of men, was shouting orders to them all. They began to leave in a flurry of activity. His pitted face was grim as he entered the last car and left.

Beside Mac, Jorge whispered, "I counted his men. That leaves between one and four persons to guard Anna. We can leave her here for now. I know he is connected to the woman somehow. We need to know where he is going. Let us hope it is his headquarters. We have not found that yet. I can leave one man here, watching."

"But will the men harm her?"

"No. He is very strict with his men. They will not go against his orders. And also, he will want to be there to question her. She will be safe for now. My men will keep him very busy."

"Ok, if Anna's safe for now, let's do it. Let's hope he leads us to the woman. He ordered his men south. They'll have to take the main highway. We can catch up."

Jorge muttered orders into a cell phone and ran behind Mac back to their vehicles. They took off into the night, racing south.

Mac contacted Jorge as he reached Cancun.

"Where are you? Have you seen them?"

"I am just south of Cancun. We have lost them in the dark. They must have turned off onto some side road. I am sure one of the reasons he left her is that I have had

212

men raid a place where he was keeping children. This is something we planned before you got here. We got the children out. He has lost his merchandise. I hope that is it."

"OK. Where are AJ and Sheila?"

"They are at the little town, Santa Anita, where he is starting the clinic. I myself have not seen them for two weeks but they should be good. Why?"

"I need to let him know his grandmother has been murdered and his brothers are missing. Maybe even his sister. Like I told you when we met, I think Alex, Cory and Marnie must be down here somewhere. That's why Anna's here. Whoever kidnapped them is trying to lure her here, and they did. We had a plan to see who contacts her but..." Mac's temper simmered as he thought of her impulsive action of leaving the taxi..."I'm sorry I haven't explained it all. I was lucky to run into you when I did. Jorge, I have to see AJ and Sheila and I have to check on Ian Stewart. I think I can pick up information there."

"I must go down there also. I can get to AJ to let him know. I tried to contact him two days ago and got no answer. I have a man in that area who can get to him very quickly but I prefer to go myself. We will want any information you can get from Stewart. Anna will be safe enough for now. El Cocodrilo will be occupied for some days. I will make sure of that. You can count on that."

"Muy bién. I'll make contact with Stewart's camp then. I'll contact you when I get there."

# Forty-eight

...journal...

We thought I'd be contacted for a ransom. We never thought I'd be kidnapped.

I am furious and frightened and I have only myself to blame. I thought I saw Ardith and left the taxi and got myself kidnapped by a man I don't know. He wouldn't tell me his name but I heard his voice before. His gravel voice was the one who threatened me over the phone. How is it this man knew about me and my home in Wisconsin? What is his connection to all this?

I was blindfolded in the car. The man refused to speak to me during most of the ride. He got a phone call and was very angry and cold and was barking orders in Spanish. He spoke too fast for me to understand all of it but it sounds like he has some crisis he must face. Good!

I was completely astonished when he took the blindfold off. I'm in my own home. He bragged he has used it as an outpost for his men. I believe it. It's a mess.

There is only one guard here that I've seen but he's very vigilant. I'm confined to my bedroom but he comes and peers in the door every single hour.

It's been two days and no sign of Mac. I know he was watching me but he must have lost me in the crowd.

I still believe I saw Ardith, although the woman's hair was loose and she looked tired and furiously angry. I never saw Ardith tired or angry or with loose hair.

I have to get out of here on my own. No phones.

In the car, with a nasty grin, "El Cocodrilo" introduced himself. Just after we got here he showed me the disconnected wires for the house phone and took away my cell. My guard has a cell phone and makes calls now and then. I hear it ring and his voice murmuring but he goes downstairs so I won't hear what he says.

The balcony outside the window isn't barred and I'm forming a plan. If there could be some diversion at the front of the house, I could use the sheet to drop down and make my escape to the edge of the cliff and then to water. Crocodiles or not, it's the most likely way open. I can't know for sure but I'm assuming there are guards at the north and south. One more day and I'll go. I've been hoarding food and water—not much, but it will last me at least two days. The most dangerous part will be through the patio and garden. One hundred yards. A football field. So much open space.

It's night. I'll hide this journal in case anyone comes and hope they search and find it. I have to go. Every day is one more my boys are held by her, one more day Marnie is held in the vise of drugs. God only knows what else has happened or where help will come from but I must go. I must.


Stacy left the private plane at the edge of the Merida airport and swung her body into the Jeep waiting on a small dusty road.

"Let's go. You can fill me in as we drive," she commanded.

"Sure you trust me?" Vincent Grant said as he wheeled the Jeep around and headed for the highway to Cancun.

"Not entirely, but I need to do that right now and even though she fired you, I think you want to see this work out well. You're company's reputation is at stake and you don't like losing control. Or being fired."

"Damn right I don't. She's not one to take orders, is she?"

"Not when it's about her children. She's a mother bear who will protect her cubs to the death. She also has her mother's murder to motivate her. Melissa told me she used to freeze in fear but that's not what I've been seeing. She's terrified but she's become a fighter."

Grant nodded his head. "That could be good. Also bad if she won't listen to me, or you."

"She'll listen to me, Vincent. What have you found out?"

"Ok, here's what I know now. There's no guarantee those boys are here in Mexico. However, the daughter is. She was poured off the plane into a black limo and whisked away to a fancy estate on the coast across from the island of Cozumel. We're making inquiries into who owns it and what the lay of that land is. Anna was brought to the house she owns in the north. We're on the way there now. El Cocodrilo brought her there and left her guarded, one inside and four outside. The land backs onto..."

"I know what the land backs onto. It's a cliff-like drop into a huge fresh-water swamp infested with the snakes and crocs. The swamp borders the Caribbean. There are a few small islands off that coast, mostly bird habitat, no known human habitation. It's a dangerous place but someone's men got through to the cliff the last time she was here, and inside the house too. Anna felt them. It's why she had all the valuables taken away before she left. I've talked to Melissa, even though I wasn't supposed to contact her. You think you control us. You don't."

"I don't know why you two can't take orders. My men do."

His voice sounded exasperated, angry.

"Because you hire trained competent women, not wimpy ones, but then you expect us not to think. Or feel. You don't feel. That's why Melissa refused to marry you."

"Let's get back to matters at hand. We need to get inside that house."

"No, *I* need to get inside that house. You need to connect with MacPherson and with AJ, her son, at his clinic. AJ and Sheila need to get out of there. Mac has a man on the way there now but one man won't be enough if that village is attacked and I think they'll be attacked too. Mac plans to go to the Mayan dig to see what he can find out from Ian Stewart or whoever is there who'll talk. He said he has one man there he can trust."

"I don't like you or anyone planning my itinerary, Stacy. I have my own contacts to make," Grant growled.

"Too bad, so sad. You listen to me. When I was in London, I talked to a profiler. He said if it is the former office manager and she's doing this after all these years, this has to be a very calculating woman who has lain in wait a very long time, thinking she'd get Wentworth's money, and/or some unknown other reward. When she didn't, she could no longer control her fury and this is the result—a combination of brains, long planning, the three quarter million she got from him to use for her own ends, and that rage, a sociopath turned psycho. He thinks she's been in the drug trade for some time, long before Wentworth died, and has her own money from that to fund what she does. I think she may have been involved with Anna's husband years ago, part of that group who controlled the trade back then. She may even be using drugs herself by now but he said her addiction is more likely a behavioral/emotional one and not any substances.

"Foster was questioned by police over and over and he won't even touch discussing her. They think he's so totally afraid of her he won't even say her name. He just stops speaking when they try to get any information about her. It seems like he'd rather admit to pedophilia than to knowing her."

"Just how do you plan to get into the house?"

"You'll let me out about a quarter mile north of the property. You and your driver are going to create a diversion on the road outside the house. The guards are going to find the two of you drunks singing and pissing in the road. I'll sneak in while you do that."

Stacy had seen his look of fury and disgust before when she'd defied him. She didn't need daylight to know it was on his face now.

*But he'll do it. He won't let his company fail at anything or let Anna dictate to him. Or let me off the hook.*

A distant honking reached her ears and Anna sat upright on the bed where she'd been trying unsuccessfully to get some sleep. She heard the front door slam and feet running away from the house, then shouting voices nearby and of all things, faraway singing.

*Singing? That's odd. That's—what? Diversion. Opportunity! Go!*

Anna grabbed the sheet she'd torn into a long rope and her pack she had hidden under the mattress. Quickly tying the knot she'd practiced over and over, she let herself down to the garden. Without looking back she ran beyond the pool, the cabanas, into the high plantings that led to the cliff, expecting a shot in her back with every step. She hoped the thickening rows of large plants would hide her.

Hearing footsteps following her, she fled faster, leaves and branches slapping at her face and arms, breath coming hard and fast, sweat flying off her forehead. Suddenly her foot dropped into a hole and she pitched forward to the ground. Her face slammed into the dirt, she sucked in a mouthful of dust and began to choke and cough.

The footsteps stopped behind her.

*No, no. I have to get away.*

She forced herself to her feet and turned back. A brown-skinned man she had never seen before stood behind her grinning, an arm with a machete grasped in his hand rising high over his head.

Anna was bringing her pack in front of her to defend herself when the man slid slowly to the ground with Stacy's thumb and forefinger pinching his neck.

"Hi. He's out cold. Let's get out of here."

Stacy didn't miss a beat, stepped over him, picked up the machete and pushed Anna in the direction of the cliff.

Time was lost while they searched for some way down.

"Whatever stuff Jorge left out here seems to be gone but there must be a way down. I know he had men down in the swamp," Anna told Stacy as they struggled through now thick underbrush.

"I know. Melissa told me. I've got a rope but I'd like to save that for later. We may have to grab onto bushes growing out of this hillside and let ourselves down little by little. That's risky. We could end up falling on a crocodile or bitten by a snake."

"I know how to anchor the rope and loosen it later. I taught it to my...kids..." Anna's voice broke softly, "when they were little."

"Don't let yourself go there right now, Anna. Focus on getting us out of here."

Anna chose a solidly anchored tree, made a knot around it and motioned Stacy down first.

"You're lightest. Go"

Tense minutes crept by until she heard a soft splash, then she followed, her pack slung on her back. At the bottom she gave a quick double yank and the rope dropped.

"I'm sure not prepared for swamp," Anna whispered as she slapped a mosquito.

"I am." Stacy tossed her a tube of repellent.

"What's happening? How come you're here?"

"Vincent Grant. He's back on your case. Don't even think of protesting. You need him. He's doing it because he hates failure, not for you or me. Take advantage of it. He created a diversion so I could get into the property. I figured you'd take advantage of that. I knew you wouldn't sit still for long. It was a long shot but I was right."

As she spoke she pulled out clothing from a pack and shoved camouflage into Anna's hands.

"Put these on."

Two pairs of chest-high waders unrolled from the pack.

"These too."

Knives on belts appeared. Stacy's gun took its place at her waist. Hats covered heads. Gloves were put on.

"To protect our manicures," Stacy intoned solemnly, then chuckled.

She grabbed the machete and gave it a swing.

"We'll take turns using this thing. I heard you wandered jungle before and came out a lot worse for the wear. Not this time. I'm about to teach you how to navigate a crocodile, bloodsucker and snake-infested swamp and survive. Follow and learn."

Far behind them the women heard the sound of gunshots. Anna followed and learned.

Vincent Grant surveyed the results of his attack on the house. Four guards taken out and one left who would give any information he was asked to give if he wanted to live. He did. The location of the woman's island was the first bit he got. He texted it to Stacy's phone and other connections he had in place and then called in the men he'd had follow himself and Stacy.

"This house will make a good command post for us here in the north. See that it's protected," he ordered the three men with him. "We need to get someone to the coast and pick up Stacy and Anna. Let's hope they make it through that swamp."

After reconnecting wiring to the home, the three men set up their office in the kitchen and began making contacts.

Grant left, intent on finding both women.

## Forty-nine

Mac made Felipe Carrillo Puerto by mid-morning and continued west from there toward the dig. But caution stopped him from using a new main road to the archaeological site when he arrived at the turnoff. Instead, he rode his cycle onto a back trail, stashed it and walked through jungle just off the path, stopping to listen to all bird and animal sounds frequently, on intense alert for the human species. He neither saw nor heard those until he was within shouting distance of the dig. Moving warily in the late afternoon light, he edged closer to the open area west of the pyramid where workers were still climbing in and out of the pit that ran the perimeter of the immense mound, three-fourths of which was still covered by vegetation.

The small area of the vast hill that was now laid bare revealed partially crumbling stonework. Two workers perched on ledges there, carefully removing more vegetation. Below, two men sifted dirt through a large rectangular strainer. Others were setting out and photographing small items.

Ian Stewart was not one of the workers, but a tent sat about twenty yards from the northern edge and Mac could hear the faint sound of a radio playing a popular salsa tune.

The man he really wanted to meet was not visible either. He settled down to wait. His mind drifted to Anna and the one intense episode of sex with her.

*She's right. Something possesses her. And I definitely want to be with her every time it does. That was right out of old stories. Amazing. Almost frightening, that power.*

He forced himself to push all thoughts of Anna out of his mind.

*I'll lose all concentration. Have to stay on guard.*

Jorge gunned the engine of a very old Ford pickup and headed south and west for the small village of Santa Anita in the state of Campeche. His mind was on Anna and the one time he had been inside her. Now, hunger to be with her devoured him continually. He replayed his night with her again and again in his mind, fearing he would forget some small part, some moment. He steeped his memory in her musky smell when he first met her, the sweet taste of her, her erotic movements under him, her sensual responses to his brother, the electricity that ran between the three of them.

An insidious and powerful longing had filled his body in the months since he first met her, until he finally broke the promise he had made to himself so long ago, to remain away from women completely, until the ceremony in which he would play an important part.

He heard the words of Adelina.

"It is not necessary to remain celibate to carry out your part in the ceremony. Your brother has not done so. It will be enough that you know you must do this and prepare for it as we tell you."

"I want to do it this way," he had promised to her and himself.

Until Anna, he had kept that promise, even during that first time she came to the Mexico. But later, when Anna returned and the relationship between she and Ramon had expanded into wild and deep sensuality, Jorge felt his own sexuality become so intense it left him doubled up in agony when Ramon and Anna were together. Adelina had found him one night crying with frustration and hunger and gave him medicine. It helped only a little.

"You must go to your brother and tell him. He will understand. He is the same as you. He is to do the ceremony also. Anna will accept you. She must. The goddess will see to it."

So on the last night before Anna went north, he had stood on the roof and waited and watched and when he could no longer stay away, he went to her. Now he remembered every moment, every movement, every touch and taste and smell and sound.

*I emptied my body and my soul into her and I will do it again and again.*

Riding on the memory, he came to Santa Anita to find her son.

Sheila, disinfecting her hands after examining her twentieth or thirtieth child of the day—she had lost count again—dried them on a soft towel and watched Jorge emerge from the truck. It was impossible not to notice his erection and his attempt to hide it by adjusting his pants. She smiled, thinking of AJ, now her husband.

They had told no one of their marriage. They had gone one week to a beautiful lake in the mountains, where, naked and alone, they had made love for days. At the end, they made their own ceremony and vowed their lives to each other.

AJ had remarked, "Mom will kill me. She'll want a ceremony in a church with all the trimmings, but I can't wait for that. You're the only woman I've ever wanted to be with forever."

Sheila had pretended to be jealous of the other women he'd had. She made him talk about their faults, extracting comparisons that put those women in a bad light, pretending she was jealous. Then she laughed at his efforts to pacify her.

"I don't care about them. Jealousy is silly. I have what I want most right here."

She opened his shorts and grabbed what was closest at hand. What was closest at hand responded by becoming larger and closer, to the delight of both of them.

Smiling at the memory, Sheila forced her mind back to the present.

Now she watched as Jorge hesitated, started for the door, turned back to his car, took a deep breath and turned toward the building again, and set his face in a mask that hid the hunger she'd seen in it moments before.

Jorge entered the small building that was used as the temporary clinic until a larger one could be built.

"Buenos tardes, Señorita. I have serious news for AJ. Is he here?" he asked in Spanish.

"No, he is gone to a settlement on the river to see about someone who is sick. The brother of the man came for him this morning. What is wrong? I can see something is wrong."

Sheila steeled herself.

"There is very very bad news."

Jorge paused, took another deep breath and wiped his sweaty palms on his pants.

"Es muy malo. I have news from his mother. She has been trying to reach him for days. His grandmother has been murdered and his brothers kidnapped. His sister may also be in trouble, possibly a hostage. Our information is that there is at least one cartel involved and possibly two who are collaborating. His mother is also a captive now but safe for this moment, I hope."

"Oh no! Oh, Jorge, I can't get hold of him! Our cell phones died and we couldn't get them recharged. We were going to leave tomorrow and go to the house up north and stop on the way to pick up news when they were working again. Here is where he is."

She walked to a hand-drawn map on the wall. Pointing to the wavy line representing a small river, she touched a dot next to it.

"There's a tiny village—just a few huts and a communal fire. It's only about four miles away as the crow flies but much longer walking over rough terrain. He could be staying there or on his way back already.

He's been treating a man who came in with a broken wrist and a dislocated shoulder and he was worried about bad infection in some cuts and scrapes the man had."

She turned back to Jorge, tears in her eyes.

"Jorge, I can hardly take in all you said. His grandmother was murdered? His whole family kidnapped or...? What's been going on? Why?"

Jorge repeated all Mac had told him.

"Señorita, you and AJ are in danger. You must leave. Señora Anna is held hostage in the house in the north. We, Señor MacPherson and I, believe that perhaps you will be harmed also. The woman who is doing this will stop at nothing. She is perhaps insane. Who knows?"

"Anna is hostage? In her own house? What is being done to help her? We must get her help!"

"Help is on the way to her soon, Señorita. The man I work with made calls to bring much help."

"Jorge, you can call me Sheila, and also Señora. AJ and I have married now."

"Congratulations, Señora. That is good to hear. I know he loves you very much."

"And I love him. I can't, I won't leave here until he returns, but we will go as soon as he gets back. Will you stay until he returns?"

"No, Señora, I must go. I must return to help free Anna. I came to bring this news to you and also to collect news from others about the movements of the cartels. Do you feel safe here?"

Sheila smiled and he thought, *she has the smile of an angel.*

"Of course. The people here have been very welcoming and are planning the clinic with great enthusiasm. We have encountered very little opposition. You see there are many women and children here and a few old men. We are no threat to anyone."

Jorge left after drinking the tea and eating some small cakes she offered him.

AJ trudged through the thick vegetation, hacking away with his machete. He had avoided the main trail in favor of a more direct route.

The man had been healing well except for his infection and AJ had cleansed and dressed the wounds. There were more than one and they looked suspiciously like cuts made by knives but the man denied that, saying they were from sharp spines on a plant. At the request of a grandmother, AJ then spent time checking the children. He had planned to remain overnight if necessary but he sensed the few people of the village did not want him there. Something was off but he could get no information from them.

It was near sundown as he walked into Santa Anita and stopped dead. He felt the evil, smelled the blood, heard the flies, and his entire body turned cold at the overpowering silence.

No bird sang. No dog barked. Nothing moved. He ran into the small space of the clinic. Blood all over. Medical supplies tossed around, ripped open, lying on a dirty floor. He ran to their small quarters. More blood. More mess. He ran from building to building, passing the corpses of three small children as he went. A dead woman lay sprawled in one hut, her legs spread, and he read the rape and murder on her face and body. Another had been dragged out from under the house where she hid and killed there. More children dead. No men. No Sheila.

He turned colder and began his hunt. Slowly he made his way around and around the village in an ever-widening circle. He found the bodies of two old men and another woman. She had been pregnant. The body of her child lay half-in, half-out of her abdomen where it had been cut open. No Sheila.

The circle widened and he began to think of where she could have gone. Where would she run to? Where could she escape to? The cave. There was this small cave. He headed to the cave and found one child there, alive but mortally wounded and unconscious, bleeding out. He couldn't save her. Who had taken the child to the cave? No Sheila.

There was a small pool to the east and south. When he got there it was already dark but the moon shining on the water showed it black-red and two bodies lay half in-half out. Still no sounds. No Sheila.

He found her, a long time later, crucified to the side of a hill, stakes in her hands, her body mutilated with obscenities etched with a knife into her skin, the lines dark against her skin where blood oozed out and clotted. He threw himself over her to cover her nakedness, his entire body shaking violently with grief and anger and horror.

In the morning, he dug her grave, holding his mind carefully together by focusing on each shovel full of dirt, carefully counting each one, carefully laying it aside.

He bathed her and put on the dress she'd worn in the mountains and laid her in the grave and carefully counted the shovels of dirt as he gently laid them over her. He piled stones on top at the head and the foot of the mound of dirt.

Then he quietly welcomed Insanity and wandered into the jungle.

The spirits of Rage and Revenge smiled at each other and followed him, waiting.

# Fifty

In the darkness, Mac dropped between the huge green leaves of the plant and moved silently under them on his elbows and knees to the edge of the cleared pit twenty yards from the pyramid. He slid into the pit and moved through it to the corner where it met the pit on the western side. The man to whom he wanted to speak stood guard halfway down that side. When Mac was just yards away he brought the lighted marijuana cigarette, cupped in his hand, into the open, sucked in a mouthful of the smoke and blew it in the man's direction.

He watched as Eduardo came carefully and slowly more alert, squatted down to the ground and quietly breathed out, "¿Qué?"

"Manana, cinco, helipad."

"Sí."

Mac laid the cigarette on the edge of the pit, silently returned the way he'd come, then carefully skirted the camp, followed the road to the top of the mound that held the helipad, tucked himself into the crotch of a tree at the edge of the open space and went to sleep.

Eduardo retrieved the cigarette and relaxed into his sentry duty once again.

5 a.m.

Eduardo, with a sly grin, sneaked up on the tree that held the sleeping man. Just as he got under the man and was ready to poke him with his rifle butt, Mac growled, "Poke me and I'll piss all over you."

Mac extracted his legs from their position wound around a limb and dropped down next to Eduardo who began to speak as Mac opened his pants and pissed into the dirt.

"There are three cartels operating. We know this now for certain. They are more or less cooperating with each other at the present to increase profits but the leaders are never to be trusted. One is a woman and she is slated to die. El Cocodrilo has told one of his men this. He plans to take over her business. She has been in control from behind the scenes for many years and he did not think her any challenge because she always had men who did the work, made the contacts, men who appeared to be in charge. Now, she is running the business and El Cocodrilo resents this. He does not like women. He believes they bring bad luck."

"Who heads the third cartel?"

"We do not know. Whoever it is stays very very far from public view."

"What else have you heard?"

"There was an attack on several small villages in Campeche where Mayans united to oppose the cartels. Many women and children were killed and one old man was captured, tortured and paraded through villages as a warning to others. We do not know which cartel did this. We think again that they cooperated in this. It is said a gringa died there also."

"What villages?"

Mac felt the dread begin in his stomach and make its way up to his heart.

"I do not know."

"Who will know?"

"Antonio Escobar and his brothers. They are part of the men who were hired to do this."

"Antonio! That scumbag. He's sold his sister to a cartel."

"Sí, and his own niece, the small daughter of his sister. But he will never talk to you and probably not even to me."

"Where is he?"

"He hangs out in a cantina in Puerto. If you go there, be very careful. They are all cartel soldiers in that place."

"Listen. A friend of mine is a doctor who has a small clinic in the village of Santa Anita. I need to get hold of him. He's a gringo and his woman is Native-American. If you hear of them, get back to me. His family needs him. OK?"

"Of course. And muchas gracias for the cigarettes."

He left, singing softly to himself, slightly adjusting the words of *La Cucaracha*...

"*...porque tienes, porque tienes, marijuana que fumar...*"

## *Fifty-one*

*I have been very stupid! I broke my connection to her. Now I need to find her and I cannot feel her.*

For the hundredth time, Ramon Aguilar beat himself up for shutting Anna out of his consciousness. As he sat in the bow of the small craft making its way along the edge of the swamp, he prayed to all the gods he knew to keep her safe. Jorge had called on the special cell phone only they used, alerting him. Now his companions, cousins who fished these waters, watched with him for any sign of Anna. The tide was high at the moment and he could not imagine how she would survive. If it was lower, she might find places to walk or at least wade, but these deep waters, with their powerful undertow, were impossible.

Still far into the swamp, Anna and Stacy waited, in darkness, perched precariously on the limbs of a large thick bush, watching for signs the tide was turning.

"It's good we have to wait," Stacy said, "because crocs hunt at night. We're safer this way."

Both women listened for night sounds.

Anna squirmed into another position to ease the cramps in her legs. Sweat dripped down her body under the layers of cloth and the waders. Hunger prowled around her stomach. Fear sat in her heart. Anger fueled the neurons in her brain. Hope had faded into a faint fog off in the distance. She tried for a connection with any of her children. Nothing.

"Even if we make it to the edge of this, what then? We need a boat," she said.

"Grant has a boat patrolling for us. When we get far enough to the edge of this hellish place, out where the salt water and fresh water meet, we just need to wait until they find us."

She pulled out her phone. "Oh damn! It's dead. I was hoping we could give him a GPS reading or text him."

She fiddled with it for a few minutes. "It won't work. I don't know what else we can do but we'll think of something. I know he'll be looking for us. We'll just have to get very lucky."

After leaving Anna's house, Vincent Grant had sped south to a small cove where two more of his men waited with a fast cigarette boat.

"Let's go. There are miles of swamp edge to search."

He settled himself into his seat and the motor, carefully engineered to be as silent as possible, purred to life. Easing it out a hundred yards from shore, he gunned it and sped north again.

The woman known as Ardith had been watchful and her spies had kept her informed. Now, she sat in the cabin of her small yacht waiting. After luring Anna into the hands of El Cocodrilo, she had not gone, as she had told him, to her island off the northern coast of the Yucatan peninsula. She had ordered the yacht to pick her up at the harbor on Isla Mujeres. The yacht now was slowly trolling the waters just beyond the last of the swampy vegetation, waiting and watching. She knew he would leave Anna at her home. She had spies watching his every move. She knew Anna. Anna would not sit still for long. Even if The Crocodile left her guarded, Anna would escape.

More, the woman's spies had informed her of the "diversion" although it puzzled her who had done it.

*Another player in this game. I shall find out soon enough who that is.*

*Anna will not get out on land. I know that. She must come this way. I want her alive. I want her to see what I have done to her children before she dies. For years I had to listen to her brag. Cory did this. Alex did that. AJ is doing so well in med school. And the beautiful, beautiful daughter. Not so beautiful now. Staggering drunk and stoned! Delightful!*

She smiled her satisfaction. Accomplishing that had been easy. Her friend and client, Aristide Fournier, the wealthy French politician who owned homes in France, Mexico City and the Yucatan, had literally salivated at the opportunity to keep Marnie as his possession. The drug Rohipnol would make sure he had total access to her body.

At the northern end of the swamp, El Cocodrilo, on a cell phone, ordered six canoes with two men each into the swamp.

"Go in now while this tide is high. Get as far as you can into it and watch for this woman. Bring her to me! Do not fail!"

He remained in his boat, waiting.

The canoes glided into the swamp, each covering an assigned area.

Hours after they had fled, Stacy and Anna watched as the waters slowly went down, revealing tree limbs, roots, even some wet sandy spots. In the east, a pale light began.

"Let's go. Stay close together. We could hit patches of quicksand so we'll have to go slowly, testing this mud."

"I'm right behind you, wishing I could be in northern woods. I'd know how to get through so much better up there."

"Watch out!"

Stacy smacked a tree just above Anna's head with a staff she'd made as they waited. A snake dropped from the branch inches from Anna's head, hit the water with a soft splash and slithered away.

"That's a cantil! It's deadly!"

Anna, frozen motionless, shook herself and forced a deep breath into her lungs.

"Thanks. I never saw it."

"Easy not to."

The water in which they waded had receded to knee deep and they made their way toward the lightening east where the sun had not yet come above the horizon. Vegetation was no longer thick. Anna could see it thinning even more ahead of her and knew they were nearing the edge of the swamp. The water had become salty.

Concentrated on watching every step, she didn't see the canoe as it glided toward her or the net as it was thrown over her. Another net flew into the air and trapped Stacy. Both women were dragged, kicking, through mud and water, and hauled into the canoe. Entangled in the nets, struggle became useless. The shouts of both women were quickly silenced.

Another canoe arrived and Stacy was transferred to it.

One man spoke only to give orders, the canoes swung around, headed out of the swamp and turned north.

"There they are!" The woman pointed as she watched through her binoculars. "Kill the men. Sink the canoes. Bring me the women."

Anna, from her position lying face down in the canoe, heard a roar of engines and shots. A man landed full on top of her body, knocking the breath out of her, and he didn't move. At first, she thought maybe he was protecting her but the shots died, low voices began, his body was lifted and she heard it splash into the water. She was dragged roughly from the canoe, transferred to the deck of another boat and it sped away. She could see Stacy lying next to her. Both of them were bounced and tossed up and down as the boat they were in slammed wave after wave.

Slowing down, they came alongside a yacht and were again jerked roughly up. The nets were removed.

"Climb! Vamos! Up the ladder!" A man's harsh voice ordered them.

Stacy grabbed it and climbed. Anna followed.

When they stood on the deck Anna looked around. They were out to sea, the swamp just a thick line in the distance. She lost her balance and fell as the yacht began to move. Rough hands grabbed her and forced her to her feet.

Above her she heard a voice she recognized.

"Welcome, Anna! It's so good to see you at last. You've come to join the others in your family I suppose."

"Take off those muzzles. I'll want to hear what she has to say," she ordered one of the men.

Ardith stood above them on the upper deck. Her blond hair was loose, flying around her head in the wind. Her outfit, a casual top and matching pants, was impeccably white, expensive, tailored. On the third finger of her right hand she wore a large diamond ring, matching the earrings in her ears. Her eyes were blue hate, her mouth a thin red gash cut into her face.

Stacy glanced at Anna.

"This is Ardith, I presume."

"Never call me by that name!" the woman snarled. "Put them in the hold until we reach the island!"

She turned and disappeared into the wheelhouse.

Alone in the locked hold, Stacy and Anna were left unbound. Stacy immediately began searching for anything they could use as a weapon or means of escape. She found a short length of cord, some scraps of paper, pulled on boards to try to get them loose. Finally, she turned to Anna.

"Well? You know her. What do you think she wants?"

"Me. She wants me. She wants me to see what she's done to my children."

"Why, Anna, why? What's between you that you haven't told anyone about?"

Stacy's look mirrored the distrust in her words.

"Nothing. All I can think of is that Conrad was between us, but Ardith and I never even had a verbal spat, much less a fight, never even disagreed on anything. I truly don't know, but I'm going to find out. I have to go with her wherever she takes us. I have to find my sons and daughter and I have to know what this is about.

Anna was silent briefly then continued.

"This isn't your fight, Stacy. You don't have to stay with me. If you see a chance to escape, take it. I have to see this through. I won't follow you if you go."

It was, or seemed like, hours before the yacht slowed and the sounds of mooring came through to the women in the hold. A door opened and bright sunlight blinded them as they were ordered to the deck.

When her eyes cleared, adjusting to the sunlight, Anna saw they were moored in a large bay. To the north an island rose out of the water and Anna could see a home built atop a hill. Below the hill, tilled fields lay and tiny figures moved in them. Beyond that whole scene, a mountain rose.

Her attention to the island broke as she heard a shout, running feet, and a splash. She turned and there were two men looking over the side. Stacy was gone.

"Leave her. The sharks will get her. It's almost their feeding time. They expect large chunks of meat."

Ardith's voice conveyed her amusement. She looked down on Anna.

"I've trained the sharks here to expect human and other meat at certain times of the day. Your friend is as good as dead. You will be too if you follow her, but I don't think you will.

"Bring her up to the house. I have much to show her," she ordered the men.

When he reached the northern end of the swamp, El Cocodrilo turned his boat. Four canoes had reported. Two had not. He waited long for them, then sent out his men to search. They were not found. He cursed and waited even more, but his wait resulted in nothing. Just after midday, he gave up and ordered his yacht to her island, leaving four men to continue the search.

Ramon and his cousins searched up and down the length of the swamp all day. Once they saw two men in a canoe. From a long distance they looked like gringos but it was hard to tell. When the next tide came they rode as far as they could into the swamp but they found nothing. It was night when he left his cousins in Puerto Juarez and called Jorge.

Vincent Grant saw the yacht through his binoculars and the blond woman standing on the bridge.

*That's the woman! I'll bet my whole operation that's the woman who's after Anna.*

He changed to his camera with its long powerful lens. Her face loomed into his sight and his stomach turned at the hatred he saw there.

*Anyone who crosses her is dead. I know some police who will want to see this.*

He took several pictures of her in profile and then waited until she turned toward him and got a frontal.

Removing the camera card, he slipped it into his computer and spent a few minutes sending information out to his central command, where they directed it to London police, Interpol, the FBI, DEA and to police in Green Bay, Wisconsin.

*Somewhere, sometime, lady, someone knew you. Time to find out who you really are.*

"Follow that boat carefully. We want to know where it docks."

Later, when Stacy sliced headfirst into the waters of the island's bay, underwater divers were waiting and swiftly sped in her direction.

Far out to sea, a tall man stood on the deck of his very large yacht, receiving ongoing reports of the activities of Los Serpientos and Los Cocodrilos. He was especially attentive to the activities at the edge of the swamp.

"Do ya'll want us to intervene in that mess?" drawled a shorter blonde man with a thick West Texas accent, twirling the ice in his drink.

A long silence followed.

"No. Sooner or later, one of them will be a victim of the other. Have our operatives keep track of every move. Document every weakness you can find, in their supply lines, in their methods of managing the locals, and keep me updated on their earnings once a week.

"I want you to go back to Wisconsin and insert yourself into a position to get info on police activities regarding this woman's delivery system there. My bet is she'll go down first. Let's see if we can take over that path to Canada."

"You'll need to invest lot of money to do that."

"I pay good money if the investment is worth it. That path is well worth it. Pay any bribes you have to. There'll be an extra bonus for you when you finish that job."

Remembering his own time in Green Bay, the man smiled.

"It should be easy to infiltrate. All you have to do is be a rabid Packer fan and you can get anyone to do anything."

"Hell, man, I can do that easy."

## Fifty-two

The blonde woman sat in the high-backed maharani chair at the far end of the main room in her spacious white stucco home. Wide windows revealed the scene far below her on all sides. It had been built to her specifications by the slave labor she kept in the caverns below the small mountain on her island. Three sides of the room looked out on blue-green seas.

On the eastern side, the Atlantic, calm at the moment, sparkled in the distance, deep blue in sunlight.

On the western side of the island, the ground on which her house sat dropped some fifteen feet to a large plateau where the hangar held her planes—a small helicopter for quick travel, a large helicopter heavily armed and kept ready for fighting if such should be necessary, and the prop-driven plane she used to travel to her new Lear jet which was based at the Merida airport. The landing strip stretched into the distance and dropped abruptly at the edge of a five hundred foot cliff, where, far below, waves from the sea wore away at the rocks that lined that shore. Across that sea lay Mexico, at the moment slightly shrouded in fog.

North, the peak of the mountain rose, some eight thousand feet above sea level.

To the south, the land fell in many layers where her slaves tended gardens and a small farm which provided her with food for her table. A sheltered harbor held her small yacht and the boat in which El Cocodrilo had arrived a short time ago.

The room was furnished with European antiques of the seventeenth and eighteenth centuries, preferably French, but with some Italian acquisitions. The floor was covered in carpets from Turkey, Iran, and Iraq in shades of her favorite color, wine red.

All chairs and settees were upholstered in dark red silk or velvet. The walls and ceiling of the entire room were matte black.

The Crocodile had been most impressed with her taste and he had joined the woman today to savor her newest acquisition, and to carefully monitor her. He knew obsession when he saw it and knew she was caught in this one. He watched her glittering eyes, her look of triumph, and saw the passionate hatred ooze out of her as she viewed the large closed circuit television screen in front of her.

On the screen, in a dim room in some unknown place lay the unmoving bodies of two young men he knew to be from the Kinnealy family.

"Have you killed them already or are they alive?" he asked, his voice kept very casual.

She turned her head sharply to examine his face. Seeing indifference, she relaxed slightly. She would tolerate no interference from him, even the mildest sort. He knew that.

"They are alive, of course. Sedated. What fun would it be if they were dead? I want to see the look on her face when she sees them this way first. Our plan worked perfectly. She saw me, she left her cab, she was captured by you. A woman like her has no cunning, no guile, a lamb to the slaughter."

She gloated, smiling, seeing in her mind the look she knew would be on Anna's face.

He eased slowly just out of her line of vision.

"When will you have her brought to the house?"

"I won't yet. I want her to wait for days, wondering, hoping and then losing hope. I want her in great emotional pain wondering where her boys are. Has the daughter arrived yet? Where is she?"

"She is at the home of Fournier."

"Is she using drugs, alcohol?"

"Sí She is very addicted."

"Good. Leave her there for now. My plans are not yet complete."

"What about the son who is the doctor?"

"I want him here when you find him."

She stood up abruptly and shut the television off.

"In the meantime, we have other business. You think I am obsessed with this and that this will prevent me from attending to our businesses. You are deluded if you think that. What do you hear from Ian Stewart?"

"He is cooperating. Since we began to fund his dig, since we built him his new road, he cooperates beautifully. He is obsessed with his archaeology, just as I am obsessed with many things in my life, and you are obsessed with the Kinnealys. It does not seem to prevent us from doing any business," he said, hoping this would ease the tension he saw in her.

He did not tell her he had no trust in Ian Stewart, nor would he tell her about the Canadian who had been seen near the dig and had been nosing about in Felipe Carrillo Puerto, and who had then dropped out of sight in a very professional manner.

Rumors about the man told many things and nothing. The man is a drifter. He works for the Canadian government, looking for oil, looking for gems, looking for..., not looking for..., just hanging around places. El Cocodrilo's network of informants, created with meticulous care and very extensive, came up with shadows of this man.

This did not sit well with The Crocodile.

Meanwhile, to business. The art trade was proving very lucrative. He reported their successes to her.

"Have you located the art from the Kinnealy home?" she asked.

"Yes. Sotheby's has stored it. I don't have enough connections to consider looting them. It will have to be very carefully planned if we decide to do that. In the meantime, we do have some via our Mexico City dealers ready for our select group of collectors. We must also discuss the trade in women from Serbia. That will net us much more."

The meeting lasted well into the afternoon, after which both repaired to the rooms where they satisfied themselves with the humans brought by The Crocodile for the occasion.

After a late supper, when she knew he had returned to his bed, the blonde woman returned to the television set.

*Yes, tomorrow I will show Anna what she is missing, what she will forever after miss.*

*The ending of the story will be "and she lived sadly forever after." She will come to know what loss really is, just as I have.*

## Fifty-three

Anna stood in the middle of the room, seeing the view out over the island. Outside on the patio stood the woman she knew as Ardith and the man with the pitted face she'd seen for the first time as he had pushed her into his car.

Far below in the bay were two boats, a yacht on one side and another smaller boat anchored at the opposite end. In the center, she could see rowboats where men threw objects into the water. The waters churned and splashed and now and then a fin showed.

*Feeding time. This is what she was talking about. Oh god, I hope Stacy got away!*

She didn't see how that could have happened. Ardith had ordered the feeding to begin immediately instead of waiting for the regular time.

Anna felt cold nothing. Death oozed through the air and walls of this place, killing all emotion, all sensation. She examined her surroundings.

*Black walls. Oriental rugs. Elegant but all darkness. The furniture bleeds red. A huge television screen. Why would she have such a big screen? An enormous black desk with nothing on it but a statue...oh, my god, it's the sculpture of the woman and child we found at the dig. How did she get this? I was told the police took it as evidence! It's so out of place here—love and kindness in this cruel room.*

"I see you recognize my acquisition," the woman said as she entered the room. "You've seen it before, I know. Ian told me how you all found this. He's very cooperative now that I'm funding his excavation of the entire area. His name will go down in archaeological circles for the finds he's making there."

"It doesn't belong in this room. The setting isn't right. I thought you had better taste."

"Oh, it won't remain here. It's to be sold to a very wealthy collector. I just thought you'd like to see it once more, to remind you of your children perhaps. You must be wondering where they are."

Anna remained silent.

The woman's face flashed with a moment of annoyance when she heard no reply but she quickly obliterated it.

"Why don't you speak? Surely you have questions."

"I don't know what to call you."

A puzzled look appeared on the woman's face.

"I don't know what to call me either. Isn't that amusing? I never even knew what my real name was. I chose to be Ardith but that was not it. I chose to be several other names in my life, but they aren't real either. I suppose...no, I don't think there is any name I want you to use."

El Cocodrilo, obviously at home in the room, had arranged himself on a settee, his legs sprawled out in front of him, one arm flung over the back. He had lighted a long thin cigarillo and held it between thumb and forefinger. The faint sweet smell of it drifted to Anna. Marijuana.

He gazed unwaveringly at Anna and seemed about to comment but didn't. Silence took over the room.

The woman sauntered to the huge desk that dominated one wall and sat behind it. She opened a drawer and took out a remote and clicked it.

On the screen, in the dim light of some sort of cavern, bodies lay on the ground, some curled, some sprawled, some moving slowly, others still. The camera zoomed in on one body. Anna could not make out at first what she was seeing—a young man she thought. Then she froze and her stomach tossed and turned. In the dim light she saw Cory, his face bruised and cut, his body hunched inward, his hands raw and bleeding from cuts, red round marks on his arms, cigarette burns. He moved slightly and groaned.

Anna came to lying on the patio in a pool of cold water and the sight she'd seen etched itself into her mind again. Sounds came from the television in the room. She heard the lash of a whip and the scream as it hit someone. Anna knew that voice. Alex's scream.

Crocodile boots appeared at her eye level and he grabbed her hair, pulling it until he forced her to stand. He pushed her back into the room and forced her to watch.

Anna went numb. She tried to sense one finger against another and couldn't. She tried to feel any emotion and there was nothing. She tried to remember the world she knew but it was gone. She had the absurd thought that the cold water had frozen her somehow.

It was the emptiness of all feeling that allowed her to ask the question. "And the others? What have you done to them?"

The screen changed suddenly to show her Marnie stretched out on a bed, naked, unconscious, with an old man standing over her and gloating.

It changed again and Sheila lay crucified to the side of a hill, her body slashed with deep cuts.

"I regret that we haven't found your son AJ as yet. He seems to have wandered off into jungle. But we will. All who knew you will also be gone. No one left.

"Why?"

"Why? Why?" the woman snarled.

"Because *I* was the one who should have gotten everything from Conrad. I waited for years. He thought no one survived. But I did. I survived and I am his rightful heir. I. Am. His. Sister. Sister! Sister! I am his sister! Do you hear me?"

## Fifty-four

Anna awoke to the sensation of a creature with small claws crawling over her neck. She couldn't move at first. There was mud under her right hand and one of her fingers slowly made circles in the coolness of it. Her brain didn't work at all. There were no commands in it that said sit up, or look around. She could only lay there.

After an unmarked time, a vague formless terror seeped in, oppressing her, pushing her into the ground. Eventually, after not breathing for a time, her reflexes sucked in air and the memories hit and she shook violently and uncontrollably. That too passed, and she was left with despair.

Despair is strange—a chameleon that turns gray as it creates ashes in the spirit. Or, sometimes it is colorless, emptying the spirit out, like a dustpan or wastebasket. Other times it takes on the deep red fire of rage, burning itself into a force that propels a person to move. Feeling the heat of the red energy is how Anna finally found courage to sit up and look around. She discovered herself in an underground cavern amid bodies of women and children. Leaning against the wall, she surveyed her surroundings. The cavern that held Cory and Alex came to mind and with it came that horror of all horrors, faint hope. Anna shut that down quickly. It was far too painful.

Moving slowly, supporting herself along the wall, she began her search. Words took form in her mind.

*The island. Am I still on this island?* Then...*Who are these people? Prisoners. Obviously prisoners.*

When she was finished, she had counted twelve children and thirteen women. No young or old men.

The spirit of Hope drifted to a far corner, mocking her.

In one place she had seen light coming from a hole above her head. She returned to the place and smelled sea air. Sea air brought furious indignation that it was just out of reach and rage again brought energy for action. Anna began to think of getting out. A tap on her arm made her look down.

Shorter than Anna by at least a head, broad and sturdy, a small woman with a dark brown face stared up at her. She pointed to the hole and pantomimed Anna lifting her up.

Anna nodded and smiled and a set of white teeth gleamed back at her in the dimness. Anna bent and grasped the woman around her waist but that was clearly not going to get her high enough. Anna knelt and the woman climbed on her shoulders. Slowly, wobbling unsteadily, Anna stood. The woman grabbed the edge of the hole, stood up on Anna's shoulders, then slid herself into the hole and disappeared, sending scratching and scraping sounds behind her.

*Now what do I do? Will she come back? Will she be killed?*

"¡Señora! ¡Tráigame los muchachos!" came the command from above.

Anna grabbed the nearest surprised child and pushed her upward. The woman pulled and the child disappeared.

By the time the children had all been lifted up, women stood at Anna's feet. All were small, native, Mayan. One by one they crawled to her shoulders and they disappeared.

Anna was left alone. She sat down, exhausted. Despair returned as the images of her own children ate their way back into her brain.

Hope faded into deep shadows.

## *Fifty-five*

An unmeasured time later, two men arrived to find the women and children gone. Cursing and swearing, they sounded an alarm, grabbed Anna roughly and force-marched her out of an opening on the mountain and down to the house.

Anna glimpsed one yacht in the harbor. No other boats. The Crocodile was not present in the room when they forced Anna to her knees. The woman barked orders into a cell phone.

"Search the whole island. They can't get off. They must be somewhere."

Her voice rasped with hostility and the face she turned to Anna was vivid red with malice. A vein pulsed at her throat.

"So, once again you have attempted to destroy my profits! There is nowhere for them to go. All your efforts are in vain. Once I've found them, you will die and your children after you. Or, maybe I will have them killed as you watch. Have you been hoping your sons are here?"

She laughed.

"They aren't here. You know that. You searched for them. I watched you. They are in those precious northern woods of yours but even if you were free and flying north, you would never find those boys in time to prevent them from starving."

Anna stood up, wobbly but determined. The guard tried to keep her down but the woman waved him back.

"Let her stand. She's a fighter. It makes her a worthy opponent for me. Soon she won't be able to do that. I will enjoy watching her fall to her knees and beg for mercy."

Anna took a deep breath, remembering Mac's breathing lesson.

"Why?" she asked. "Conrad isn't enough of a reason. Why?"

The woman stood silent for a long while and Anna thought she was not going to answer.

Her scornful bitter voice finally broke through the empty silence.

"Your male chauvinist husband betrayed both of us. I have fantasized for years making sure he paid for that. He and I were supposed to run this together but he got greedy. Then he lied to me. He betrayed Big John O'Keeffe too. Big John looked at Art as the son who made good, nothing like the wimpy son that crazy wife of his birthed. But Art betrayed us all in the end. You must have realized by now the body in the plane was not his, but he is dead. Oh, yes. Very dead. We left him in a place where he could not escape from the hungry jaguars. Yes. He is long gone. Much as I would like to kill you with my bare hands, I will leave you there too. Maybe his ghost will comfort you as the animals rip you apart. Maybe not. I don't care. I have a business to run. I am in Phase Three of my business plan and I need funding. You will turn over all the assets you have to me."

Anna listened to the woman as she detailed the entire plan.

*She sounds so logical and reasonable, like a normal person, but she's not. This is crazy. She's crazy. Was this what she was like when Art was alive? Did he see this? Did he take over? Did he really work with her to run the drug and other smuggling trades? Might he have escaped? No. Not possible.*

*I must escape. But how? Why won't she give me a name to call her? She must have had a name. If she really is Conrad's sister and survived the Nazis, how did that happen? Who helped her?*

The woman became more excited as she went on, sometimes looking out over her domain, sometimes pacing back and forth as she spoke of the great extent her "business" would reach soon.

Anna began to edge closer to the desk which held a a large and thick glass ashtray. The guard's eyes were on the woman, a combination of admiration and fear in them, almost transfixed.

When distant shouts began to come from far away, Anna glanced outside. Down in the fields workers were running toward the huts at one edge of the area. Another boat was speeding into the bay and there were small boats and men on the shore.

The woman was still talking, but turned to look where the sounds were coming from. She froze.

Anna grabbed the heavy ashtray and hurled it at the woman's head. It struck her just long enough to stun her and Anna hurled herself after it, slamming into the woman. Both landed on the floor, Anna on top. Not for long. Ardith's strength was powerful. She twisted, kicked and punched Anna with intense force. Shoved off balance, Anna rolled to her left and came to her knees, then to her feet, partially crouched, ready to attack again. The woman came to her feet just as fast.

Anna gave quick thanks for the skills Stacy had made her learn, both defensive and offensive. The women grappled, struck, parried, hit, and slammed each other across the room and back to the desk. Anna was almost pinned backward against it but dodged out from the woman's attack just in time. The move sent her to the floor and Ardith dropped on top of her. Anna was struggling when she felt the glass ashtray under her hand and brought it up aiming for the woman's temple.

Instead it hit her back as Ardith rolled and sprang to her feet. Anna dove for her ankles and brought her down again. The woman screamed for her guards, kicked free, sprang to her feet and ran for the doors to the patio. Anna followed, caught her hair and slammed her into the glass of one door. The woman screamed and stopped. Embedded in her right shoulder was a long shard of glass.

A guard suddenly appeared, aimed his rifle at Anna and was about to shoot when the woman grabbed his arm, pulled herself up and ordered him to get her away. They disappeared briefly, then reappeared as he drove a golf cart away with the woman in it. A helicopter was warming up on the helipad.

Anna ran to the edge of the patio but knew there was no preventing the woman's escape. She turned back to the room as Vincent Grant and Stacy burst in, followed by Jorge and more men.

"She's getting away! Get her! She knows where Cory and Alex are! She says they're in the north woods. She didn't tell me where. Get her!"

Grant and the men ran over the patio but machine gun fire burst from the helicopter and they took cover, then crept along on elbows and knees. Before they could go far, the helicopter took on the woman. Her guard crumpled to his feet, shot. Spouting fire, the copter sped toward the house, then abruptly veered out over the fields and the bay, spraying death along the way.

The wild sounds died, silence grew, broken only by a few moans and brief cries. Grant and his men stood up and he ordered them into the lower fields to survey damage.

One did not rise and never would. Grant stood over him and swore.

Stacy pushed Anna down on the settee and sat beside her.

"What else is here, Anna? What have you seen?"

Anna opened her mouth and spoke. The voice that came out was strange. *I don't sound like that. I'm not me.* There was some disconnect, some break between herself and the words and the sound.

"There is a cave inside the mountain where she kept women and children. I lifted them up to a hole but I couldn't reach it myself."

Anna's voice sank to a whisper.

Stacy stood up.

"Grant, there's a cave in the mountain, maybe more than one."

He walked into the room.

"We'll search this island inch by inch."

He stood in front of Anna.

"Did you find out her name?"

"No. She refused to tell me. She seemed not to know her real name but she said she was Conrad Wentworth's sister—that she survived when the Nazis took their family, just as he did. She believes she's entitled to all his fortune. She also said she was betrayed by my late husband years ago and he was left somewhere and killed by jaguars. She said the body in the plane all those years ago wasn't him. AJ was right."

Anna's voice became a whisper as she spoke, following her mind into the time warp of more than eight years, seeing again the charred crumbling remains in the morgue.

Jorge Aquilar, standing next to the inside door, saw her spirit drift slightly away from her body, saw the jaguar spirit hovering, saw the fragile connections among the two spirits and Anna's body. He heard Adelina's words to him when he had told her of AJ's disappearance and of Sheila's death.

"You must tell her what happened. You must go to her. She can go either way when you tell her. If she tries to leave, you must hold her. Take Ramon if you can, if he is near. Give her this."

She pressed a small vial into his hands.

Ramon had been in Cancun, not near enough to get here.

Jorge walked in and knelt in front of Anna, taking both her hands in his. He was frightened by the vacancy in her eyes.

"Anna, I have news for you. We have news that AJ is alive. But his mujer, his esposa, she is dead. AJ is in the jungle somewhere. We do not know where yet. Anna, we need your help. Please stay with us."

He continued to speak as Anna tried to pull her hands away but he held them tighter.

Suddenly Anna swayed, caught her breath and fell into his arms. He held her and began rocking back and forth, humming a slow chant. Brushing the hair across her face aside, he gently kissed her eyelids, then her mouth. She shuddered.

He struggled with one hand and got the vial out of his pocket.

"Open it for me, por favor," he said to Stacy. She did. He took it and dripped a gold liquid into Anna's mouth. Little by little, her body relaxed. A small sigh escaped her and she suddenly slumped down completely into his arms.

Stacy and Grant thought she had died. Jorge laid her gently on the floor and kissed her again. Anna curled into a fetal position and slept as a quiet snore floated from her into the air.

Stacy was the first to move.

"Let's find out what else is here."

She and Grant left.

Jorge remained with Anna.

## *Fifty-six*

The search of the island and questioning its inhabitants took three full days. True to his word, Grant had his and Jorge's men cover it inch by inch, take apart the house, probe the mountain and drag the bay.

Anna slept for two of those days. When she woke, she had to see the tapes on the screen all over again and hear of Sheila's death and AJ's disappearance again. Mexican Federales and Interpol came and questioned her.

Jorge gave her Adelina's medicine again and the spirits merged into her body. The jaguar lurked inside her, hungry for blood and revenge, but her grief held her immobile.

On the third day, the Federales brought a Frenchman to her. He was handsome in a wearied sort of way, deep lines of care etched into his forehead and around his mouth. He stood before Anna and gave a short formal bow, took her hand to shake it and instead, held it in both his hands.

"My name is Etienne Charboneau. I am so very sorry to meet you under such circumstances, Madame Kinnealy. This is not what I would have chosen. I will be brief.

"I am acquainted with your daughter. I am from France. I met her when she first came to Chicago, and in fact, I care about her very much. I am seeking her. I know she was drugged and taken here to Mexico. I have news of where she is being held and I have the cooperation of the federal police in removing her to France and then to Switzerland to return to the clinic. I am wondering if you would give your approval of this plan. I should let you know that even if you don't, I will carry it out. I intend to marry her, you see, someday. That is, if she will recover and have me."

He had the grace to look somewhat embarrassed by his frankness.

Anna looked at him, read his spirit and nodded.

"Yes. You must do that. You know that she may reject you in the end?"

"Oui. But I must try."

"Good. I have others I must find and care for. I am pleased to have your help with Marnie. She will not listen to me. If she comes to the point where she will listen, tell her I love her. Please keep in touch with me."

"But of course."


"Stacy, will you call Jorge and Ramon here?" Anna's voice rested quietly in the air, floating, disembodied.

"Anna, Mac is here too."

"Yes. I feel him. Bring him too. We need to plan how to find the others."

"Anna, you have to include Grant on this."

Anna sighed quietly. "Fine. Him too."

An hour later all were assembled on the patio.

The vista over the fields was calm, sunny, hot, and deceptive. Tensions reverberated through the air as those who had been enslaved told stories to each other, and families were reunited or informed of the deaths of their loved ones buried in unmarked graves—graves discovered only because of the loose dirt and the memory of one or another who had been forced to bury the corpses. Of those eaten by sharks, the desaparecidos, there would, of course, be no news.

Ramon and Jorge sat at opposite ends of a couch, hunched forward, elbows on knees, watching the dark energy swirl around Anna, aware of the jaguar's presence. Mac too was aware of an animal energy emanating from Anna, but not an animal he had known in his northern

Native ceremonies. This animal was very dangerous if uncontrolled. That he knew without being told.

Vincent Grant was oblivious to all this but sensed Anna had changed. He hoped it was for the better. Better, in his mind, meant that she would finally be more cooperative.

Stacy, watching Anna and seeing Grant's expression, knew "better" would not please him. Anna was changed, and was definitely more dangerous, more ready to fight. It had escalated in the swamp. It was even stronger now. Stacy was ready to back her all the way.

"Thank you all for being here. I probably wouldn't be alive if you, Mr. Grant and Stacy, and you, Jorge, hadn't shown up when you did." Her voice was calm, firm, quiet. She inclined her head to each one as she named them.

"Jorge, thank you for bringing Adelina's medicine. It has helped a great deal.

"Now. All four of my children are in grave danger or may be dead. I have Monsieur Etienne Charbonneau who will find Marnie and care for her. That's very good because she withdrew herself from me and into drugs. She will refuse my help. He will get her away from this country and return her to the help she needs.

"AJ is lost somewhere in the jungle. I need you, Jorge and Ramon, to find him and help him. You know this land, speak these languages, and know people who can help.

"Mr. Grant, I am rehiring you to help find Cory and Alex. Ardith said they were in the northern woods but didn't give a hint as to where. We certainly didn't find them on this island. I want you to know and believe that I am going to be very active in this search. You can't find them without me. I am the only one who can do this. I want you and Stacy to come north with me.

"I'm sorry if it sounds like I'm dictating to you but I will never rest until I find my sons, dead or alive, with or without you." Anna's voice hardened as she spoke these words.

"Mac, I need you to stay here and find out where Ardith went to ground, and get more information from her. Right now she's the only one who knows where the boys are. We have to find her.

"I hope you will all help me."

Ramon rose, walked to her and took her hand.

"He is my brother, my friend. I will find him. You are my love. I will find him." He kissed her cheek.

He returned and stood by Jorge.

Jorge rose and repeated the same words in Spanish, and kissed her also.

Together they left.

Mac stood, pulled her up and took her in his arms.

"I would never let you face this alone. We'll find them." He kissed her.

Vincent Grant, for once in his overconfident life, was actually confused. *She can't be lovers of all three men!* He looked at Stacy.

"I'll explain later," she mouthed silently.

"Of course we'll help you, Anna," she said out loud. "Grant will even offer his private jet to get us up there quickly, won't you, Vincent?"

"Of course, of course. It's ready at any time."

Anna moved to shake his hand.

"Thank you. On the way you can fill me in on just what resources you have that can be brought to bear on this search."

The meeting adjourned. Hours later, a helicopter flew them to the private jet. When they were in the air to Wisconsin, Anna told him how she knew where her children were.

He nodded in seeming understanding. Privately, he thought she was overwrought and quite possibly hallucinating.

She saw his disbelief and didn't care.

# Part Four

## *Fifty-seven*

Far to the north, Alex held Cory's head in his lap and cried, remembering Cory's torture and his own, seeing in his mind the marks of the torture on his brother's body.

"Don't worry, Cory. Mom's coming," he repeated over and over. "She's coming. I can feel her. Hang in there, man, she's coming."

Above them, in darkness, a bear snuffed at the ground and pawed at it. She could smell the humans faintly but was puzzled. She had never smelled live humans under the ground before, or dead ones either for that matter.

When her two cubs caught up with her, they snuffed as she had, but all three moved on when a more delicious smell reached their noses. Somewhere in the waning night, hints of honey from a hive wafted its way in their direction. Breakfast!

Underneath them, hunger pain shot through Alex's stomach and he thanked the unseen stars Cory was unconscious and didn't have to feel that pain too.

High in the air over Texas, Anna felt a pain in her stomach and wondered if she had picked up a bug in Mexico. Then she grew still and for the first time in an eon, Hope came out of hiding and hovered nearby.

*I'm coming. I love you. I'm coming.*

## Green Bay

### Fifty-eight

Vincent Grant unrolled the large map on the dining room table of The House. It encompassed three states: Minnesota, Wisconsin and Michigan.

He looked at Anna. The faraway look in her eyes annoyed him. *She's in her own world again. This is ridiculous.*

"You heard her say the northern woods. That's a hell of a lot of territory. We've gone over the house where you found Alex the first time and we've found nothing. The tapes she played for you looked like it was happening in some kind of dim enclosure like a cave. We found no sign of any cave on that land. We must narrow this down."

Anna remained silent, seemingly inattentive.

The group gathered around the table—Stacy, Caroline and Rob, Cait, Ben and Greg and Iron Mike—gazed at the vast expanse of territory with dismay.

An FBI man, Frederick Banning, stood to the rear of the group. He was not happy. His orders were to be in charge. Between the weird Kinnealy woman's strange insistence that she'd know where her sons are and Grant's arrogance, he was completely unable to function. He had decided, in silent fury, to stay out of it and let them all fail. It would be on their heads.

Greg Klarkowski spoke up.

"I think it's got to be Wisconsin as a first priority and maybe into Upper Michigan. It seems to have been her path of choice for smuggling her wares. Well, maybe not, but it's the one we know best right now. I've contacted other police forces. They have only bare bones information we can definitely say is part of this, but there's been a serious growing drug problem in towns up this way."

He moved his fingers up the highways 141/41 and along the highway leading through the Menominee Reservation that lay to the west.

"Of course, she could have built other routes, but these are most likely."

Greg glanced at Anna.

*She's on hyperalert. Like an animal. She's feeling them. I'd bet anything she's feeling them. Why doesn't she speak? And tell us?*

He looked at Grant and Banning and knew why.

*They'd refuse to believe her and she knows that.*

Caroline watched Anna and knew she had changed and felt a tug of fear. To her surprise it was not fear for Anna, but fear *of* her.

*She's dangerous. Something about her is dangerous. I want to slink out of here. Why?*

Cait stood with a half-smile on her face.

*Once before she was like this when we were in fourth grade and Jon O'Keeffe tried to bully her. The only reason he never reported the bloody nose he got was because he was ashamed of being beaten up by a girl.*

Anna remained silent while other voices chimed in with opinions, most seeing Wisconsin as the first place to look.

Finally she bent over the map, took a red marker and drew it around several counties, naming them as she went.

"To Ardith, if she said north, since she lived in Green Bay for so long, it would most likely be this territory she thinks of as north—Brown, Oconto, Marinette, Shawano, the Menominee Reservation, Forest, and Florence counties. In Upper Michigan I think she would have used a route through the counties of

Menominee, Iron, Delta, Alger and those leading through the locks at Sault Ste. Marie."

"I agree," Iron Mike said. "Police know Marinette and Menominee, on Highway 41 north, are having a hell of a problem with drugs right now. It's as bad as any big city ghetto. She probably transported a lot of stuff up that way by small trucks, vans, U-Haul trailers—vehicles no one would look at twice. Trucks can't bypass the Marinette-Menominee towns so there's huge truck traffic right through them. She also could have gone up through Coleman, Pound, up 141 north."

Stacy spoke. "That made sense to Mac. He told me that since he visited and has seen the territory, he believes 41/141 is the main route she uses."

"Anna, where do you sense the boys are?" Cait asked.

*Whether Grant likes it or not, or anyone believes her or not, I know she's sensing them. She won't talk because she knows they won't believe her.*

"My sense of where they are is too diffused right now. We have to narrow it down. I think of all the possible routes, I want to check out the most likely first and that's the territories between northern Highways 41 and 141 in Wisconsin and the route to either Marquette or Sault Ste. Marie in Upper Michigan. Or both."

Anna turned to Grant.

"Can you fly me over those in a helicopter or low-flying plane? Or can we drive those routes? I know that will take time and I must tell you all," she looked around at the others, "that I can hardly feel Cory. I feel Alex more strongly. She tortured Cory and his mind is..." her voice broke. "His mind may be gone."

"Oh, my god!" Cait breathed out.

"Anna, are you sure?" Caroline had tears in her eyes.

"Yes."

Grant moved impatiently but stopped dead when he caught Stacy's warning look.

"Here's a plan we can try," she said. "Vincent, why don't you get the equipment up and see if you can detect and map human presence where it's not supposed to be— like in rural areas. We're probably looking for two b..., people together in or under something. Anna, if we drive up those highways and through the territory where she had that home, would you be able to sense the boys more strongly?"

Anna nodded.

"What if she's stashed them in a town or city? Then what?" Greg asked.

"Then we go there." Grant stated, "but we have to get started now, do something now. We can't wait. Damn, this is still a lot of territory."

"I'll feel them if I get close."

"Anna, what can we do?" Rob asked.

"Pray. Just pray. Just keep yourselves safe. Ardith is still out there somewhere, wounded, still hating. There's no telling what she's doing now."

# Mexico

## Fifty-nine

"Get us out of here," she snarled at her pilot.

The shard of glass grated on the bone of her shoulder blade when she reached for the handle to pull herself into the copter. The man who had accompanied her to the plane reached out and helped her in. She seated herself and turned and shot him.

"Just dead weight," she said to herself.

The pilot took off.

"Cozumel," she ordered, "Fournier's house. He has a doctor who can treat me. Notify them."

The pilot did as he was told.

Hate is a powerful motive. Hate had kept her alive long ago and hate kept her alive now.

"I will make her sorry for every move she made," she vowed, and replayed the fight in her mind to count the moves.

They arrived at the island and transferred to a yacht, then crossed the channel to the mainland where they taxied up to the dock. Fournier's doctor met them and she was transferred to a gurney and moved up the path to a small but well-equipped clinic

She had been a guest before. The native servants did not like her. If there were jarring bumps and stops and starts along the way to the house, it was only to be expected. She shut her eyes and gritted her teeth and didn't know the way was actually smooth.

Some hours later, partially sedated, she lay at rest in a sumptuous bed. Monsieur Fournier stood beside her.

"You need to rest, mon cheri. You lost much blood."

"I need to murder, mon ami. I lost my island home to that woman."

"I have had inquiries made. You have indeed lost it but I think El Cocodrilo will retake it for you. He has enough influence with the Federales to get them to vacate it when they are through examining it all. Of course, the people will be gone. You will have to build up your slave population again, but that is easily done."

"What of the girl, Marnie? She satisfies you?"

"Oui. She is most satisfactory for now but I shall want her to be more willing and not on Rohipnol. That will come in time when she realizes she can't escape and she might as well have pleasure."

She smiled.

*She will be of even more use when she realizes she is a slut now and shame takes over and I can taunt her mother with that.*

"Leave me. I must sleep."

"Of course."

*I must make sure El Cocodrilo does not take my house and my island* from *me instead of for me.*

She fought passing out as she thought this but lost the battle.

Fournier returned to the bedroom where a drugged Marnie lay, naked on the deep blue velvet cover, her long black hair spread out beside her, the short black hair that covered her pubis curling softly onto the very top of her thighs.

He sat in a nearby chair, gazed at her body and sighed. His old penis did not stir, had not stirred even at first sight of her. He was no longer capable of that. Even medication had not helped but no one would know of his failure.

Nor would anyone believe her if she said she'd been raped. He had told her that, that he had raped her. He wanted her to believe she was no longer desirable to other men and that he was in full control. Then he told her she had also given herself to him of her own accord when she was drunk and on drugs. She believed all of it when she saw herself naked in the mirror over the bed. She believed it because she felt and saw the bruises where he had pounded her body in sexual frustration.

Would she even remember what he had told her, what she had seen? Maybe not. Rohipnol and Ambien erased memory. But then, he had the tapes.

He did not plan to allow anyone to have a chance to talk to her. She now belonged to him—a trophy, a prize, a beautiful possession like his art collection, the rare animals in his small zoo, and the other women he kept at his secret place in the French Alps.

The few paparazzi still waiting outside his home would soon give up. The rumors on the internet would die. They always had. The four other women he kept had been forgotten after a while. So would this one.

*France*

## *Sixty*

One week after the dinner party for Anna, Louie De La Vergne had been sitting at her Louis Quinze desk and mulling over the list of guests she had invited that night. It was her habit to keep a detailed account of all the dinners she gave and parties she attended—flowers and décor, food and guests. Her reputation as a gracious and attentive hostess depended on it.

One name stood out. Andre Lemaire. She had invited him at the request of a woman of wealth she knew only casually. There had been complaints about his behavior, including Anna's casual remark that he seemed irritable. Another friend had questioned why he was invited at all and mentioned his poor reputation among certain circles and rumors of possible illegal activity.

Louie had delayed any action until she was informed that Marnie left the treatment center and France. Today she picked up the phone and called a certain number at Interpol. When she was finished with the conversation, she was thoroughly frightened and horrified.

*Had Andre been watching Anna? Does he have anything to do with the disappearance of Marnie? Where is Marnie? Where is Anna?*

Fear and horror were not strangers to Louie. A childhood with an alcoholic and violent father taught her a great deal, not the least that fear and horror lost much of their power when strong action was taken to confront these bullying companions of one's own spirit. Louie did not play victim to anyone or any circumstance, or her own fears.

So it came to be that she saw the internet rumors about Fournier, gathered information on Marnie's contacts since she had arrived in France, learned of the count who had fallen in love with her, and pulled a few strings to endeavor to meet him in Mexico.

"My dear Robert, you know I must do this."

"Oui, oui. I know you. You will not rest until you put it right. If you need help, remember I was once a member of the French resistance although I did not do very much, being only twelve at the time."

"A twelve-year-old who blew up a train. That was, and is, quite good enough, my love. I will call you from Mexico. Perhaps we can vacation in Cancun once I have gotten her out of there."

"What a wonderful idea! Do be careful."

"But of course"

Louie picked up the phone again and called Stacy.

*There is always foresight in getting to know the persons who work for your friends. It is good that I got her cell number.*

That is how Louie came to know more of the story.

"So," she said to Stacy, "Anna will have to be in the USA. Well, then it is perfect that I will be in Mexico. She cannot be all places at once and I can move in higher circles without suspicion. Lower circles too, when I choose."

She packed her elegant summer clothes and her American jeans and t-shirts, her Mayan dictionary, her maps of the Yucatan, and landed in Cancun the next day.

A few words dropped in certain ears of the rich and famous, and a certain French politician with a penchant for young girls became very interested in inviting a well-heeled, popular, and lusciously endowed hostess to a party at his estate, hoping she would stay for a week or two as his guest.

After that, Louie and the French count met with the man named Mac, who seemed to know everyone, to plan a reverse kidnapping.

## Southern Yucatan

### Sixty-one

Eight men walked slowly through the village of Santa Anita while hordes of flies buzzed up from each corpse they neared, and resettled on that body after they passed. The flies had gorged, mated, laid eggs, watched their offspring hatch and become maggots. Birds had feasted on the maggots. Other animals had come in the nights since the killings to feed on the sweet flesh.

Ramon turned aside and threw up. Several other men did the same.

After a while, one by one, they stopped walking, unable to make their feet move, to feel, to smell, to see, to think. Jorge dropped to his knees, bent over and laid his forehead against the earth. Perhaps Mother Earth sent him some healing because he was the first to move again.

He stood and looked around as if for the first time.

"Find them all. Bring them to the center of the village. Find shovels. You, and you and you," he pointed to three men, "begin digging."

Slowly they found what was left of the children, the women, the old men. One grave was found, with stones at the head and feet. Ramon knew immediately who had dug the grave and who was under the soil.

"I have to find mi hermano. He is lost."

"Sí. Comprendo," Jorge replied.

Ramon took Alberto and they melted into the jungle. Jorge and the men buried the others.

Jorge called a meeting.

"We must stop this. We can no longer live this way," he said quietly. "We will make this our camp. Go and tell the others. It is time. This will be our headquarters. Do not wash the blood from the walls and floors. It will be our reminder. The Maya were once warriors. Now we are again."

After the men had dispersed to spread the word, Jorge, heart weeping, eyes dry, stood for a long time at the foot of the grave of the woman with the angel's smile.

## Northern Wisconsin

### Sixty-two

Alex ate dirt. They had stopped the food a day ago, whoever "they" were. The food had just appeared somehow. Alex didn't know how. The pain in his stomach was annoying. He found he didn't need much dirt. He was an expert on this.

His first memory of eating dirt was at age three when he wanted to find out if dirt had taste. It did. Some of it. After a while he lost interest.

At age ten, after bragging about that incident to them, his classmates dared him to eat a pile of dirt. He got through about one cup of it when a teacher stopped them and hauled them all to the principal's office. His mother was called.

He spent several days in embarrassment while she and the doctor poured water into him and monitored his poop to be sure there were no bad results. There weren't.

The worst problems now had become thirst and his worry for Cory and his own growing sense of losing his mind.

Which is why, when, somewhere in the misty recesses of his brain, it came to him that they were not without air, he sat bolt upright.

"We should have been without air. Being buried alive should mean we're without air," he said aloud.

Cory stirred.

"Sit up, Cory. Wake up!"

Cory rolled to one side and groaned. A sharp pain in his right leg made him hiss in breath, then expel it again as the pain hit him again.

274

"Shit!" His voice was a rasp from a dry throat.

"Cory, we have to look for an out. There's fresh air coming in from somewhere. Wake up, dude."

Cory heard Alex's voice out of the blackness, which was all he could see.

"Shit! I'm blind! Alex, I'm blind, I can't see!"

A cold fire of fear seared the pit of his stomach.

"It's ok, Cory. It's ok. We're in total darkness right now. Sometimes it gets lighter. There must be a hole letting daylight in somewhere."

"Where are we? I don't remember getting here."

"We're underground. If it is daylight when the light comes, and I'm pretty sure it is, then we've been here about three days, maybe four.

"Cory, are you in pain? Cory, uh... uh... she had you tortured. Me too."

Alex's voice shook slightly as his mind supplied pictures of what they had endured. He forced himself to get the words out.

"She filmed us," Cory answered. "I remember that. My mind is missing some of it, I think, because it's not making sense to me. I see bits and pieces. Mostly it's like I'm some other person looking into the scene now and then, not seeing it all. God, my mouth is so dry."

"Scrape some dirt off the floor—sand or small pebbles—and put it in your mouth. Just hold it there. Maybe it will start some spit."

Alex heard Cory scrape. After a few minutes he heard, "Mmm. A little. I can say an s without sounding drunk. I feel like I'm drunk. My mind isn't working too well. Something's wrong with my right leg. If I move, I get a sharp shooting pain. My skin burns too. What did she have her bastards do to us?"

There was a brief silence.

"You don't want to know, man. You really don't want to know. Look, we've got to get us out of here or find a way to let someone know we're here. I think we might be in a cave."

Alex stopped talking for a bit.

"Yeah, that could be it. I got glimpses of where they took us after the long time on the plane. There was a car, then a short time in a dark room, then a really long ride, then the place where they tortured us, then..."

"Torture. Oh, god, yes. Oh, god..." Cory gasped. As memory he returned, his chest imploded with pain and he began to moan.

"Oh god, oh god, oh god."

He curled up in a ball as horror shook him. He saw the lighted cigarettes coming at him and the belt hitting him.

Alex reached for his brother and held him as they both rocked and cried.

"I'm sorry! I'm so sorry! I shouldn't have said that! Shit, shit, shit, shit! I shouldn't have said that."

Later, Alex felt Cory's body relax into sleep or "...or maybe you passed out." He curled himself around his brother and hoped for sleep too.

He woke to the time of the dim light and his own cold anger.

"We are fucking getting out of here."

Leaving Cory, he began to explore the entire place, beginning with the space they were in, a small cave. He found the opening where the light came in but it was indirect, very dim, as if it was coming into yet another space and being reflected into where they were. He began to wiggle through a small passage where the air was freshest and then realized that if Cory woke and found himself alone, he might panic. He wiggled back to his brother and shook him.

"Wake up, Cory, it's time to see if we can get out of here. Wake up."

Cory didn't move. Panic!

Then Cory groaned and grumbled, "It's too early. I don't have school yet."

"Come on, man. We have to get out of here."

"Oh shit! I can see you! Sorry. I don't mean that the way it sounds. I mean, there's a little light in here. I can see. God, you look awful!"

"So do you. We have to explore this place. We need to find a way out. Come on."

"I've got stomach cramps. Alex, I've got diarrhea. Oh man! I've messed my pants."

"Cory! Focus! That doesn't matter. Come on. We've got to move. If we stay here, we'll die here."

"Ssssss!" Cory jerked and moaned, then gasped, "I moved my leg the wrong way."

He lay panting until the pain let up.

"Alex, it could be broken. Check it, please."

Alex moved his hands down the leg feeling for broken bones, or something out of joint. All felt well until he came to Cory's calf which was sticky and wet. Even in the near-darkness he could distinguish blood. There was a long tear in Cory's pants and his calf muscle was ripped and torn.

*He can't walk. That muscle won't support him.*

"It's not broken but your calf muscle is hurt bad. If you move at all, you'll have to crawl. It's going to hurt a real lot. I'm going to rip up part of my shirt and bind it so it won't get any worse.

Alex stood and moved around the space.

"I'm looking for something to use as a splint but I don't see anything. Will you be ok if I go in search of something? I'll keep talking the whole time so you can hear me."

"Yeah, ok. Just do it. You don't have to talk."

Alex began to crawl on hands and knees, reaching into any dark places and feeling around. In the end there was nothing he could have used. A few stones, a small charred piece of wood, some old dry papers.

"Good. Someone's been here before and there's no dead skeleton which means they didn't get trapped here."

He sniffed again at the place where the air came in and wondered aloud where it went out.

Returning to Cory, he took off his shirt and tore the lower half into strips. Working as gently as he could, he bandaged the calf. Cory lay with clenched jaw as pain raced up his leg over and over. Both sighed with relief when it was over.

"Ok. I'm going exploring. I've got to find a way out of here while we have some light. So, do I follow the air or the light? Light first."

It proved a good choice. The passage was low, narrow, but manageable and when he had wiggled and clawed his way through it he found himself in a much larger space. Some ten feet above him was an even lighter area. He saw a slanting round tunnel about two feet wide that looked like it might open into another space. The air was fresher, stronger.

"That's man-made. This has to have been used for something. I've got to get Cory this far."

He wiggled back to Cory and explained what he had to do.

"I'll have to move backward through the passage and drag you by your hands. It's going to be bad, Cory. Really painful for you but it's better than here. You might be able to help with your left leg if you dig in with your heel and push where the space allows that."

"Let's do it then."

Excruciating pain plus movement through a narrow uneven passage equals an infinity of time. Cory's equation.

When they were finished, the light was dimming again.

"Alex. Leave me here and go up that passage if you can and see what's there before the light goes. If I have to face another night here, I want to know there's some hope for getting out. Maybe it's there."

"Ok. I'll be back"

Climbing to the opening high up in the wall proved impossible.

278

"I'll have to gouge places into the wall for finger and toe holds. The good news is I can try using that piece of charred wood and I've found a metal trowel head that has no handle, but is usable. I'll make holds until we lose light and then we'll have to wait."

Cory began to shiver.

"No. It'll have to wait. You're in shock. I need to get you warm."

Alex lay down and wrapped his arms and body around Cory.

"Just try to sleep."

# Green Bay

## Sixty-three

A frustrated Vincent Grant paced the long hall of The House on the second day of the search.

"This is impossible. There's too much territory to cover. We've got to narrow this down somehow. We need more information. We can alert police forces everywhere, we can pore over these maps, we can fly over the whole damn territory, and we've driven the two highways, but we need more information. It's taking too bloody long.

"Anna, I brought a copy of the tapes from the island. I know watching them will be hard for you but can you take a look at them again and look for details, anything that catches your eye?

"Greg, can we get someone who knows the geology of this land? From what I saw on those tapes, it's got to be some kind of cave. There was an echo in the sound, like it bounced off walls. The light was dim. If we can have someone pinpoint places where that kind of configuration can be found we can narrow down our search a lot.

"Stacy, call the London police again and see if they've found any more information on small planes that left the country for destinations in the Midwest US or Canada. Maybe we can pinpoint a destination that gives us a clue."

Anna sat, her head down, her body tense and alert. Images poured into her mind from the tapes.

"I don't need to see them again. I'll never forget them. There was only one clue I remember. In a few of the frames in one sequence I thought I saw a kind of cart in the background, like those carts that run on tracks that

they have in mines. Northern Wisconsin and Upper
Michigan have many old mines, most of them closed.
Some are open and give tours. There are caves too,
where...like you said, cave systems maybe."

She sat up suddenly.

"She wants my money. She wants the inheritance.
That's the bait. We need to hold out the bait. She's
injured. Where would she go if she was injured? Where
would it be safe for her? With El Cocodrilo? No. Not if
she's vulnerable. He'll kill her and take over her business.
Can we get the names of people she's been associated
with, people who she visited in Mexico, people she
socialized with, if any?"

Banning came upright from his slump on a living
room couch. *That's more like it. Now maybe she'll follow
our procedures.*

Grant stopped pacing. *I wish she'd keep her mind
in one place, dammit.*

Banning spoke. "I've already got people on the
watch for her. I have a list of some social contacts but it's
not very long—politicians and a few wealthy businessmen
who go to Mexico looking to satisfy their sexual appetites.
I'm expecting a call from Mexico soon with an update.

"I like your idea, Anna, of luring her in. We can set
a rumor going in Mexico that you're willing to pay to find
your sons. Let's see what cockroaches that brings out of
the woodwork. I saw that cart on the tapes too. It's a
start. I'd still like you to scour those tapes for anything
else that might help us. Meantime, we'll pinpoint every
possible mine and cave system and make those our
priorities."

*She could have tortured them in England, Europe,
anywhere. Those tapes may be all wrong.* Banning knew
they might never be found.

Anna rose slowly from the living room couch
where she had been sitting.

*This feels like some insane dream, something I've made up. I can feel the boys. They're still alive but so far, so dim, so remote. Why can't I feel them more strongly?*

Her cell phone rang and she excused herself, went into the library and closed the door. A slight feeling of relief spread through her at being alone. She glanced at the name on the phone. Louie. Yes.

"Louie, hello, how are you?"

"My dear, I am perfectly fine, as always. I know you are not. I have some news for you. I do not have much time so you must listen and not interrupt. I will give you the bad news first. I have found Marnie and she is at the Mexican home of an old French pig named Fournier. I will be there as soon as I have all possible plans in place. I am so sorry to tell you that it was because of one of my dinner guests at the party you attended that she is in the hands of this disgusting man.

"Do you remember the man you disliked? Well, I have found out he is, to put it in common terms, a pimp. He arranged for your daughter to be taken and she was drugged. I am here with Etienne, the man who loves her. He says he met with you. We will be rescuing her within the next few days. You must not concern yourself. We will take her back to the clinic and to freedom and health.

"There is more. I have been contacted by another friend of yours. He calls himself Mac. He has brought me up to date on all that has happened to your family. He has been tracking this woman who is your enemy and she has also been brought to the home of Fournier. A doctor was called and attended a woman who was cut badly and lost much blood. It seems she procures young girls for Fournier. This is not good news. She is evil. If she knows that Marnie is in that house, she would not hesitate to want her tortured and may even kill her.

"Robert has much influence with, and is my link to Interpol. We will work with them. This 'Ardith' must have been from Europe originally. He is attempting to trace the woman's origin. He will try to find out if Conrad's sisters actually survived. Personally, I think she is what you Americans call 'nuts'. Robert will also arrange for transport of Marnie to Switzerland without all the red tape.

"I have the greatest hope this will all work out well because we are very good at this. Now you must find your sons. If I find a way to make this bitch talk, and I know many ways to do that, I will find out where they are for you. Make sure your cell phone is charged. I will be keeping you up to date.

"Au revoir, my dear Anna."

The transmission ended.

Anna stood, phone in hand, mouth open. Hope did a short but sweet dance in the corner of the room.

"Well. Ok then. Au revoir."

The animal inside her raised its fur and Anna glided into the hall and announced, "Ardith is at the home of the French politician, Fournier, in Mexico. That's also where Marnie is being held. There are three people on the way to rescue her. Yvette-Louise de la Vergne, the woman who just called me, and Etienne, a Frenchman who has fallen in love with Marnie, and Mac. Louie—Yvette-Louise—will try to find out where the boys are. Interpol will be involved. Robert de la Vergne, her husband, is having them dig into Ardith's background in Europe.

"In the meantime, Vincent, I would like to be taken to any abandoned mines that still have fairly easy access to the surface. Eliminate those where tours are offered. Police can search caves and cave systems for evidence of inhabitants.

"Please, Greg, can you arrange for me to see Clayton Foster? I want to see if he will talk to me.

'I'm sorry I couldn't seem to work with you all before. This has been very difficult but I have myself under control now and would like to cooperate with everyone. We will need every possibility checked out. The boys are definitely up here somewhere."

"Mr. Banning, will you take charge of offering a ransom, of getting that word out and monitoring any responses? I'll offer $1,000,000."

A gasp went around the room followed by a silence.

Finally Greg broke it by moving to the living room to make phone calls.

Cait mouthed to Caroline, "RoBARE? Yvette-Louise?"

Caroline shrugged.

Marthe, who had been watching from the hall, moved to the kitchen to make lots of coffee and tea.

"Holy shit!" Greg's voice exploded from the living room. "That's impossible! How could anyone get to him? Who screwed that up?"

He appeared at the living room door.

"Clayton Foster was found dead in his cell early this morning. It looks like murder."

## Sixty-four

Silence ruled for some thirty seconds until Cait exploded.

"Good! The dirty old man is gone! Kids everywhere can relax now."

"Except, we don't know what else he knew."

Greg flipped his phone closed with a snap. He shot a dagger look at Cait, and an apologetic one at Anna.

"We don't know how it happened and who did it, what kind of connection with him and others on the drug scene the person who murdered him had, and if it had anything to do with these kidnappings. His voice is permanently silenced. Needless to say, a thorough investigation is in progress."

Another long silence.

"Anna," Grant said. "Why the mines?"

"Because I've remembered a long ago conversation about our vacation. We were taking the kids to the UP and were considering the mining tour in Vulcan, Michigan. Ardith wasn't normally interested in what we did but she asked a lot of questions about that place and I thought it odd or maybe that she was just being polite at the time. It was before Art died, a few years before. We were at a party to raise funds for some charity. It's a very long shot, I know, but I can't stand any inaction. I have to do something."

"Then let's get started."

"There's one more thing I have to say. Cait and Caroline, I'd like you to back away from this. I know you want to help but I'm terrified you'll be targeted more than you already have been. She'll stop at nothing, kill anyone. She shot the man who helped her into the helicopter before he could even try to climb aboard. She may even be the one who ordered Clayton killed. Who knows how far her reach extends? I'm sending you away too, Marthe. I can't lose any more people I love. Please. Please."

Stacy nodded.

"She's right. You're all at high risk."

"We'll agree only if we can do what we want. We have a proposal," Caroline said with hands on her hips, jaw firm.

"There have to be clues to what these people were doing for years and no police force can possibly have the time to find them. We want to. That's what we came here to say. We want all the files, notes, letters, etc., and the computers, from both law firms, for the last twenty years at least. Besides the coding you found, Anna, somewhere in all those records there must be more clues, hints, whatever, that point to what was going on and who was doing it. We can take the whole lot and go somewhere safe and read it all, page by page. No one else has that kind of time."

"Anna, you know what you discovered just going through Art's files," Cait said. "Greg, you know you haven't even begun to get through all that information."

Iron Mike agreed with enthusiasm. "I'm all for it. The whole police department together wouldn't have that kind of time."

"Done and done," Greg agreed. "Let's get Arnie on the phone. I bet he'll agree."

He walked back into the living room, phone to his ear.

Grant was obvious in his approval. *Fewer people to distract Anna and under my feet.*

"Well, who will make the coffee here?" Marthe asked.

"Not you. You'll come with us," Caroline demanded, "because someone has to keep us awake reading all that boring legal stuff. I'll be at home packing. Put us up at a resort somewhere, Stacy, where we can take swimming breaks and eat well. But not Mexico. Please, not Mexico."

Stacy grinned. "Done and done."

"I want to help too," Lindy said. "Anna, I insist on staying here to help. The boys are the brothers I never had. I have to be here. I know Tai Kwon Do. I can defend myself when I have to. or..." she stopped and stood still, "...or I'll go to Mexico and try to persuade my father to leave, and pick up information on the cartel."

A chorus of "No!" exploded around the room.

Cait stepped to her side and took her arm.

"No way you're going alone into that hellhole down there. Better the hellhole up here that we know. I've got plenty of ideas about what you can do, including teaching my boys some of that Tae Kwon Do. Think of me as the kind of mom you never had."

"Lindy, I need you up here," Anna said. "Cait, I want her with Stacy and me. The House is our headquarters for now and we'll need people on alert constantly, phones answered, everyone kept in contact with each other. She can speak Spanish and French when calls come from Mexico. I want as much contact from there as I can. Lindy, I want you to establish that. With Louie, with Jorge, with Adelina, with everyone we can trust there and here."

"Damn good idea!" Grant said. "Anna, we have to get you out there looking for those boys. I'll pull in people who can set up our best computer-phone system and..." he turned to Lindy, "...you're multilingual?"

She nodded. "French, Spanish, English and a little Portuguese and Italian."

"Damn! I'm hiring you. Fantastic! Stacy, alert the plane. We'll text coordinates after we pinpoint all mines in northern Wisconsin and the UP. Lindy, take all cell phones right now and program them so we have instant access. Stacy, can you call our group in Mexico? They're headquartered at your house there, Anna. I forgot to tell you that...and alert them too and have them send everything they know by encrypted email.

"Stacy," he began again but she stopped him.

"I'm not working for you, Vincent. I'm working for Anna. I'm setting up secure shelter for these families first and then I'm with Anna full time. I've got Melissa on the phone..." she waved her phone in the air, "...and she's in Mexico. I'm having her make contact with Louie, Anna, and she'll be going in with her to Fournier's lair, a fourth person with some very needed skills. She's also keeping tabs on El Cocodrilo. Or rather, Jorge and his men are. They're keeping him busy with some little diversions so he doesn't ally himself with Ardith out of a misguided sense of opportunism."

Grant hit his fist on the woodwork in the doorway.

"Women! I'll never understand why they just can't take orders!"

Six pairs of women's eyes in the room turned on him at the same time, with no smiling faces under them. He shut up.

Greg returned from the living room.

"Arnie's all for it and I've added everything we've just planned. Stacy, if you can let him know where you'll base these families, he'll have all legal files sent there. The only thing is, Cait, he wants to keep Sean and Mike here. They know the streets and the players. We need them here. Andrew and Seamus are still underage and they go with you. Liam will be safe where he is."

Cait shot him her dirtiest look but gave a reluctant nod.

"I can't control Sean and Mike. They're legally adults. But I don't like it."

Ben, silent for the whole time, went over to Cait and put his hands on her shoulders.

"Believe me, they are very street smart and they'll be fine. I need them at my back, Mrs. F."

Anna drew Stacy into the library.

"Is there any news about AJ? About Ramon? And what about Pete?"

"No. Nothing. Jorge only said there are many people from the villages searching for AJ. The London police will call if they find Pete, but, Anna, I don't hope for that. He's probably dead."

Anna's eyes became wet but her tears never fell.

"I'm so sorry."

*Mexico*

## *Sixty-five*

Aristide Fournier thought of himself as a man of impeccable taste and the perfect host, so it came as no surprise to his butler that planning for the visit of Madame de la Vergne was given close attention.

"Put her in the Guest Wing, the Blue Room Suite. She will be in one room and Count Charbonneau in the other. Check to be sure all cameras are working. Their dalliance will be most entertaining and possibly a source of good income. She will not want her oh-so-influential husband to know of her activities. Of course, you may also benefit from this, my dear Leo."

Leo, all simpering caramel smiles, made a small bow of gratitude. Leo thought of the money he was putting carefully away for the day when he could get out of the position of serving this arrogant white man.

"Of course her secretary, this Melissa somebody, although she is somewhat attractive, will not be in that wing. Put her in the Utility Wing and most definitely keep our blonde patient there. See to it she does not even hear of my dinner tonight. Keep them apart at all costs. I am hoping for El Presidente and his wife. I want nothing to spoil this gathering.

"And the other man, the swishy one who is clearly stoned on something. We'll have to put him in the Guest Wing since he's somebody in Canada, but find him a boy to keep him occupied, will you? He will no doubt make it an early evening if he finds out someone luscious is awaiting him in his room."

290

In Cancun, Yvette-Louise, in an elegant pink silk dress accessorized with glittering high-heeled Jimmy Choo sandals and matching bag she'd had made especially for her, an Hermes scarf in rainbow colors and Chanel No.5 perfume floating en l'air, and Melissa obediently walking two steps behind, entered the architect's office smiling and holding out both hands.

"My dear Gerhardt, you have not changed a bit! It has been far too long since I have seen you. I have heard you have a new wife, your fifth or sixth, is it not? You old rogue, you! The pretty young ones are never safe from you, are they?"

Gerhardt beamed and soon they were relaxing, drinks in hand, in his beautifully appointed office.

"Now Gerhardt, I know my dear Aristide might not approve. He is so jealous of his houses. But Robert and I want to build here and I must have the expertise you lavished on his house to help us. Can you not show me the specialties of the design? It will help us so much in deciding what we want. What is more, if Robert approves, perhaps he will want to hire you as our architect. Yes?"

His architectural business was in a serious slump. Louie had checked that carefully beforehand.

Gerhardt beamed even more. One must court the rich, famous and influential to maintain the style of living he chose and Gerhardt had not chosen well in his latest wife. She was not very willing to court and please the rich and famous men he introduced to her. She was very willing to spend as much of his money as possible. Louie had checked that out as well.

Melissa took notes as they looked carefully over the house plans Gerhardt had ordered brought to his office. She took pictures with a small camera as well, although Gerhardt was not aware of that. Yvette-Louise could be very distracting.

"Dear Gerhardt, you are so clever. I am sure Robert will want to know of the very special amenities you had built in to Aristide's house."

291

She turned to Melissa.

"Do you have the list of those, Melissa? Do you have all you need?"

"Yes ma'am. I will fax this to him tonight."

"Merci beaucoup, my dear Gerhardt. Au revoir."

She touched one of his cheeks with hers and then the other, leaning her chest just enough into his to give him a slight thrill.

"It is such a privilege to know brilliant men like you. So delightful!"

In their car, Melissa sent the pictures to Mac and Etienne, who prepared prints and laid out a map of the house on the long table in the luxury hotel in Cozumel where Louie had gotten them rooms.

As night fell, Mac rented a motorcycle and made his way to the countryside. At a small house behind a wood fence he knocked on the door.

"Hola, Tomasita. Buenos noches. Is she here yet?"

"Sí, Señor MacPherson. She has been here for three hours. Come in. Would you like café con leche?"

"Just café negro, por favor."

"She is in the back room."

Mac walked into the small back room, sniffing at the smells that lingered on the air. Many herbs. Fresh.

"Ah, Señor Mac. It is good to see you again. This time you look much younger than the last time I saw you. An improvement I think."

Mac laughed.

"I hope so. I am so sorry but I must not linger. Are the preparations ready? Will they work as I asked?"

"They are ready. They will work just as you want them to and leave no memory, no trace. You will get any information you need. I have other information for you now that you will find helpful. I hope you will not leave too soon."

Tomasita entered with a large cup of black coffee.

"Muchas gracias, Tomasita. I will be able to stay awake tonight much more easily."

He lifted the cup in a salute to her.

"De nada, Señor Mac."

She turned and left, closing the door.

"I have names of those who will help you at the home of this man. There are those servants who must work there to live, to eat, but hate what happens there. If something goes wrong, you will have help, but they must keep those jobs so they must be very careful."

Mac spent a half hour memorizing names and positions. When they were done, he hugged Adelina and wished her well.

The night was moonless, dark. He made his way carefully on back roads until he hit the city lights and then sped to the rental agency, returned the cycle and headed for another meeting.

Mac believed there should always be Plan B and even Plan C, just in case. When he was finished both were in place. Interpol had been briefed. One trusted Mexican police capitan was in place.

Later, at the hotel, Louie, Mac, Melissa and Etienne memorized everything they could about the house and its staff.

In the cool of early morning a limousine carried them to the large villa where effusive greetings were exchanged between Aristide and Yvette-Louise. Introductions were made. Guests were attended to by a flock of servants carrying refreshments and small gifts of welcome. Bags and guests were sent speedily to rooms in the beautiful wing allotted to prominent people.

Melissa found herself with one young servant girl moving in complete silence down a corridor with many closed doors. The girl unlocked and opened her room, left the bag at the door, turned and fled. Melissa smiled.

"Yes!"

She texted the word to Mac and the others.

293

She spent the next half hour finding every camera in her room and the main corridor and made sure she could disable them all speedily when she chose.

A phone call summoned her to luncheon at one. She dressed for it and a servant came to lead her to a large patio in the main section of the house.


Shown to his room, Mac, acting just on the edge of a little too high and mumbling to himself in French Canadian, by "accident" blocked off all but the camera trained on the bed. When a young boy was brought to him, he acted even more stoned and sent him to the kitchen with a note listing his "special dietary requirements", leaving Aristide, watching on a small screen in his study, amused at this inept man's misunderstanding of the "gift". The sous chef was grateful to get the list and went on alert, recognizing the coded words in the message.

Mac took himself and a bag to the nearby desk, now out of camera range, and made plans for a visit to a certain blonde woman. When his call to lunch came, he was on the balcony carefully memorizing shrubbery on the grounds.

Etienne, not trained to seek out and disable cameras, left his room after the valet unpacked for him and began to wander the house.

Aristide joined him within minutes.

"Aristide. I must say your objets d'art are wonderful. And the architectural details. They are every bit as excellent as those in my ancestor's chalet in France. When you return to France, I must have you as my guest. Now, tell me, where did you get this painting? It's breathtaking!"

Putting his arm around Aristide's shoulders and flooding the man with questions and observations and praise for the beauty, the perfection, the incredible taste, etc., etc., etc., Etienne managed to keep his attention for the remainder of the morning.

Etienne observed that Aristide carefully kept him away from what he called the Utilitarian Wing.

"It is all practical, nothing artistic there, just the useful parts of the house."

They ended on the wide patio with a very good wine at hand.

After lunch, Louie insisted on having her secretary wait on her, which was fortunate because upon touring her room to be sure it was "suitable" for her, Melissa spotted several camera possibilities.

Louie kindly stopped the servant from unpacking more of her things.

"Please, my secretary knows just what I want and she will help me. Do not trouble yourself."

A sum of money pressed into the maid's hand and a gentle steer out the door left the room to the two women who proceeded to find three cameras focused on the bed, one in the bath, and another centered on a chaise longue near the French doors to the balcony.

In Portuguese, which she knew Fournier would not understand, Louie observed, "He obviously wants to see me naked and having sex. Well, naked I will be but sex, no. I draw the line. However if you and Etienne...No? Ah well, dear Aristide will be so disappointed in you both. But not in me."

She began to fling off her clothing, dropping it piece by piece on the floor after her, parading semi-naked back and forth as she prepared for her shower.

"You do your thing while his eyes are on me. Study the house layout again and decide where we must look first. He will most certainly not be watching you."

After picking up Louie's clothing with much rolling of the eyes and disapproving lifts of the brows, Melissa slipped into camera view, ostentatiously picked up her I-Pad and moved to the gardens where she "did work for the madame" as she told a curious waiter, who brought her an iced juice drink.

From time to time she would set down her "work" and wander the grounds, admiring all the trees, bushes, flowers, sculptures, and memorizing all the doors that opened to the outside from the wings of the estate. She always left the I-Pad long enough for it to be examined by the man, which either bored him to death with all the feminine trivia she and Louie contrived to program into it or aroused him intensely as he viewed the "secret" porn of two women having sex. The women were not Louie and Melissa however.

And so the day passed.

## Sixty-six

Dinner came and went. Aristide was indeed a gracious host. After other guests left, he proposed an evening walk with Louie on the grounds which lasted for over an hour, Louie being an accomplished flirt.

Mac, true to his character, had, almost immediately after eating, succumbed to the wine and whatever he appeared to have taken earlier. Aristide was very happy to see him go.

Melissa was sent to Louie's room to "see to my clothing for tomorrow."

Aristide was treated to a hidden view of a secret tryst between Etienne and Melissa, romantically staged in the orchid greenhouse.

Louie had been most persuasive with them both.

"We will need the diversion. I am good but his attention span is too brief. There must be more for him to see," she had said to Melissa.

Now she told him, "I knew they could not help themselves, Aristide. It is so romantic here. One cannot resist your secret little places. It excites you, yes? Of course it does, but I bet you have other treats for yourself for later. You are a man of passion. You must have them."

"Well-l-l. There are pleasures, of course. Would you like to partake of them, too, my dear? You are also so passionate, so sensual. You enjoyed your bath, did you not? Perhaps an end to this evening in my hot tub?"

"Oh! What a lovely idea but I am still feeling the effects of jet lag and am not at my best. But tomorrow night, ah, then, I will be full of energy, ready for anything. You comprehend?"

She lifted her eyes to his with half-closed lids underscored by her half-open mouth where the tip of her tongue just peeked out between her pink lips.

Aristide's breathing came quickly and he even felt a bit of stirring in his lower regions.

"I look forward to that, my dear. Yes, very much so."

When she left him he hurried to check on his model, who was sound asleep, and then to view the camera tapes from Louie's room, savoring what was to come.

He completely forgot to check on the blonde woman.

A single word of text from Louie sent Mac sliding through the moonless night, a ghost of a shadow. He entered the utilitarian wing, found an unoccupied small room, changed to medical whites and a short brown wig, and slipped into the kitchen where he found the tray he had hoped would be ready. Carrying it and a small medical kit, he approached the one door where a guard was posted.

"Could you open the door for me, por favor?. The doctor has sent me to bring some food and also to check on her. He is worried about infection in that shoulder."

The guard lifted the cover on the tray and checked the fruits and other snacks there, then opened the medical kit, looked in and closed it again.

"Are you new here?" he growled.

"No. I usually work during the day when you aren't on duty but we may have to set up an IV for her and I am the one the doctor has do that. You might have to help me."

"Sí. I must watch you while you work."

"No problem."

The guard laid the tray on the table near the bed.

Ardith appeared to be sleeping soundly, possibly sedated.

298

Mac shook her and she came to a groggy consciousness. He began his examination, taking the woman's pulse, listening to her heart and lungs. She asked for a drink and Mac handed her the specially prepared juice in a small glass.

"Tell the kitchen I want my juice in a large glass next time."

"Certainly, madam. I must take a quick look at your wound."

"Yes, yes. Get it over with."

Mac unbandaged the wound which sat high on her shoulder. He looked worried. She saw the look and attempted to move her head to that side to see but cringed in pain.

"What is it? What's wrong?" she asked.

"Infection, I'm afraid. I can either give you a shot or a longer-acting IV. The IV will attack the infection with more effect. Which do you prefer?"

"The IV. I want to be out of here as soon as possible."

"Certainly. The best choice, of course."

Mac quickly re-bandaged the wound and had the guard hold a portion of the stand while he set it up.

With little trouble he inserted a needle into a vein at her wrist and watched as she relaxed into sleep again.

"I'm going to have to monitor this for about a half hour to be sure she remains comfortable. Can you keep the time for me? I'm beat. I worked all day and now this. I might fall asleep."

The guard grinned and nodded.

"Easy to do, even when you get sleep. I have to walk to keep awake. I'll be back when the time is up."

He returned to the corridor where Mac heard the sound of his boots as he paced.

Mac made sure the camera was covered, injected certain drops into the IV and aroused her enough to have her answer his whispered questions. He put her to sleep again and when the guard returned later, he appeared to be nodding off.

Jumping up as if startled, he rechecked Ardith's pulse and breathing.

"Everything looks good. I'll be back in early morning to check her again."

"I'll be off duty then. Someone else will check you into her room at that time."

Mac waved a salute and left the corridor. Changing quickly in the small room, he slid again into the night.

In his room, he sent a brief text message north with the ending words, "more to come." He dared not risk a long message in case Aristide's sophisticated monitoring equipment included cell phones. He had discovered no equipment of that sort in his nighttime prowling but that didn't mean all was safe.

## Sixty-Seven

Marnie came to semi-consciousness in dim light, her mind fogged and unresponding. A vague urge to pee began in her body and she looked to her left and saw an open bathroom door, the edge of a tan toilet bowl in view, it's lid upright. She tried to rise from the bed but her body fell into an uncontrolled roll and she landed on the floor. She tried to stand and her body wouldn't obey. Slowly she rolled and half-crawled across the floor.

By the time she hit the cool bathroom floor, her arms began to work and she got herself onto the toilet. When she finished, she fell again and crawled into the shower. Clawing at the tiles, she stretched to reach the handle of the faucet and turned it. Cold water hit her with a shock and her mind began to function.

Huddled under the spray, she looked around her. The room was no place she could ever remember seeing before. Her last memory was of sitting in a group at the hated clinic where she was being educated on the symptoms of addiction.

"I'm too young to be addicted," she had told them. "I don't use that much. Just for fun and games. Not like these other people."

She had looked with disgust at the people in the group around her.

She didn't remember leaving. There was the really cool man who was driving the red convertible and drinks with another man whose name she didn't know.

"Yeah, yeah," she said to herself. "We went to Orly and took off for..." but where they had flown to escaped her.

Marnie looked down and, with sudden horror, she realized she was naked.

Then she laughed.

"Of course I'm naked. I'm in the shower."

She continued to laugh at her joke.

After a while, she stood and turned the water off.

"No towels. Why don't they have towels here. Where is here?"

Holding onto the wall as she went, she made her way back to the bedroom. An unsteady search of drawers and a doorless closet yielded no towels, no clothing. None. Nothing.

Marnie sat on the foot of the bed, puzzled. Another unmeasurable block of time passed before she looked up and saw the camera focused on the bed.

*Why a camera?*

It was then that fear crept into her mind and her stomach knotted. Shame sent red flame to her face. She pulled her long wet hair over her breasts and tried to make the ends cover her pubic area. They didn't quite. A little too short.

One sheet was on the bed, tucked under the mattress sides. She stood up, jerked out the sides, pulled the sheet up and off and wrapped it around her.

It took her only one try at opening the door to realize she was a prisoner in a locked windowless room.


Far across the Atlantic, in Berlin, Robert de la Vergne sat sipping brandy with an old friend in an unmarked office where stacks and stacks of old files filled shelf after shelf of the room next door.

On the mahogany desk were three files the man had pulled from those stacks.

"They did not survive. I remember Wentworth. We didn't have the information then but it's here now. His family all died in Auschwitz. There were no survivors of that group of people at all. None. The Nazis in charge tried to destroy records but didn't have time to get them all burned, so I am sure about that. All of them are listed."

"Who could this woman be then?"

"Perhaps an orphan found on the streets of some European city and adopted. There were so many of those. However, not all were adopted. Many were placed in mental hospitals or orphanages. The trauma of that war affected millions of ordinary citizens, not just military. She could be one of those.

"Mental illness was epidemic after the war. There are still survivors in nursing homes and assisted living facilities, who have what is now called post-traumatic stress. It is chronic with them. It doesn't go away.

"There are records of the lost people, of course, but it will take forever to find them. She could be from any wartime country, even one that was under Communist domination during the long Cold War. She could have fled East Germany over the Berlin Wall.

"I tell you what. You get me a picture and some DNA and I can try running it through my databases but don't get your hopes up."

Robert rose to go.

"Well, thank you, old friend, for the brandy. I won't take any more of your time. I will get you that information. She's caused quite a disturbance in several countries and is very dangerous."

"I will be happy to help if I can."

*Northern Wisconsin*

## *Sixty-eight*

Alex chipped and chopped at the wall until at last, he could insert the tips of his fingers and the edges of his toes into the sides. Slowly he made his way upward to where the shaft slanted toward some lighter space. Cory watched from the floor where he lay.

"I wish I could help you."

"No. Save your strength. You're going to need it if I find something to pull you out of here. I'm going to try to find rope or something before I come back, anything to lift you up, so don't panic if I'm out of sight for a while. I'll keep calling back to you as long as I can."

He wiggled himself up into the shaft until his entire body lay in it and then wormed his way onward. At the top he flopped himself into the place of light. It was another cave and the light, a bit stronger now, came from still another passageway. He called this information down to Cory.

"No rope here. No anything. I'm going on."

Cory shut his eyes. Fear gripped him as he realized he would never get out if something happened to Alex. He tried to think the horror away. Finally he let it wash through him and when it subsided somewhat, he had the thought that he could use his fingers and one toe to do the same as Alex had done. Pain would be excruciating.

*But I must. I must. We've climbed higher than that wall before. I can do it.*

He rolled himself to the wall, hauled himself onto one knee, then pulled himself slowly up to one foot.

"If I fall..." he muttered. "No! Don't think that!"

304

So he began his agony. Once he slipped, his muscles quivering with fatigue. He held himself close against the wall, imagining he was melting into it, waiting, waiting until he could move again.

His arms cramped. His good leg cramped. In his mind he clung there for hours. The worst was when he had to haul the dead weight of his lower body, dragging his bad leg, up into the shaft. It battered again and again at the wall before his whole body was supported. He thought he lost consciousness for a while. He forgot all about Alex.

Finally he continued inch by inch along the slanted tunnel, grateful for the few rocks sticking out of the dirt where he could hold on and pull himself along.

It was only at the top, when he peered from the opening, that he remembered Alex. There was no sign of him and no answer to his call and at least fifteen feet to the opening across the floor where the light was now waning. Cory got himself out of the shaft entirely and realized he could go no further. He had no strength left.

Alex moved easily through three more connected spaces, each lighter than the one before, all empty of any sign of life or people, before he reached the full light. He found himself on a stone ledge jutting out of a very steep hill. Far below, a small creek edged its way through brush. The hill was barren, dry. Severely eroded, it looked like it had been clear-cut. Looking up he saw the top of the hill some thirty or so feet above him.

"When I lose daylight, I'll never be able to find my way up or down. I have to see what I can see now from the top of the hill."

Once again he began to climb. It wasn't as easy as he thought it would be. The soil was loose, fine dust, almost sleek and shiny. He slipped back three times before he made it a dozen feet. After four more tries he made it to the top and stood up. Miles of nothing but this hill and others, some barren and others still treed, and far down below, a small cabin jutting from behind a huge rock.

Hope filled him until he realized that if he went back to tell Cory, he would have to slide feet first down the loose soil. He could end up sliding right off the side of the hill, tumble right past the ledge.

"Cory!" he yelled as loud as he could. "I have to go for rope, Cory! I'll be back as soon as I can."

Deep inside, Cory heard the voice but couldn't make out what Alex said.

"Cory!" He heard it again. "I'll be back."

He knew Alex was leaving him. Despair crawled over him and pinned him deep into loneliness. Darkness came.

Sometime in the night he heard the sound of wings, a large whoosh, and the clicking of a beak. He never saw the bird but was sure the bird saw him and waited there, watching him.

"Thanks, bird," he said out loud, grateful for the companionship. Clicking sounds replied.

Much, much later he heard the bird take off and leave and the depths of loneliness flooded him again. In total darkness, he could not trust his mind or senses anymore.

Moving carefully down the slippery slope, Alex made the tiny cabin before night fell. A quick search yielded a small bottle of water, a dirty blanket, a length of leather thong—about seven feet, he thought—a claw hammer, and two screwdrivers in a drawer.

He drank the water, feeling guilty at how good it tasted going down and thinking of Cory. Lashing everything to his body wrapped in the blanket, he crawled back up the slope to the top but the light gave out and he saw with despair that he could not see the ledge.

"No moon, no damn moon! Shit, damn and hell!"

The night became colder and he shivered, unwrapped the blanket and covered what he could of himself. He passed out sometime during the night and woke into dim and cloudy dawn light when a stab of pain ripped up his leg. He sat up, hissing, and startled a turkey vulture who flapped his wide wings and hopped a few feet away. The bird turned to eye Alex, hoping his chosen food was not alive. Looking around, Alex saw another emerge from the opening where the ledge jutted from the side of the hill.

"Oh god, Cory!"

Carefully he plotted his way backward down the dew-wet slope.

"I'll use the screw drivers in my hands, like pitons, let myself down slowly, aim for the widest part of the ledge."

He tore a piece of blanket, lashed the claw hammer to his right foot, and tied the rest to his back. Before he'd gone six feet, a wall of pouring rain began to drench the hill and the mud became even more slippery. He used all the strength he had to drive the metal screwdrivers and claw into the earth but even then he began to slide slowly downward. At the last, he fell onto the ledge and almost toppled over the side, just barely catching himself.

It was with immense relief that he crawled back into the still dark caves and made his way down through them. In the fourth cave he stumbled over Cory in the dark, shocked, thinking he'd made a mistake, thinking he was hallucinating. Cory groaned and muttered. Alex shook with relief.

"Water."

The word was a hoarse whisper.

Alex staggered back through the caves and lay on the ledge, getting the blanket and his clothing wet with rain, holding the can out and wishing the rain would come faster. He got his wish. The rain came in sheets.

He made his way back and dripped water between Cory's lips by wringing out his clothing and the blanket. Then he used the precious water in the can. Cory drank reflexively but remained unconscious.

Alex dragged Cory to the mouth of the cave and gathered more water slowly for both of them as the cloudy day lightened. When he could finally see the terrain, discouragement washed through him.

"Oh, no, Oh, no."

Looking up the slope and downward, he knew they couldn't leave. The hill was awash in mud. In places mud even slid down in small waves They couldn't go up. They couldn't go down.

He shivered, watching the cold rain batter the hillside. Hypothermia loomed as a serious threat.

## Sixty-nine

Vincent Grant stood next to his plane at Austin Straubel Airport watching the downpour. Ground teams had been checking out old mines all day in five counties in the Upper Peninsula and three in Wisconsin. Nothing. He and Anna had flown as long as weather permitted, into late evening, up and down major highways running north and south and all the lands around them. He was convinced she was deluded. He was convinced the boys were dead. He had finally left the house, unwilling to be there with any of them. He had his men make a list of cave systems that might have been used to stash two bodies and start a search of them.

He called Mexico.

"We have a partial report for you. We were just waiting for more confirmation and more details regarding the team inside Fournier's home. Mac located the woman named Ardith. He got some information out of her. We've got a map here on computer and we've just sent it to you.

"There's an old lumber camp in Florence County in the township of Commonwealth on the edge of the Spread Eagle Barrens where the townline road runs. Look for County N south out of the town of Florence and Johnson Creek Road going east. He says look for clear-cutting on some of the hills. There's a cave system accessible from just east of the camp. It's extensive. Sorry we can't get more specific. He was pressed for time. All hell is breaking loose at the Fournier place. We've sent help and the Federales are with our guys but they may not arrive in time."

"Finally. Get our people there if you have to drop them from a helicopter. That woman is too dangerous and Fournier is her patsy."

Grant clicked buttons on his phone.

"Stacy, get everyone ready. We're going north as soon as this weather clears."

"I've got us ready. I just got the news too. Lindy will stay on computer to Mexico. I'm coming with. I've already sent Anna's brothers and Cait's boys north by car. We need searchers. The FBI is sending people and the sheriff there has been notified. He says the area is quite large but he's pretty sure he can get hunters who know the area to begin searching. He knows of the cave system."

"Stacy, why the hell send the old men and the boys? I can order in more personnel."

"Because they're friends and relatives, Vincent. They love those kids. It's a done deal. The weather service says the rain will let up in an hour. It's already stopping up near Florence. I'll have us at the plane in a half hour."

"How did you get this news so fast?"

"Lindy has been texting Mac. He's been texting it back bit by bit for about an hour. He had to be very cautious. Several times he had to break away in mid-sentence. We've been piecing it together. Mac got caught before he could get more accurate information from Ardith. I don't know what's happening down there right now. We've lost contact temporarily.

"There's some good news. London police found Pete. He's in a hospital there. I'll fill you in later."

"Ok, just get here and we'll take off as soon as I can get clearance. If we're there by two or three a.m., we'll be able to begin searching with morning light."

In the sitting room in the central part of the house, three of Fournier's guards held guns pointed at Mac. He had lost the brown wig in the fight and his long hair, in a ponytail, hung down his back. He was still in medical whites. He had tried again to get information from her and he had gotten caught. She had been waiting for him this time.

The door opened and Ardith slowly walked through, shoulder bandaged, arm in a sling, but looking steady and in control.

Mac studied her carefully, watching for any sign of weakness.

Another door opened and Etienne, his hands in the air and protesting loudly, stalked stiffly at the point of a rifle, held by yet another guard.

"But this is absurd, outrageous! I am a guest here, You do not know who I am. I am Le Comte de Charbonneau. I am a friend of Monsieur Fournier. I will not be treated like this."

Ardith regarded him with scorn.

"Tsss! Shut up! You are no one! Nothing! Sit down!"

The guard prodded Etienne into a chair.

She turned her attention back to Mac.

"So. The mysterious Canadian at last and a French count. Now all we need is the stupid French politician and the Swiss bitch who thinks she is a princess. We will wait. No. We need one more. The American model. Perhaps she's out of her drugged state and able to walk. We shall see. Is that why you are here? To rescue the Kinnealy brat?"

Mac remained silent.

"You won't talk? Perhaps not now but in time you will. It's a good thing I trust no one and have my people placed everywhere. I have taken control now."

Ardith turned to the guards.

"Where is the secretary and her mistress. I told you to have them here. Go and search. You! Go to the guest wing and you, go to the other wing. Find them now!"

Only one guard remained and Mac began to edge toward him.

311

"Stay where you are!"

Ardith pulled a pistol out of the sling.

"I said we will wait."

She wavered slightly out of balance but caught herself quickly, her face an iron mask, showing no pain or weakness.

She continued to hurl questions at Mac, her voice becoming more demanding, higher in pitch, until she finally was near screaming.

He waited—still, silent, voiceless, watching her lose control of her emotions.

She snarled, "I will find out. I have ways."

Pointing her gun at the remaining guard she yelled at him, "Call the others and see what is taking them so bloody long!"

Mac tensed to attack. *She's on something. I know she's on something. I'm the one who gave it to her but it's having the opposite effect. It's increased her agitation.*

A door was pushed open with force and Marnie was hurled into the room, clinging to the sheet wrapped around her, stumbling as it caught under her foot. She looked up and around, saw Etienne and blushed with embarrassment. When she looked the other way, she raised her eyebrows in surprise.

"I know you. You are, were, Mr. Wentworth's secretary. Why are you here? Why am I here? How did I get here? What is this place? I demand to leave now."

"Ah. The Kinnealy primadonna. Just like your mother, like you own the world. Well, my little slut, I own you now. And your brothers. It's only a matter of time before I own your mother's world entirely—her stocks, bonds, cash, art, all of it. Even her precious self."

Ardith's voice became more brittle, escalating again.

The guard's cell phone rang and he put it to his left ear. Turning and plugging the other one so he could hear, he tucked the rifle in the crook of his arm.

Mac moved silently and swiftly, got him from behind and turned his body, using it as a shield.

Ardith broke off her rant and fired wildly, backing toward the door. It opened behind her and Melissa karate-chopped her. Ardith slumped to the floor.

Mac struggled with the guard to wrest the gun from him. A shot went through the ceiling.

Etienne dived for Marnie, knocking her down and rolling her away and behind a couch.

Mac wrenched the weapon out of the guard's hands and knocked him cold with the gun butt to his temple.

"I thought you'd never get here," he said calmly to Melissa.

"Shut up and come with me. Louie is with Fournier and some more guards and she's trying to talk her way out of danger."

She motioned to Etienne, who was again on his feet and to Marnie, who was struggling with the sheet.

"Tie the woman up, sit on her if you have to. Don't let her get away. She's very dangerous. She will kill you if she gets a chance. We'll be back."

Etienne picked up a corner of the sheet, tore strips from it and tied Ardith's hands and feet and put a length of cloth around her mouth.

"I have heard enough from her. More than enough," he said through his teeth.

He did the same with the guard and then turned to Marnie, who was trying to wrap more of the sheet around her.

"Now I will tell you where you are and how you came to be here and what has been happening here and what has been happening to your brothers and to your mother. You have much to learn."

He sat her down roughly on a nearby straight chair.

Marnie had no choice but to listen. After a long while, the grace of shame came to save her from her arrogance.

In the main sitting room, Yvette-Louise held out her arms to the Mexican police officer.

"Oh, my dear Generale, I am so happy you are here. Monsieur Fournier is very ill. He must leave here as soon as possible. We so much need your help. It is his heart, I think. He is old, weak, and he has been under such stress. You are a servant of the people. You will know how hard it can be at times. I have sent one of his servants to pack so I can take him back to France."

"I am here to have my men search this place. I have heard there are people held here against their will. I insist on an extensive search." The officer stared coldly down at her.

"But of course, you must carry out your orders. I will have my secretary and my other assistant show you everything. Ah, here they are!

"Melissa, will you please assist the police in their search, and where are our other guests, le Comte Charbonneau and his fiancé? Mac, be a dear and go and have them come here immediately. Here, take this police officer with you. He will be a great help to you. There are so many bags to carry."

She pulled one of the men near a window into the center of the room.

The soldier smiled and followed Mac, who recognized the nephew Adelina had described perfectly to him.

"Please assist him in every possible way," Louie called after the soldier. He did.

A loud groan issued from Aristide whose face was a pale shade of green.

Louie floated to him.

"Oh my poor Aristide, we will get you home in the greatest comfort we can."

314

She pressed a button on her phone.

"Robert, my darling! Do you have Aristide's plane waiting at the Cancun airport? Oh, mon dieu, you are so efficient, so organized. Yes, Etienne and his fiancé, our assistant Mac and my Melissa, and of course myself."

A door opened and Mac ushered in Etienne and a well-dressed Marnie. He nodded quickly to Louie.

She continued speaking to Robert.

"Our baggage is already on the way, and you and I will have our vacation here as planned. Au revoir, my love."

She ended her call.

The officer drew himself to full height.

"We must examine all baggage before you leave."

"But of course you must and Mac will have it all brought here for your men to examine, won't you, Mac?"

"It is on the way to this room now," Mac said with a small bow. Moments later servants arrived with bags and bags, setting them down in the middle of the room.

"You see, mon Generale, how efficient we are for you."

Two police officers began the search and Louie crossed the room to the general, took his arm in hers, making sure he felt the swell of her ample breast, and chattered on as she steered him to the library.

"And now, mon Generale, for all your work you need something refreshing and Aristide keeps a wonderful bar in his library."

Her voice continued to float back to the others.

"What do you mean, you are not a general? But that is impossible. How can you be effective if you do not have the proper rank for such important work? Robert and I will be having El Presidente and his wife as guests in Cancun in a few days. You must come. I will most certainly let him know how efficient you are at clearing up these matters. My husband will be so glad to meet you, to thank you. He is in banking you know."

Mac and Melissa helpfully assisted police in their search of the baggage and the house. All was peaceful, neat, and clean.

However, certain information made its way via very secure internet to Interpol and to other police and north to Wisconsin.

Many hours later, across the ocean, Interpol and London police took charge of a certain piece of baggage that somehow had escaped unexamined.

## Seventy

"Anna, your brothers and Cait's boys have a police escort now. They'll be there soon. What can you tell me about the boys?"

Stacy was on the phone to those driving north and held the phone to Anna's ear. The drone of the plane's engine made it difficult to hear. Anna took the phone and turned it up as high as she could, then blocked her other ear.

Anna had been withdrawn while they waited for clearance to take off, in her own world, and now, in the air, she dragged herself out of it.

"It's muddy. There's lots of mud, a mess, both are together, some sort of underground but not quite, I don't know. When Alex was little he ate mud. Absurd. Why am I thinking of that? It was so long ago. Alex is thinking of mud? I'm not sure."

She shook her head, trying to clear the confused picture in her mind. She handed the phone back to Stacy.

"Sorry. I can't get a clear picture."

Later the plane dropped into the dawn at a small airport and its occupants raced to the waiting helicopter and were in the air again moving southeast over forest and the small side roads and isolated homes of the Barrens.

"Anna, get on the mike and describe what you see to the sheriff's guide."

Vincent handed her the mike.

"Anna, my name is Billy. I know these Barrens. Tell me what you see."

Anna told him. "Mud. Lots of mud. And they're in a series of enclosures, caves, I think, but I'm not sure of that. I know that's not much help but if I get closer, I can tell you more."

"Ok, I'll keep in touch. I know a cave system in those hills. Part of it was always natural and part was dug out as a possible bomb shelter during the Cold War. God only knows who or what's been there since. There are four large hills that were totally cleared of trees and brush. A big mistake. Because of this rain the land will be a mess, a real sea of mud. We'll concentrate our search there. Your pilot has the coordinates. Call you later."

Within a short time Vincent announced, "We're over the four hills. We're beginning to fly a grid pattern now."

Anna sat up, alert, feeling Alex.

"I can feel them. They're down there. They're down there!" She pointed to her left.

Alex stiffened and came out of a slight doze to the distant chop-chop-chop of a helicopter, getting louder.

"I can feel mom," Cory whispered.

Alex staggered to his feet.

"I have to get to the mouth of the cave. I need your white shorts, fast."

He tugged at Cory's jeans, now loose from loss of weight.

"I'll try not to hurt your leg. My shorts are black. They won't see them."

"I pooped in those. They won't be all white."

"It's enough. Hurry!"

As they worked to get his jeans off, Cory's hopes dropped as the sound of the helicopter faded.

"Get back in your jeans. I'll be back to help you get out of here," Alex ordered.

On the ledge he searched the dawn sky for the chopper, waving the shorts, hoping it would pass over again.

In the air, Stacy, binoculars at her eyes, yelled, "I see him. There he is. He's on the side of that hill." She pointed to her left.

The pilot turned and began circling back and down, homing in on the white flag.

Suddenly, Alex slipped and fell, yelling.

Cory crawled to the mouth of the cave and saw Alex sliding helplessly down into and through the wet mudslide.

In the helicopter, Anna yelled, "Alex!" feeling his panic.

Cory looked up. "Mom! Help!"

He pushed himself over the edge toward Alex.

On the helicopter intercom, the guide's voice could be heard directing the rescue trucks "...within 350 feet of..." static "...the southern hill on the east side above..." static "...Creek." The rest was lost in more static.

Anna caught sight of a parade of vehicles below rushing along a small road to the foot of the hill, red and blue lights flashing, coming to an abrupt halt, and men pouring out of them.

"Anna, look!" Stacy ordered and gave her the binoculars. "There they are. One is farther down than the other."

Anna found Alex, then Cory.

"Of course, playing in mud. Still playing in mud." She began to laugh and cry.

"Where can we set down?" Grant asked the pilot.

"There's a clearing about a half mile up this road. Nothing closer, I'm afraid."

"Good enough. We can cover that on foot in no time."

Due to the messy soil conditions, no time turned out to be over an hour before both boys were brought down.

Finally at their side, Anna fell to her knees and cried.

319

Medics examined both and all three left in the county medical helicopter

Grant and the sheriff stood together in the rain that had begun pouring down again.

"We were lucky this rain let up long enough to get those boys out. My question is, did that woman use this cave system as part of her drug road? I'm going to have it searched from one end to the other," the sheriff said.

Grant stood, hands on hips, eyes squinted and he looked around.

"It's a real possibility. If you need any help, I've got men who can assist you.

"I'll take you up on that. Come on. We can't do anything until this rain stops. I've got hot coffee for all."

The old man sidled up to Stacy. A thick miasma of pain accompanied him.

"We'd like to go to the hospital where the boys are. Can you get us there?"

Next to him a taller old man, his face lined with fine wrinkles, stood straight as a lodgepole pine tree, a halo of white hair ringing his head, dark blue eyes reaching to infinity.

Stacy was unable to speak. Sadness shivered and reverberated in the air, and clung to both men. She merely nodded in the face of such pain and motioned them back to the SUV.

The ER at Florence became a sea of muddy clothing, blankets and footprints while both boys were treated. Finally a doctor came to Anna.

"Your son's leg will need major reconstructive surgery, probably several surgeries. Physical therapy too. He'll need the best of care. I can give you some referrals if you need them."

Anna stood up.

"Thank you, doctor, for all you've done. I'll be taking my sons home and then to London. They will have the best of care."

She turned to go back to the room where the boys both lay. They had refused separate rooms.

A tall old man stood in her path.

Anna stopped breathing. "Jamie."

Jamie stepped out of the shadow in the corridor where he had been standing. Pat stood just behind him, tugging at his hair.

"My girl. My girl."

Anna moved closer, step by step, unable to take her eyes from his.

"Thank you for saving me, Jamie."

Jamie raised his hand and touched her cheek where a tear slid down. He brought his finger to his lips and licked the salty water.

Anna's eyes widened.

"You did that when I was little. You drank my tears. I remember that. I had forgotten."

She caught his hand and pulled it to her cheek and put her hand on his cheek.

"And we used to do this too, when I was very little."

He nodded.

"You were more my Da than Da was. I thought of you as my other Da. I felt terrible when you left."

"I was afraid to leave you. I was afraid Ma wouldn't take good care of you. But I had to go."

"I know. I know. You don't have to leave any more. That's over. Will you help me bury her?"

"Aye. That I will. We'll find your other son as well. There's life in this old man yet."

He wrapped his arms around her and two minds thought the same.

*I'm home. I'm home.*

In London, Etienne, Marnie, and Melissa had arrived at the apartment.

Melissa handed a phone to Marnie.

"Your brothers Cory and Alex have been found and are as well as they can be, given what they have suffered. Your brother AJ is still missing. Here is your mother's cell phone number. I suggest you call her.

"Tomorrow you will be escorted by security to a plane I have hired. You will fly to Switzerland and you'll have a private car to bring you to the clinic. Any questions?"

Marnie looked down. "No. No questions."

She moved into the small sitting room and sat down, looking at the phone. Etienne waited. Melissa waited.

Finally she keyed the phone. "Hello? Mom? It's me, Marnie."

## Seventy-one

...journal...

The funeral was yesterday, a Wednesday, at St. John's. Cory and his band sang. Jamie joined them in the songs. He has a fine voice. I never knew that.

Marnie was not here for it. She's returned to the clinic. We've made a small start at connecting, but the barrier remains, an emotional minefield neither of us know how to cross right now.

It was a quiet ceremony, friends and family only, and I had the announcement put in the paper afterward.

Still, Greg had police there and Stacy has security surrounding us.

Ardith is in custody in London and charged with kidnapping. She will face drug charges here and possibly in Canada. Cory and Alex will have to testify in England. Vincent Grant is taking them there.

I gave them one of Mom's lectures at the airport this morning as we waited, with Pete, who had flown here from England.

"I just had to extricate myself from the cartel's clutches, Mrs K, and it took a while. I wasn't badly hurt. A flesh wound and a few bruises. I hear you have some experience in that area."

"Yes. Yes, I do."

A new bodyguard, Stan, replaces Harry, who will need more time to recover.

"When you see your sister, please don't come down on her too hard," I cautioned Alex. "No one ever born has not made mistakes. God knows I have. Go to the clinic and visit her and give her hugs for me."

Cory was practicing wheelies on his crutches, whirling around on one and landing on the other.

"Why can't we go to Mexico with you to find AJ?"

"Your leg, for one thing. Will you please stop that? You're scaring me. You're looking at several reconstructive surgeries for that calf muscle before you can walk without crutches. I have a very good surgeon waiting for you."

"Mom! He's our brother. We want to be there," Alex protested yet again.

I ignored him and continued.

"You will have to testify for another thing, and I want you where Mr. Grant can post security and have tight cooperation with the police who know your story. We don't yet know who might still be working for Ardith, who might carry out her plans. I also want you both in counseling for the trauma of the torture.

"If I need help, I'll send for you. Mac will be with me and Stacy, and everyone down there who loves AJ. I'll keep you updated daily. You know AJ is skilled at survival. Of the four of you, he's the last one I'd worry about. We'll find him."

Greg was waiting for me in an unmarked police car when I left the airport with Stacy.

"Police escort, ma'am," he said as he held the door for us.

"What does the drug scene here look like now? Has all this made one iota of difference?" I asked when we were on our way.

"It's hard to tell yet, but the number of ODs have gone down and we're keeping Design Imports open as a front to see what else we can catch. Cait's boys are on the street again for us. Sean has decided to take police science at NWTC. He'll make a good cop."

"Yes he will."

"What about Mexico? Who will help you there?"

"Jorge called. He and Ramon have men out looking. There are rumors of a gringo wandering the jungle but all leads have been false ones so far. Unfortunately, the offer of a ransom made that worse, drawing out every sleazy opportunist in the entire region.

"Jorge has a growing underground Mayan army to oppose the cartels, mostly to sabotage their lines of distribution wherever they can. Grant will fly down there to expand his own network after delivering Cory and Alex to London and securing that scene. Mac will go down with me. He's at the house now. And Stacy, of course," I added as she cleared her throat.

"Good crew, that. Cait says to tell you they'll examine everything and if there's anything to help you, they'll find it."

"It's more likely they'll find something to help you. Where are they?"

"I can't tell you because I don't know."

"Seriously? Stacy hasn't even told you?"

Stacy began humming an off-key tune.

"Nope. She placed them somewhere in Wisconsin. That's all I know."

"Wow! Very cloak and dagger. Well, good. I want them safe."

"Exactly," said Stacy.

...journal, later...

I am alone, well, as alone as I can be with Mac and Stacy and a security crew here.

I have told Grant to be sure the boys remain in London. I've been completely unable to make any connection with AJ. I believe he's dead. I don't want my sons finding their dead brother.

Lindy is gone. Her note said she went to Mexico. No word of when or how she went. No protection.

One more to find.

## Seventy-two

The Texan stopped and laughed out loud. He had stepped off the plane at Austin Straubel International Airport in Green Bay, walked into the terminal, and was passing a window when he glanced over the tarmac at another terminal where a sleek private plane caught his attention.

"And there she is," he said to himself, "and her boys. My luck is right on. It won't take long to find out what's happenin' up here."

"Did you say something, sir?" an airport attendant walking nearby asked.

"Just hopin' them Packers stay in good form this fall season. I want to see me a great game or two."

"Yes, sir. Don't we all." The attendant moved on.

He labelled Stacy as security immediately, then lingered behind to see Vincent Grant take the two young men to the private plane. One, the redhead, was on crutches.

"So Grant's in her stable as well. A formidable opponent. That other chick he employs, Melissa somebody, must be around too. El Capitan will want to know that."

Three days later he had made the necessary police contacts, one in the Brown County Sheriff's Department and another in the Green Bay Police Department.

After that he made his way to the apartment of the man who was next in line to take over the drug scene in Wisconsin.

"She's in the custody of the London Police. You'll be taking over up here but El Capitan will be calling the shots."

The thin man took a long drag on his cigarette, held in the smoke, then let it out slowly, but never turned from the window where he was watching pedestrian traffic on Broadway.

"I don't think so. He's been gone from here too long. He doesn't know the scene anymore. There is one other thing he doesn't know. She's not in London police custody any longer. She bought herself a high price solicitor and is out on bail, which she paid easily. Tell him to back off."

"Your agreement was loyalty to him. You really want to change those terms?"

"Why not? He did."

"He didn't have much choice back then. Now he does. You can't match anything he's got in place. He owns whole towns, whole states in Mexico, and other countries as well. I warn you. You'll end up dead."

"Are you going to do that for him?"

"I'm no hit man. I don't like the killing part. I just like a lot of money. If you turn El Capitan down, you won't make half as much as you could."

"We'll see. Tell him I'm reorganizing things up here and I'll get back to him when I've got something solid in place."

The Texan was silent for a time, waiting, then shook his head and left.

On his phone, he reported to El Capitan.

"Fine," came the reply. "Let him alone for now but stay there. I want to know every player he's got, every contact. Work with the police. Tell them you're DEA under deep cover. I'll be sure your cover's tight. Keep me informed."

"Expect the Kinnealy woman and that Canadian down there soon. The crazy bitch had her son's wife killed and her son's gone missing."

"Which son?"

"They call him AJ."

"Where are the others?"

"Her sons Cory and Alex are in London. Cory's under care of some high-priced plastic surgeon for repair of a bad wound. The bitch had both of them tortured."

"And the daughter?"

"She's a drug addict. She's at a treatment center in Switzerland."

There was a long silence.

"Boss? You there?"

"Yes. Just keep me informed on them all."

# Epilogue

The jaws of the crocodile snapped shut on the unsuspecting fish. Above the water, on an overhanging bank, a jaguar crouched, watching.

The scene repeated again.

And again.

And again.

Anna, her feet mired in mud underneath the water, struggled to escape the scene, looking to left and right, but it repeated, in every direction, same scene, again and again.

She tried to walk away. No.

To move sideways. No escape.

Only one option. Walk through the water, step on the crocodile, walk over it and meet the jaguar.

Behind her the spirits of Despair and Hope were fighting silently with each other and shoving at her back.

Above her, Rage dripped its poison on her until, around her feet, the water turned blood red.

Thirsty, her throat parched, Anna tried to cry for help. Sound floated from her mouth slowly, turned into flames, burned into ashes and drifted away on the wind.

From the bloody water a black cup rose.

"Drink, you bitch!" Ardith's voice commanded.

"Drink!" grated the voice of El Cocodrilo.

"Drink!" came Art's voice.

"I drank it, Mom. You have to drink it too," AJ whispered from the mist on the shore.

Anna drank, walked over the crocodile, stepped on the shore and felt her body enter the jaguar.

In her bed, Mac felt strong arms pull him over her, felt her open her legs and wrap them around him.

"Drink!" she commanded.

Addiction to her fired its indelible path into his brain.

He drank.

# Cast of Characters

*From the author: December 2013*

I have been told it's not the fashion these days to have many characters in a book. I read somewhere that modern readers have no patience for depth of detail, complicated plots, and long descriptions. I don't think that's totally true.

It certainly is not true for me. I've lived long and have heard many life stories. I have learned that no person's story is told without a list, most often a long list, of those who influence our lives, directly and indirectly, in large and small ways.

I grew up reading books that, to me, seemed based on this view. The books I read were rich in characters, plots and sub-plots, detailed descriptions and settings. I loved that because it meant I could live in their lives deeply. I lived one whole summer in Galsworthy's *The Forsyte Saga*. The book, not the tv series. I lived this past summer in the series by Stieg Larsson that begins with *The Girl with the Dragon Tattoo*. The book, not the movie.

I aim to make my books a space on the continuum between those above and the current fashion of quick solutions and one-hour mysteries on television. I've created many characters, prominent and minor, and a complicated plot, but I think I've written them in a way that moves with enough speed and action to hold the interest of the modern reader.

However, to help readers sort them out, here's a list of the characters.

## *Betrayal by Serpent* Character List

The House, Anna's home for many years. It became her safe place and her business office as well. The House came to have a character of its own so I include it in this list.

*The Kinnealy Family*

<u>Anna O'Neill Kinnealy</u>, age 52, mother of five children, four still living, wife of <u>Arthur Kinnealy Sr.</u>, who died in the crash of his small plane in the Yucatan seven  years prior to the beginning of the story.

<u>AJ, or Arthur Kinnealy Jr</u>, age 27, oldest son

Daughter, name unknown, died of SIDS

<u>Marnie Kinnealy</u>, age 20

<u>Alex Kinnealy</u>, age 17

<u>Cory Kinnealy</u>, age 16

The ages of these characters were each minus seven years when Art Sr. died.

*The Bradleys*

<u>Robinson Bradley, Caroline Bradley,</u> and their twin sons, <u>Jake and Jim</u>, (age 16) live across the street from the Kinnealys

*The Fitzgeralds*

<u>Caitlin DunLeavy Fitzgerald</u> and her five sons: <u>Sean, Michael, Liam, Andrew and Seamus.</u> Cait is Anna's best friend from childhood. They live in the West   side neighborhood where Anna and Art grew up.

*Old Mr Houlihan*, a protector and friend from Anna's childhood

*Relatives*

<u>Katherine O'Neill</u>, Anna's mother, known as <u>MomKat</u>

<u>Aunt Carrie Brennan</u>, married twice and divorced once, or the other way around, the family "black sheep" and sophisticate

*Friends and acquaintances*
Big John O'Keeffe, owner of a large construction
company and friend of the Kinneallys for many
years. Jon O'Keeffe's father
Jonathan O'Keeffe, Art's law partner and co-founder of
their firm
Jennifer O'Keeffe, Jon's twin
Mary O'Keeffe, Big John's wife

*Boarders at The House*
Marthe Grimm, Anna's first boarder and now surrogate
grandmother and friend
Lindy Stewart, student at UW-Green Bay and like one of
Anna's own children, daughter of Ian Stewart

*The Law Firms*
O'Keeffe, Kinnealy, Soderstrom and Moss. The firm
begun by Jon O'Keeffe (Jonny O) and Art Kinnealy
Sr. Sometimes called The Firm.
Andrew Moss, deceased partner
Samuel Soderberg, former partner, deceased
Susan Jane Soderberg, his wife

Wentworth and Foster
Conrad Wentworth, Anna's lawyer
Clayton Foster, his partner
Ardith Seacrest, Conrad's executive secretary

Abigail Woodman, from a law firm in Appleton, WI.

*Others*
Greg Klarkowski, Green Bay Police Department,
Detective
Thomas Rudmann, Brown County Sheriff's
Department, Detective
Ben Bennett, former classmate of AJ's and now a police
officer with GBPD

*Mexico*

Capitan Jesus Arispe Sandoval, investigator of Art's death

Sandy, a worker sent from the American consulate to help AJ and Anna

Ramon Aguilar, guide and friend, becomes Anna's lover

Jorge Aguilar, his brother

Adelina Sálazar Díaz, housekeeper, elder, advisor, cousin to Jorge and Ramon

Tomasita, Adelina's helper in housekeeping

Ian Stewart, Lindy's father, an archaeologist

Kevin MacPherson, "Mac", mysterious investigator of the drug cartels, Canadian and Native American

Walton Herder, American consulate representative

Matthew Simoneska, archaeologist sent to check out the archaeological dig by the funding organization, Cross-Cultural Archaeology Institute (CCAI)

Hernan, Jaime, and two others. Mexican workers on the archaeological dig


## CHARACTERS ADDED TO *In Crocodile Waters.*

*Wisconsin*

Myron "Iron Mike" DeLorme, Green Bay police detective

Arnold Schwartzkopf, Green Bay police captain

Father O'Doul, pastor at St. Pat's church

Mr. Black, drug pusher

William "Big Bill" Holworth, camp director, Sitting Bear Summer Camp for Children

Rich Wolcott, sheriff

Vincent Grant, owner of a worldwide security firm
    Employed by Grant: Melissa, Stacy, Pete, Harry, and assorted others

*Europe*

Gabrielle de Launay, administrative assistant to Robert de la Vergne

Robert de la Vergne and Yvette-Louise de la Vergne, Swiss banker who administers Anna's financial holdings in Europe, and his wife, who is called "Louie"

Aristide Fournier, French politician

Etienne Charboneau, French count

*Ireland*

Pat and Jamie O'Reilly, Anna's older brothers

*Mexico*

The Crocodile, El Cocodrilo, head of his own cartel

El Capitan, head of a third cartel

The Texan, employed by El Capitan

# ABOUT THE AUTHOR

Judith M. Kerrigan is the pen name of Judith Kerrigan Ribbens, a visual artist, amateur photographer and writer. She holds a Bachelor's Degree in Human Development, University of Wisconsin-Green Bay; a Master's Degree in Expressive Arts Therapies, Lesley University, Cambridge, MA and is a Licensed Professional Counselor in Wisconsin. She has been a counselor for over twenty-three years, including thirteen years as a crisis counselor.

A mother, grandmother and great-grandmother, _In Crocodile Waters_ is her second novel.

Born in Green Bay, she was a longtime resident and has an extensive family background there. She now resides in the Wisconsin countryside.

The first book in this series, _Betrayal by Serpent_, is available on Amazon.com in paperback and e-book forms. It can also be ordered through Barnes and Noble.

The third book in the Anna Kinnealy series will be titled _The Jaguar Hunts_. Tentative publishing date is 2016.

*** 

Judy holds a limited number of expressive arts playshops each year for groups who wish to arrange these.
Contact 920-471-8500
Please arrange six months in advance because she works four days each week as a creative arts therapist in the fields of mental health and addiction.

*** 

Book signings may be scheduled at least one month ahead.
Contact information:
Email: jkerriganwriter@yahoo.com

**Websites and Blog:**
For much more on the writing of her books,
their characters, settings, events, and illustrations of The
House and Mayan art, go to
www.judithkerriganribbens.com
\*\*\*

For online galleries of visual works:
www.artid.com/judyribbens
\*\*\*

To purchase prints and canvases of selected works:
www.fineartamerica.com/judyribbens

\*\*\*

Other connecting points include LinkedIn and Facebook.

A big thank you to all who have purchased my work. It is the great reward of my old age to be able to use every talent I've been fortunate enough to have received, and to give back to the world some little bit of what I've received from others. Most especially, I give thanks to the many mystery writers out there whose works have inspired me.

Made in the USA
San Bernardino, CA
20 March 2014